C000165693

....perback

Sentence Adjourned

After leaving Bristol University, Paul Genney worked as a dentist for six years before becoming a potato merchant. He stood twice, unsuccessfully, for parliament in the 1980s before becoming a criminal barrister.

He now divides his time between his homes, in Grimsby and London, and his chambers in Hull.

He is the author of two novels: *Pleading Guilty* and *Sentence Adjourned.*

Sentence Adjourned

by

Paul Genney

Dedalus

Published in the UK by Dedalus Limited
24-26, St Judith's Lane, Sawtry, Cambs, PE28 5XE
email: info@dedalusbooks.com
www.dedalusbooks.com

ISBN 978 1 903517 96 3

Dedalus is distributed in the USA by SCB Distributors,
15608 South New Century Drive, Gardena, CA 90248
email: info@scbdistributors.com   www.scbdistributors.com

Dedalus is distributed in Australia by Peribo Pty Ltd.
58, Beaumont Road, Mount Kuring-gai, N.S.W 2080
email: info@peribo.com.au

Dedalus is distributed in Canada by Disticor Direct-Book Division
695, Westney Road South,Suite 14, Ajax, Ontario, LI6 6M9
email: ndalton@disticor.com   www.disticordirect.com

First published by Dedalus in 2010
Sentence Adjourned copyright © Paul Genney 2010

The right of Paul Genney to be identified as the author of this work has been
asserted by him in accordance with the Copyright, Designs and Patents Act,
1988.

Printed in Finland by WS Bookwell
Typeset by Marie Lane

This book is sold subject to the condition that it shall not, by way of trade
or otherwise, be lent, re-sold, hired out or otherwise circulated without the
publisher's prior consent in any form of binding or cover other than that in which
it is published and without a similar condition including this condition being
imposed on the subsequent purchaser.

For my children Joseph, Eleanor, Lewis and Adelaide.
For their kindness in putting up with the first.

Chapter 1

Did I go to Pauline's wedding? Pauline had been ringing me with that glorious indifference that only self-obsession can bring.

Why not? There was nothing to lose. See how she looked. Mingle with the guests. Drink Tomkinson's wine. Sample the catering for free.

But I would have to buy a wedding present. Nothing's ever for free - but I'd try to finish on top. A chance to wear my rather elegant dinner jacket that I found in a charity shop. A chance to get off with one of the bridesmaids. Man's eternal hope. I'd heard of people seducing bridesmaids in a room of a posh hotel. Once incredibly the bride. But my chance with a bridesmaid? It must be a million to one. Good enough for me. Better odds than classes in adult learning or lonely nights in the pub.

I gazed at the fancy invitation where it had rested on my blotter for several days. Tomkinson, who had never been to church for years, but whose ancestry was vaguely connected to the Church of England had no difficulty in persuading his local village church to stage his wedding to Pauline who had never been to church at all.

A gold embossed card. RSVP. Of course I will you bastards. Delighted, I wrote, to accept. At least I was the only one in Whitebait Chambers to receive their especial call. I fingered the thickness of the card and tilted back in my chair.

But I wasn't. Of course I wasn't. Everybody had got one. Giles was pleased to inform me.

"We're hiring a charabanc."

"What do you want a coach for?"

"Everybody's going. Looks bad to refuse. Anyway should be plenty to drink. There's the present of course …" he scratched his head, "… a picture. Something in oils. Commission a local artist. Give him fifty quid."

Pauline was never off the line.

"The wedding list's at Harrod's. Do you know where it is?"

Christ, I've lived in this country all my life. A boast or an admission? I couldn't quite decide.

"I know where it is."

"Or Selfridges if you prefer. That's near Oxford Street."

"It's on Oxford Street."

"Who cares. Make sure you get something nice."

Now I know what this invitation was about. Another tribute to be placed on the pile. A payment for former favours. A recognition of value. A monetary reminder of what I had lost.

"Who is doing the catering?"

I couldn't care less, but needed something to say.

"My mother's banging up some sandwiches. Not really, before you ask. Charles's mother has taken over. Sorry to disappoint you; no pork pie. But what a lovely church in the village. Met the vicar, a lovely man. Saxon or Norman or something" she laughed, "… the church not the vicar. And then off to Warburton Chase Manor, assume you know where it is. Morning suits. Don't forget."

I was getting tired of this.

"Why spend so much money?" I couldn't work out the price. "What's the point?"

"Different world tiger. This time I'm doing it right."

I thought about her first marriage to Barry. Gazing out over Morecambe Bay in a headscarf, blinking into the wind.

The creaking springs of the mattress. Running the gauntlet at breakfast; up and down the prom in a gale.

"No more on the cheap."

I'd heard the story. Barry playing bingo. Barry getting drunk. Barry objecting to some imagined familiarity with an artiste in a bar. Barry getting angry. Barry getting randy. Barry falling over. Barry ordering his full English breakfast. Barry farting and snoring in his sleep.

"I've done Blackpool. Walked up and down the front. Pretending to enjoy myself. Pretending to be in love."

I said nothing.

"Make sure you get something nice."

So I bought her a carving in wood. An abstract of sinuous curves. Fashioned from a knurl of walnut by some tosser with a beard and shavings in his hair. £350. For what? A recognition that I'd lost.

I drove my car to the little country church and parked up on the grass verge next to the hawthorn hedge. One of the first there. I nodded to a group of women waiting by the gate.

"Lovely day for it." They turned and weighed me up.

"Yes. Turned out nice again."

I cupped a cigarette in my hands and fiddled with my zippo. A guarantee they'd leave me alone.

"Shall I carry a bouquet of lilies?" She'd asked me in her umpteenth call. "Or would a bible, a white bible, make a better effect?"

Why not a cheque book? A white cheque book. You could wave it over your head.

Tomkinson had arrived before me and was standing with his manicured friends at the church door throwing their heads back and laughing at something he'd said. I edged down the path towards them. Shake the hand that shook the hand that touched the bride that .... But he saw me coming and turned away, with one last joke that set them laughing, he slipped away through the porch.

I followed him inside. It was cool, and very pretty. Whitewashed walls; the occasional protuberant stone; a gallery over the brass pipes of the organ; the carved oak of the choir stalls, I looked around at the cascading flowers, the old stone font, the pulpit draped with a gold embroidered cloth, the twinkling lights from the stained-glass window playing on the limestone flags of the floor.

Was Tomkinson a Christian? Was Pauline? Was anybody? Religion had become an entertainment. That's show business. A lovely venue for a wedding where once they prayed to God.

I watched as the audience gathered; the pews slowly filling up.

Pauline's family to the right, wearing their morning coats and fancy waistcoats and those ridiculous wing collars jutting out over garish cravats. Men's hair with brylcreemed partings, the women fresh out of curlers wearing hats, fascinators, shawls, capes, jackets and corsets under the white, yellow and strawberry of their straining silk - turning their heads at every new arrival to smile or nod or frown.

I gazed across at Tomkinson's ensemble. Less Brylcreem; less curls but the same ridiculous suits. A few medals, a mayor with his chain of office, his consort beside him with replicate gold and brass.

And was that the Recorder? The Honourable Recorder of Hull. Immaculate as ever. Striped trousers, black waistcoat and military tie. He'd never been in the Army. An ex-member of chambers I'd plotted the course of his career with a combination of jealousy and regret - but I did my share of nodding, as he ushered the pink bubble of his wife to a reserved seat at the front.

Giles arrived with the rest of chambers and squeezed in beside me pushing me over towards the wall.

"Why didn't you wait for us? Why didn't you come in the coach?"

Why did I come at all? I looked at the printed Order of Service that some enthusiastic public school-boy had thrust into my hand.

'The Lord is my Shepherd.' How original.

'Palladio for Strings' Tomkinson's younger sister on the recorder. Interesting.

The Lesson - 'Corinthians'. Pauline's cousin primed and panting in the traps.

Why not Barry? That would be original. Barry giving his blessing in an alien dialect in the strictures of an alien tongue. Oh the tales he could tell! My mind wandered. Putting up a screen. Fiddling with the projector. "A few clips from a film … Pauline as you've never seen her before …"

But where was Pauline? Where was the star of the show?

'Here comes the bride. Here comes the bride.' The organ struck up the Mendehlsonian chorus and Pauline and her father appeared at the door. Face downcast, eyes slanting upwards in mock subservience, she seemed satisfied with the turnout and edged her modest way forward between the rival factions of supporters leaning unnecessarily upon her father's arm. God I don't believe it. Carrying a bible. Yes a white bible. A heavy reverent hold upon a book she'd never read.

'Here comes the bride. Here comes the bride.' Tomkinson turned and grinned at her, and she - what an actress - shyly, eyes demurely, furtively, turned upwards, sweetly returned his smile.

A bridesmaid took her bible setting her free to concentrate on the ring.

Giles elbowed me in the ribs. "Looks nice don't you think? Good looking woman. I wouldn't mind a bash myself."

She stood beside Tomkinson. Shy, tentative, banal. That staring upwards look again. "Do you take this woman to be your lawful wedded wife?"

Tomkinson threw back his shoulders and stuck out his chest. "I do."

"Do you take this man to be your lawful wedded husband?"

Pauline in a whisper. Exercising what she thought was restraint. "I do."

"To love, honour and obey, for richer for poorer, in sickness and in health, forsaking all others till death do you part?"

"I do."

The best man produced the ring from his waistcoat pocket and handed it to the vicar who slipped it on Pauline's supplicant hand.

"I now pronounce you man and wife. You may kiss the bride."

Pauline inclined her lips upwards, and Tomkinson looked down the master of all he surveyed. He had cleared away the undergrowth, expelled the trespassers, applied a new lick of paint. He placed his hand behind her neck and stooped to embrace her while Pauline closed her eyes.

Well mate, you can play to the gallery all you like. Seal a contract with a kiss. I kissed her long before you and maybe will again. My eyes also shut, lost in my own cocoon of pleasure, Pauline I daresay pretty much the same.

They moved off to sign the register. Pauline, Tomkinson, Tomkinson's parents, Pauline's father and mother, bridesmaids and best man and, for some reason, the Honourable Recorder of Hull.

Giles elbowed me again and nearly knocked me off my pew.

"Dear boy, it might have been you."

"Thanks for reminding me. Never would have guessed."

We made our way to Warburton Chase Manor - a long convoy of assorted cars, limousines, and roadsters wending their way along the winding country lane listening to birds crying from the hedgerows and smelling the oppressive summer blossom, fleetingly disturbed by our passing, as if by the slightest breath of wind.

I was jammed in beside Giles. He jerked his head towards the yellow Rolls Royce containing the happy couple, the convoy of bridesmaids and relatives keeping their distance behind.

"Not bad looking those bridesmaids. Any idea who they are?"

11

"Tomkinson's sisters. Elder sisters."

"Married?"

"To the ushers."

"Looks like I'm in the same boat as you."

We swung past the gatehouse into the drive, and set off through the park. Deer and chestnut trees, a row of limes winding through the valley, until finally we caught a glimpse of the house. Tudor chimneys, wisteria clinging to a mullioned window, we ground to a halt on the yellow gravel before a double stone staircase leading up to the entrance where Pauline and Tomkinson arriving before us were already stationed, waiting to greet their guests.

I joined the queue with the rest of Whitebait Chambers and shuffled forward to pay my respects.

"Henry. How good of you to come. And Giles! And Mr. McIntosh. Can I call you Jock?"

I thought about it. Should I kiss her with intent? My lips raised in anger crushing her mouth to mine. A gesture of insolent defiance. A portent of what might be to come? She deftly pushed me sideways and past her, my lips barely brushing her cheek.

Giles having been despatched in similar fashion joined me in reception and we looked around for a drink. Waitresses were lined up against the walls holding trays of hors d'oeuvres, champagne and wine.

Giles beckoned them across.

"What do you call these?" He was looking for a slice of pork pie.

"Smoked salmon, dill and mascarpone on blinis. Prawns in tempura with a little tapenade." I knew the menu already. The continual adjustments; the little touches and changes; the endless discussion and debate; the product of her mocking phone calls during the weeks before.

"Feta and olives with anchovy on honey-flecked wild oatmeal biscuit."

Giles took two glasses. "I'll settle for a drink."

Whitebait Chambers gathered in force in a corner, we began out of habit, greed, the want of something better to do, to attack the champagne.

Pauline waltzed across. "Isn't it lovely? Charles insisted on the venue. Insisted on Bollinger. Help yourselves. Remember to use a glass."

A string quartet in the corner played Bach's concerto for two violins, guests mingled, Pauline floated amongst them - Tomkinson at her side, his hand planted in the small of her back - he guided her away towards his friends encamped strategically in the centre - a staircase to the minstrel gallery at their backs.

She threw back her head and laughed up at Tomkinson, her hand stroking his arm. I saw her wave at her guests - her family and friends ranged along a wall.

"Ladies and gentlemen. Your attention please. My Lord the Honourable Recorder of Kingston upon Hull and his lady. The Right Reverend Bishop of Holderness. His Worshipful the Mayor of Hessle and his consort. Professor and Mrs. Ragwort. The Chairman of the Justices of Bransholme. The Master of the Humber Bridge. The Head of Whitebait Chambers ..."

Giles nodded his huge head.

"Ladies and gentlemen, please be so kind as to take your seats for the wedding breakfast. Along the gallery if you please, and across the courtyard. The marquee can be found in the central quadrangle, your seats indicated on the plan."

We filed away, Giles smiling at the bridesmaids, and took our seats under a flapping corner of canvas at some considerable distance, to Giles annoyance, from Pauline's table at the top.

He studied the menu.

"Must be costing a fortune ... What's this? Spider crab on celeriac with strawberry jus, crown of lamb with pak choi and jellyfish roulade ..."

I looked around. Twinkling glass and white linen; the glint of silver. Lanterns twisting in the evening breeze, the soft murmur of conversation, the discreet pop of champagne. The string quartet struck up a Brandenburg concerto, crickets sang from a distant corner of the meadow, waiters glided amongst the tables, Tomkinson must have made another joke, I caught Pauline's distant brittle laugh.

McIntosh lit a cigar and tilted back in his chair. Giles beckoned to a waitress, who obediently topped up his glass. The soft lapping of conversation suddenly, inexplicably, came to a stop. A woman stood up and began screaming as men from two adjourning tables began to fight. Bach faltered as the violins trailed away.

McIntosh and I stood up for a better look. I saw a bottle shatter on somebody's head.

Giles pulled away from us and bounded away through the crowd. I saw Tomkinson usher Pauline away and the Honourable Recorder of Hull slip under the awning and slide across the paddock; his good lady carrying her shoes, hobbling along behind.

The Master of Ceremonies started to his feet.

"Ladies and gentlemen please …"

Tables went over, lanterns came down, the quartet packed up their instruments and quietly melted away.

I could see Giles in the thick of things, his fat arm cradling a bridesmaid, on her yellow dress a splash of blood.

Oh dear. What a terrible shame. The English typically, now at play. It couldn't happen to a nicer couple. All that money gone to waste. The happy pair, their evening ruined by all that free champagne.

I thought of the photographs in next month's Humberside Life - the top peoples' journal - assuming their pissed-up photographer could clear the mud from his lens.

Colonel and Lady Forsythe being stretchered into an ambulance. The Honourable Archibald Cartwright wiping blood from his shirt. Mrs. Featherstone and her sister Lady Penelope picking glass from their hair.

Special photographs to remind them of their special day.

What was it all about? Who knows, who cares. Give them all a bloody medal and send the bill to Charles.

The Humberside Police eventually rolled up and, as is their practice, waited patiently round the corner until they were sure the fighting had stopped and then burst in and began making random arrests.

It was time for us to go, a bottle of Bollinger under each arm, we followed the trail of the absent Recorder over the stile into the safety of the paddock and turning to look back at the flashing lights of the police cars, we could still hear the occasional crash and shout, the sirens of the ambulances arriving, the distant sobbing and crying carried clearly to us by the still summer air.

Oh dear. Life can be so cruel. My heart went out to them. How could it have happened? What a tragedy. All that planning and effort. All that money down the drain. Pauline's big day ruined. Ain't it all a bloody shame.

Chapter 2

I went to my pigeonhole and took out a solitary brief.

What's this? Theft? Shop theft? Sent to the specialist in serious crime. Fucking Freddy and his idea of a joke? Theft of salmon from a local store. Tinned salmon. I read the instructions on page one. French loaf, packet of biscuits, frozen dinner, all in his basket - John West in the pocket of his coat. I was tempted to throw it away.

Stopped by security and offered to pay. All a big mistake. Distracted by the disappearance of his wife. I leant against the wall and idly turned the page. But what's this? Professional man. Licensed conveyancer. Intending to privately pay. No legal aid certificate. No forms to fill in. No pages to count at so much a bloody page. £1,000 on the brief and refreshers at £500 a day.

Well. This is more like it. Theft of salmon eh? Something serious. It might have been sardines.

I turned to the witness statements. The usual manager's statement written for him by the police. The lady cashier. A couple of store detectives. The arresting and interviewing police. I could spin this out for days. And that's only the prosecution - what about the defence? Our middle-aged defendant. And all the character witnesses, to say what a good bloke he was. Mates in the cricket team, grateful customers, his aged mum, the folks next door. People who would speak of his kindness, his unstinting work for charity, the esteem with which he was universally regarded, his dislike of salmon in tins.

"What are you doing with that?"

One of the younger female members of Whitebait Chambers angrily reached out her hand. Short black hair, black suit, black stockings, matching black glasses, one lip curled in contempt.

"Pinching other people's briefs?"

"It's in my pigeonhole." I tried to pull it away.

"Read the name on the front."

Another Cranmer Carter & Co. spectacular. I should have known. Destined for someone other than Wallace, she took it from my hand.

"Snooping about in other peoples' pigeonholes are we? I shall report this to Giles. That's if we ever see him again; if he ever decides to come back."

But what's this? We were surrounded by boxes on the floor. Boxes that I must have picked my way through to make the studied approach to my pigeonhole and, concentrating on what turned out to be a mirage in pink ribbon, had distractedly ignored.

Boxes and boxes. Dozens of them. Boxes containing papers. Boxes comprising one gigantic brief. Boxes from London Solicitors boldly stencilled with 'Wallace'. Boxes belonging to me. The product of a recommendation? Somebody scratching their head and thinking of Wallace. Somebody in Moghul & Co., my London solicitors. Never heard of them. Thank God they'd heard of me.

"My dear, really. Do you think I've got time for that?"

She stood looking at my boxes.

"Come on." I'd noticed the strapping thighs. "You can give me a hand with this."

So we dragged them one by one up to my room and stacked them against a wall.

"Bloody hell Harry. I'm sorry about the other. That's the biggest brief I've ever seen."

Me too.

"Oh really? Terrorist case you know." I fondly patted her bottom. "You can keep your tin of sardines."

But I didn't find it so easy. Not when I'd stripped off the sellotape and lifted blocks of paper held together with treasury tags and arranged them in some sort of order onto my thankfully empty desk.

Category A.	Surveillance.
Category B.	Telephones.
Category C.	Computers.
Category D.	Fountain Road (The bomb factory).
Category E.	Explosives.
Category F.	Mohammed Mohamed Ali.
Category G.	Ahmed Gulzar.
Category H.	Iftiqhar Khan.

On and on it went. I read the summary. Thirteen people arrested at various places in London and the home counties, at work, at home lounging around, walking down the street, waiting in a take-away – handcuffed and jerked to their knees.

"I am arresting you for conspiring in the instigation, preparation, and commission of acts of terrorism. Do you understand?"

I turned to my client's response.

"Yes."

"Is there anything on your person that could cause injury to other persons?"

"No."

"Is there anything in this area that could cause injury to other persons?"

"No."

"Is there anything in a car nearby or an associated car that could cause injury to other persons?"

"No."

"Do you have any information about anything, anywhere, that could cause injury or danger to other persons?"

"No."

"Where do you live?"

"Hoe Street. Walthamstow."

"Is there anything in those premises that has the potential to damage or injure other persons or property?"

"It is where I live. It is where my family live. My children live there."

"So it's another no?"

"Yes."

"This jacket. This jacket you have discarded on the ground. I have recovered from the breast pocket a memory stick. Call it Exhibit P.D.1. Is it yours?"

"Yes."

"Does it have a password or encryption on it?"

"No."

"So what does it contain?"

"Destinations in America."

"What sort of destinations?"

"Holiday destinations."

"So you were thinking of taking a holiday in America?"

No reply.

"I want you to know I have called a bomb disposal unit. You will remain here until they have finished their examination of the area. Is there anything you want to say?"

"No."

And they had searched his house. The home he shared with his father and mother; his brothers; his brothers' wives and children; his own wife and children; and an aged senile aunt.

At approximately midnight every family member had been removed, including children, and taken to a designated hotel in a street nearby. No one protested. They had all been too terrified and confused. Placed in police cars in their pyjamas carrying an overnight bag they had been driven round the block not knowing when, if ever, they would be permitted to return.

Next morning the team moved in. I read that the house in Hoe Street was a large four-bedroomed terrace house at the end of a commercial street containing offices and shops.

Scene plans were drawn. Bedrooms, communal rooms, kitchen, bathroom, hall, attic, garden, even an out-house given numbers and photographed by Scenes of Crime.

Computers and computer equipment were numbered, marked and taken away. I skim-read some of the exhibits.

Computer Tower - shelf 2, cupboard A, room 12.

IBM ThinkPad Laptop and battery - on top of cases, 2600 Series Switch from table, room 12.

10 mega Predator External CD/RW drive and cables - from under table, room 12.

Internal IBM DWD Rom drive - under stock of CDs from left hand corner floor, room 12.

Mobile telephones were seized, numbered and photographed.

Sony Ericsson - top shelf bedside cabinet B, room 10.

Nokia - built-in book case shelf 2, room 9.

O2 Sim card - built-in book case shelf 1, room 9.

The list was endless.

And then there was the literature on bookshelves in his bedroom, a couple half-opened under his bed.

SAS Personal Survival Handbook - shelf 1 of bookshelf A, room 3.

The Stories and Virtues of Shuhadaa of Sheeshan - shelf 2 of bookshelf A, room 3.

Dharb-1-Mumin newspaper of 13 December 2001 - shelf 2 bookshelf B room 3.

The Signs of Rahmaan in the Jihad of the Afghan - shelf 3 bookshelf B room 3.

Soldiers of Allah – shelf 4 bookshelf C in room 3.

Everything was numbered, photographed, catalogued and taken away.

Miscellaneous correspondence, bank statements in various names, audio tape, keys, expired passports, applications for new passports, a quantity of CDs, notebooks, excess baggage ticket, rolls of film, Sony digital camera, binoculars, shipment invoice in left-hand pocket of leather jacket behind door in room 3, floppy discs, leaflet concerning job opportunities at Stanstead Airport, two pepper sprays in holders under bed A in room 3, knuckle-dusters cupboard C room 3, flight tickets to Pakistan.

I read the statements and looked at the photographs. The preliminary statements and photographs. The detail would come later once the mobiles had been analysed and linked, and the computer memories broken down. Why did a young Asian Muslim need three phones, three bank accounts, two computers, two passports, a load of radical literature and tickets to Pakistan?

No doubt my solicitors would tell me. No doubt Mr. Iftiquar Khan would tell them.

But why had he said nothing when interviewed by the police for day after day after day? If there was an explanation why not give it? Why not own up to what was his and deny what was not?

Why not help the police with their enquiries if only to eliminate himself? Unless. Unless of course he knew what was in the computers and knew that his assorted mobiles might link him to all the others. Only he knew whether the bank statements pointed up unusual movements of money, what the keys fitted, what the pepper sprays were for, and what the literature contained.

Fact or fantasy? A terrorist or an impressionable fool living out a dream? I looked at my boxes with satisfaction.

Only time would tell.

Chapter 3

So where was Giles? Apparently he'd not trod the trail of the wary. Something had detained him. A sense of duty? The hope of ingratiating himself with a bridesmaid? It's something we might never know. And not something he was in a position to tell us. He'd spent the night in a cell.

An agitated Doreen rang up from reception. "It's Mr. Baring on the phone, Sir. Says he's been arrested. Wants you to represent him in court."

Cases flooding in.

I walked round to the Magistrates and went down to the cells to find Giles cooped up with many of his fellow guests from the celebrations of the night before still wearing their crumpled wing collars and morning suits, rather the worse for wear.

"What's the charge?"

"I'm innocent."

"Yes. I'm sure you are Giles. But what are you innocent of?"

"Violent disorder. Assault occasioning actual bodily harm. Assault with intent to resist arrest."

"What happened?"

I had a fair idea. Not only his legal counsel, but possibly a witness as well.

"I went over to stop the trouble. Somebody took a swing. Tried to save a lady. Misunderstood my purpose. Took a swing at me as well. Forced to defend myself. Police misconstrued the situation. Some fool put me in an arm-lock. Damn near broke my arm. I may have struggled to get free. Handcuffed and chucked in the van. Interviewed at five this morning. Denied it obviously. Charged and brought down here."

"A travesty of justice." It's what they like to hear.

"Glad you agree. I want bail immediately. I want all charges dropping. An apology would be nice."

"Yes, well. One thing at a time. Do you have the charge sheet? Any papers? Statements? A preliminary summary of the case?"

"Nothing." He looked round at the other guests. Apparently unrepresented. "Neither have they … nobody has … what fool called the police when everything was under control?"

"So what's their defence?"

"Same as mine. Nobody actually fighting. Nobody assaulting anybody. Everybody defending themselves."

I made my way up to court to meet the prosecutor, what is termed a Higher Court Advocate, confining his work to the lowest court. I seemed to recognise him. Vaguely familiar features. Yet another guest? Ah. I remembered an interview for pupillage at chambers. An unsuccessful interview, I hadn't seen him since.

"Potter. How nice to see you. Glad to see you're doing so well …"

"Hello."

"I represent Giles Baring in this nonsense. You know, head of Whitebait Chambers."

"I know."

"Wants bail. I don't suppose you've any objection?"

"No objection."

"Wants these charges dropping."

"Does he now?"

"An apology would be nice."

"Yes. And he's going to have to make it. Not that'll do him much good." He sat down in the prosecutor's usual position, the right hand corner of the front of the advocates' benches and stared stonily ahead looking at the clock.

All the personality of a gatepost. I remembered him well - and if I might repeat the simile - his wooden answers in interview with the pupillage committee; his all too predictable response.

"What made you decide to apply to Whitebait Chambers?"

"I was born in Hull."

"Ah, a local lad are we?"

"Lived here all my life."

"Yes"

"Went to school here as well"

Well he would do wouldn't he.

"Carried on to read law at university."

"Let me take a wild stab … could that be … in Hull?"

What do they know of England who only know of Hull?

"And er .. I suppose it follows … now that you're qualified you'd like to work in … Hull?"

Oh dear. I wonder where he takes his holidays. If only McIntosh were here. He wouldn't hesitate to ask. Bugger it. It was one of those things looming over us like a giant albatross about to plummet onto the deck.

"And er … when you go on holiday - if you do - where do you usually go?"

"Withernsea."

Ah. The Withernsea adventure. It's takeaway pizzas and burger bars; caravans rolling away to the distant horizon. The night-life. The seaside gardens, toy boats bobbing about in the litter on the lake. The seashell museum. The souvenir shops along the promenade. Little crowds with white faces puffing away outside the pub; only their fingers are brown.

Giles was at a loss.

"Er … do you like Withernsea?"

"Doesn't everyone?" he said.

"So, er .. moving on … now what would you say was your biggest fault?"

He seemed surprised. I didn't blame him. The pupillage committee was fond of questions like this. I think they got them from some pamphlet prepared by the Bar Council, but whatever its dubious provenance, it seemed to have him stumped. And then he remembered. A rueful grin spread over his pockmarked face. He held out his grubby hands.

"I'm afraid I bite my nails."

And he still did. They were almost down to the quick. Shuffling those papers; those dreaded papers that marked the extinction of Giles.

I joshed him along, loosening the bricks, forming a breach in the wall.

"Not much of a case is it? Bit short of evidence. Sort of thing in the old days we'd get the silly buggers to shake hands and then fuck off."

"I take a rather different view." He was holding his papers with those sullied fingers rather too close to his chest. "You do realise the amount of damage that was done? And there's a victim in hospital. A lady, plugged into life-support according to the police. Some gorilla in striped trousers smashed a bottle over her head."

So. Rather a different account to that described by Giles. Rather more like the version I had witnessed, albeit from a distance, myself. This case wasn't about to go away in a hurry. I trudged down the stone steps to the cells to break the news to Giles.

"Doesn't look too clever" I told him. "Thank God it's the only place in Yorkshire that doesn't have CCTV. They seem to think that somebody having what they regard as, a remarkably similar appearance to your good-self, bottled a lady."

"What's the description?"

"A gorilla in striped trousers. They'll be wanting an identity parade to see if you get picked out."

Giles quickened his pacing up and down.

"Surely they don't think …"

"Rather afraid they might."

"Who's prosecuting?"

"Higher court advocate. Some clown from the CPS. One who applied to our chambers. I'm afraid you turned him down."

"Jesus Christ …"

"So rather unlikely to drop it in the circumstances. But you know the score. He'll hang on to it until the last minute hoping for a guilty plea and then the day before trial he'll lose his bottle and return it to some barrister in Leeds who'll say he couldn't possibly take it because he knows you and regretfully must send it back to be passed round the circuit until some tosser volunteers from London …"

"Probably some tosser with no work. Why else would he come to Hull?"

"Precisely. And then he'll prosecute up hill and down dale like crazy in his anxiety to impress."

"Oh God." Giles sat down on the stone windowsill in the corner. "This doesn't look too good. Have you told Abigail yet? She'll be wondering where

I am. I expect she might notice the empty place at breakfast ... I expect she failed to observe my footstep on the stair ... I expect ..."

"How much do you want her to know?"

"Everything. Tell her the truth."

Yes. Well. I'm beginning to wonder what that is. And so apparently were the Magistrates when they finally filed out onto their bench to listen to Potter as he gave his account of the case.

"I'm seeking an adjournment," he told them, "the investigation is still at an early stage. The police need time to pursue their enquiries, there are witnesses to be seen, a victim detained in hospital in critical condition fighting for her life. There may well be other charges. Graver charges. There may well be more defendants. Many more defendants. But at this stage at least I have no objection to bail."

Giles strode back to chambers.

"Insufferable. Banged-up all night with Tomkinson's fucking relatives. Pauline's lot - the other side. A chamber pot in the corner and no access to a lavatory. No toilet facilities before my appearance ..." he fingered the bristles on his chin, "... and where were you anyway? You and McIntosh. I thought you were right behind me ..."

He glared around at a strangely empty chambers.

"And what about the conditions on my bail. Why didn't you speak up? Were you representing somebody else as well? Curfew 7 to 7, not to go into licensed premises, surrender passport!"

He ripped off the remnants of his collar. "I ask you. Daily reporting at the local police station, not to approach witnesses - who ever they are. Security for fifty thousand quid! I could have done better representing myself."

Much more of this and he will.

"Look Giles. We have to do this thing properly. Get you a solicitor, arrange for him to take a proof, sort out legal aid - unless you are privately paying? No? I thought not. Arrange to see witnesses, make some enquiries of our own. You know the form, we have to do it right. And by the way, where was Mrs. Baring, er ... Abigail? I don't recollect seeing her last night."

"Out with friends. She had better things to do."

Odd choice of entertainment. I wouldn't have missed it for the world. I tried to distract him, creating the impression we were working on his case.

"First things first. A solicitor. Obviously not Cranmer Carter & Co. Possible conflict. You never know what Pauline might say. What about Robin Parmenter & Associates? They're pretty good. Up-market, professional, a touch of class. They don't send us any work, of course, but this could be an introduction. Let them see what we can do."

"Why not?" Giles sat down heavily in my chair and put his head in his hands. "Oh yes why not use me as your introduction. Take advantage of my own outrageous misfortune to further your own fucking ends."

"Giles, how could you? It's the last thing I would do."

I arranged to meet Robin in the Stag at Bay for a liquid lunch, after I finally got past his secretary and explained who I wanted him to represent and what I wanted him to do.

"Certainly, old boy. What a good idea. Baring you say. Is he still your head of chambers? See you there at one."

That's a thought. Of course Giles is still head of chambers. Technically, that is. But where does this leave him? Up on charges for disorder and assault. What sort of image is that? What might the Bar Council have to say? Should he be suspended? Advised perhaps to voluntarily step down? Cede the honours of his office to another? Another beyond reproach whose conduct hitherto was blameless. I leant back in my chair, after Giles had shuffled off, and put my feet on the desk.

Another of unimpeachable reputation, with contacts in London; with one fucking enormous brief. Someone with out-of-town friends, who knew how to buy a solicitor a drink. Somebody with talent, imagination, an irrepressible touch of flair. I lit a cigarette and inhaled deeply, my hands behind my head. Somebody with persuasive powers, who could sniff the smell of opportunity a mile off, sense a trickle of blood in the water and move swiftly in for the kill. I decided to have a word with McIntosh. Was it time for somebody else?

Chapter 4

I met Robin promptly in the lounge bar and slid over a double gin and tonic with, at his suggestion, a little ice and a slice of lemon. He was impeccably of the old school wearing black and stripes and stiff collar with what I took to be yet another regimental tie; a straight parting to the left with white swept back wings at the temples, a hint of brylcreem, a touch of musk. He reached out a shaking hand to knock back the first of what turned out to be many, and gave me an encouraging smile.

"Funny thing Harry old boy, I was thinking of sending you a brief when there you were, out of nowhere - completely out of the blue - suddenly there's my secretary putting you through on the phone."

"Have another Robin?"

"Don't mind if I do. Got a wonderful client; just the case for you. A lovely girl. Name's Clematis. Clematis Fotheringham. Ever heard of her? Runs her own business. Computers, web sites, digital something or other. Bit of trouble over a car."

I'm not too sure about this. What do I know about computers and modems and what is it called? Netting the surf. Next to nothing. And what do I know about cars? Even less. On the other hand I can hardly reject the first brief he's ever offered to me. How could I refuse to help a 'lovely girl'?

"Delighted Robin" I heard myself saying. "Computers a speciality. Civil work right up my street."

"It's like this. She owns, or did own, a rather expensive car. Ferrari. You may have seen it about."

"Er ... not recently."

"Hardly surprising as some chappie's pinched it. Pushed a note through her front door along the lines that he's the owner and now he's taken it back."

"Really?"

"Yes. Funny business. Apparently she bought it from some outfit in London. Up-market sort of place. Everything pukka. She's got the log book, MOT, service record, the lot. But this chappie says it's his. Stolen from his house months ago. Looking for it ever since. Traced it somehow or other to our Mrs. Fotheringham all the way to Hull. Took it from her drive, so he must have had a key. Headed notepaper in the letterbox. Count Potolski or some such. Even left his address. Somewhere in Chelsea. What do you think? Is it theft?"

"Well er ... Robin old chap ... why not have another drink? Need to check the authorities. Need to remind myself of the law. Get back to you right away. On the face of it almost definitely – on the other hand if he's claiming ownership ... says it's his ... what if it really is? Need to sue the garage who must have purported to guarantee it. And the finance company if there is one. Sue as many as possible. Count, probably phoney, Potolski. Sue as many as we can. My advice, my preliminary advice that is, we sue the bloody lot."

"Excellent. Yes I will have another. Set up a conference as soon as possible. I'll ring her as soon as I get back to the office. Which may, of course, be some time from now. Charming girl, I'm sure you'll like her ..." he clapped me on the shoulder, "never had much time for Whitebait Chambers. Giles Baring and that lot ..." We stood smiling at each other. "It's funny, as soon as I met you, yes same again, I knew I'd got the star of the show."

As soon as I staggered back to chambers I went to find McIntosh in his room - packing up, unfortunately, getting ready to go home.

"What do you know about cars and hire purchase, guarantees and linked transactions?" I tried to explain the case.

"I'm meeting the client tomorrow. Apparently fucking furious. And, if it's possible, even more fucking rich. Wants immediate action. One of Robin Parmenter's. How should I draft the claim?"

"Stick to crime" he advised me, "a Ferrari's an expensive car. This could be tricky ... claim of right ... linked transactions ... consumer credit ...

interlocutory relief … Let's go to the Stag at Bay. Why not buy me a drink?"

That place might as well be my office. I fell once more through the door.

"And what about Giles? I've heard it might be serious. What did Robin have to say about him?"

In truth, next to nothing. It's funny how time flies.

I lit a cigarette and tried to placate what I found to be his rather surprising concern.

"Don't worry, everything's in hand. Awaiting papers. The investigation still proceeding. Managed, and it wasn't easy, to get the silly bugger bail. I was wondering … in the circumstances … do you think he should stay as head of chambers? … perhaps another … a different hand on the tiller … somebody who could command a groundswell of support … with … with a better, more wide-ranging practice … an introduction to new solicitors … more experienced, more a man of the world …"

McIntosh interrupted me with an embrace. He gripped me by my shoulders. "Of course I'll help you with your case. And thank you Harry. Thank you for your support."

What was he talking about? But I knew what he was talking about. Man's eternal dilemma. Do I make a dash for the power of office? or am I to be swayed by the whiff of easy money in the conduct of a very nice case. Possibly the first of many. Mrs. Fotheringham, the lovely Mrs. Fotheringham, a portent of what was to follow and here was McIntosh offering to do all the work.

"You could go for immediate recovery. Get a court order. Apply immediately for interlocutory relief. Take the quick route. Soon over …" he polished off his drink, "… on the other hand you can't lose whichever way you go. Sue him in damages. An order for costs and interest. Join in the garage and whoever sold it to the garage, probably the thief, and join in any credit companies, this is a linked transaction … yes I wouldn't mind another … one of them's to blame - let them sort it out amongst themselves."

I weighed up the niceties of the case as I understood it. A quick result and transitory contact with Mrs. Fotheringham regretfully reflected in my fees. On the other hand a long drawn out battle with many conferences, lots of contact with both Robin and my client - my soon to be grateful client - a huge bill for damages, interest and costs from which I could extract a wholly merited slice.

"Er … let me see … it's difficult … must do what's best for the client … better safe than sorry … yes …" I hope I made the right decision, "McIntosh draw me up a claim for damages. Join in whom you like. It may take a little time as I understand it … but I must do right by the client, and Robin of course, it won't do to forget him. Yes, I'm decided. Better the tortoise than the hare. We'll go the way of damages. You get on with it. This could turn out to be a very nice case. And er … of course …" we clinked glasses together "you know you can rely on me."

I met Mrs. Fotheringham three days later and was immediately reassured as to the correctness of my difficult choice. Robin showed her into my hastily tidied room. Dark suit, bobbed black hair, very pale skin, a flash of white teeth, a hint of sandalwood, the glint of diamonds - I shook her hand and ushered her towards my very best chair, a Victorian reproduction with cabriole legs and buttoned back. She sat down, crossed her legs, lit a cigarette and watched me with concentrated dark brown eyes.

"I want my car back. How long will it take?"

"Ah …" I made a pyramid with my fingers, "… not so easy. This Count Potolski, or whatever he's called, says it's his. We call it a claim of right. He says, presumably, and of course we've never met him, that he can establish good title and for all we know this might be right. It would therefore be expedient to include a claim against your garage and whoever sold it to them. Breach of a warranty of good title …"

I squinted at McIntosh's draft claim. I wish I could read his writing. "Breach of an implied warranty of quiet enjoyment …" What the Christ was he talking about? "Don't worry. Leave everything to me."

"That's what I'm paying for. Robin says you're the best."

"Oh yes. Very kind of you." I acknowledged Robin with a graceful wave of the hand. "Done many cases together. Can take time. You must be patient."

"Ah yes …" I spread my palms in sympathy, "the law can be regrettably slow."

She uncrossed and re-crossed those lovely legs. Size five shoes and three-inch heels. "It's worth about £150,000. I need it for my business. For God's sake, I need it to get around. What about damages for that?"

Christ this bloody handwriting.

"Breach of an express and/or implied term of the contract and/or representation materially inducing the contract. Damages for loss of amenity … interference with er … don't worry, leave it to me."

"And my husband. Rodney you know … Parmenters handle the legal work for his company …" Robin inclined his head, "…he's had a lot of extras fitted. Stuff it never had before. New music system, sophisticated satellite equipment, computers, a cabinet for cocktails ... this is a collectors item, far more than the book price. Make sure you take account of that. And of course I need transport. Had to hire another. Thought I'd try a Lamborghini - £300 a day. Don't forget ..." she kept altering her position, forever moving those legs, "...make sure you claim for that."

"I will. I will. Of course I will." I pretended to take a note.

"And then there's the contents." She flipped open a small bag, "I've got a list. It's in here somewhere. Yes. Fur coat, five and a half thousand, mobile, suitcase and contents, including jewellery box, call it another ten, camera and camcorder, rainproof jacket, leather boots - calf length of course, shooting stick, some assorted tack. Here ..." she threw the list towards me and it slid across the desk.

Christ. Oil tankers run aground for less. I looked at McIntosh's, by comparison, rather paltry claim. Back to the drawing board. He won't get my support unless.

Chapter 5

There is a new procedure. It's called an S.51, Narey Hearing. The Magistrates or District Judge (he used to be called a Stipendiary) doesn't even read the papers. That's if there are any. Serious cases, and a terrorist's pretty serious, they send directly to the Crown Court without the bother of committal. I sort it out instead.

Moghul & Co. finally gave me a call. "It's listed tomorrow in the Bailey. See you there."

I found this very disquieting for several reasons. Obviously they had no knowledge of procedure. So how much crime had they done? They were supposed to obtain a list of all cases about a couple of weeks in advance. They were supposed to read it. To check out if any of their cases were to be heard, and if so, notify the barrister's clerk. Not the barrister. The clerk ran the diary and made all the arrangements. He tried to get the instructed barrister to the case, and if this was either impossible or undesirable, made sure it was covered by another barrister and the solicitor was informed.

To ring me the day before they must have assumed I was immediately available. What if I had been locked in a trial? Was I supposed to drop everything and wave my present defendant goodbye? Did they imagine I only did one case at a time? Their case involved 13 defendants with thousands and thousands of pages of evidence, enquiries were still proceeding, any trial was months, if not years, away. What was I supposed to be doing in the meantime? It was obvious. Crouching by the phone waiting for a last minute call.

I went downstairs to the clerk's room, Jackson's old room, still unoccupied by a senior clerk. We had been advertising, arranging interviews, discussing percentages, remuneration, holding interminable meetings and here we were, months later, still depending on an office junior and no permanent appointment in sight.

I wonder what Jackson would have said. "Mr. Wallace, you want Mr. Wallace? In the morning? Did you say the Bailey? Do you realise how busy he is? Do you expect him to drop everything? Sorry, Sir. Very sorry. That's not how you do things. Not the name of the game. No, Sir. Mr. Wallace is unavailable. He has prior overriding commitments. Very serious cases. Out of the question, I shall have to try, and it won't be easy, to get somebody else to do it instead. Let me see. Mmm. I have a very promising junior. Mr. Browne-Smythe. Very highly regarded. A very busy man. I might be able to get him there. Then there's Mr. Makepiece. Happens to be clear tomorrow. What did you say, is he very experienced? Enough to do a mention in the Bailey. Enough to do a last minute case for you. What did you say? Thousands of pages. How do you expect him to read all that? Sorry, Sir. Quite impossible. You'll have to meet him early in the morning. Yes. At some corner café. Name again please. What did you say? Café Bleu. Corner of Ludgate Circus. And you'll be there will you? With a summary. And some idea of what you want him to do. 7.30. It's the earliest he can do. Yes. Yes. And in the future. Allow me to tell you. I want plenty of notice for a man like Mr. Wallace. No. Certainly not. As soon as you get the listings call me on the blower and I'll do my best to get him there. That's the way we do things. That's the name of the game. What did you say your name was? Yes. I'm taking a note. That's the way it works. No. 7.30. No. Makepiece it is. I assume he'll find you there. Sorry. No. Impossible. Out of the question. Goodbye."

Happy days. Now I found myself trying to tell the office junior that I had to drop everything and catch the London train.

"But Mr. Parmenter's been on, Sir. Reminding me about a conference. Said you told him you were available. Very important client. I've already fixed things. In court in the morning and a conference fixed for Friday afternoon. Mr. Parmenter said you insisted on it. Wanted to see the client again. For some reason wanted to attend at her house. See the locus in quo. The drive where the car was stolen; the letterbox that swallowed the note. Something to do with security and insurance, you wanted to prepare for every possibility, couldn't predict the defence."

Had I insisted on it? It all seemed a long time ago. The lovely Clematis Fotheringham and I whiling away a pleasant afternoon.

"Cancel it. Set it up for next week. Return my other cases. What? How many did you say?"

I have never understood it. However many cases I had since Jackson left, be it twenty or two, they always, inevitably, it couldn't be an accident, got listed the same day. I know he was doing his best, or at least I thought he was. But why was I free for long dreary days one after another and then every case listed in the morning, the same morning, at a variety of different courts?

"Sorry, Sir, you've got an arson in York. I'll have to return it. Yes, Sir, and a rape in Leeds. No, Sir. Sorry, Sir. There's stuff in Hull as well."

And now I've got this. In London. Unreliable and obviously inexperienced solicitors instructing me in the best case I've had for years, dragging me away to the Bailey - there was no question I had to go - and all my other cases - very sorry, Sir - I'll have to get somebody else.

I took the evening train and caught up on my reading. Evidence had been arriving every day. It would take me hours to sort it into its various categories and then arrange it into lever arch files under the various types of evidence: statements; interviews; explosives, computers, mobiles ...; miscellaneous ... it made my head ache and left my mind in a blur. I could hardly find my way to the pub. And now this, I suppose it was inevitable, but it made a dent in my fees. I read the solicitor's letter. Moghul & Co., on expensive notepaper, the list of partners, associates, specialists, consultants, subsidiaries, offices in Karachi, Dubai and New York. If only their work was as good.

"Our client has expressed grave concerns. He has heard about likely sentence from associates in Belmarsh. Are we really talking 40 years?

His co-defendants have obtained the services of experts in terrorism ... Oil Court Chambers ... you must have heard of them ... busiest chambers in the Temple ... Oh yes ... experts at almost everything ... they seem to be representing most of the other defendants ... already instructed Silks ... that's right ... also from Oil Court Chambers. No. No. The defendant and his family are very happy with you. No. No. Don't worry. But they also want a Silk. Essential. If we are to keep the case. Yes. Yes. Do an advice immediately ... Can I suggest Oil Court?"

Let me explain. When I first shot down to London to meet the client and his family, they'd never heard of Silks, what we call Queen's Counsel or a Q.C. What they wanted was a barrister and I more than filled the bill. But obviously the defendants had been talking amongst themselves. They had little else to do. And sooner or later one of them, or more likely a solicitor, had suggested they appoint a Silk. And why not? If this case wasn't a Silk's case, what was?

The prosecution would certainly have a Silk. A Silk leading several juniors, and certainly the most prominent, the most heavily involved, defendants would have both a Silk and a junior. Now it seems, just like children in a sweet shop, everybody wanted what someone else had got.

So Mr. Khan wanted a Silk did he? Just like all the rest. No skin off my nose. I had rather wanted to do the case personally. Outshine all the rest with the quality of my cross-examination ... I sat back and watched the countryside fly by ... my erudition on the law, the complexity of my submissions, the glory of my closing speech ... Now all this was to be snatched away from me as I was relegated to the second row. Crouched behind the lever arch files of my own making watching some exaggerated ponce displaying the paucity of his talents while I did all the work.

I might as well admit it. I've got a thing about Silks. It's not because I'm not one. Actually I've never applied. Too many forms to fill in and too much money up front. Jackson had tried to persuade me in the days when he thought I might be some good. He'd sent away for the forms and handed them over to me to complete.

I remembered sitting in my lonely room leafing through the pages. I'd actually made a start. Set out your gross annual income for the previous five years. Recite in the space provided your ten most important cases in ascending order - not forgetting to include the result. Nominate five referees from currently sitting judges familiar with your work. I was beginning to have misgivings. Describe on one foolscap page why you wish to be a Silk. Include on no more than two foolscap pages, examples of your legal submissions from named cases made in either the Court of Appeal or House of Lords.

Set out any leading cases in which you have been involved which substantially changed the law. Provide a list, limited to ten items, of papers and publications you have either researched personally or to which you have contributed.

I remember crumpling up my application and throwing it at the door.

Thus I had never applied for Silk, and every year was flabbergasted when I read the list in *The Times* and *The Daily Telegraph* on Maundy Thursday of those appointed - not surprised at their promotion, but that they had ever applied at all

What a mob. The gall of these fellows. The self-important narcissism that had induced them to laboriously fill in their forms, curry favour with the judges, suck up to their referees, fill in their giant cheques. Now of course they could discard their stuff gowns, throw away the ordinary clothing of lesser mortals, and parade in their Silk with shiny waistcoats and enormous cuffs. The public flaunting of their mundane talents rewarded by the return of monstrous fees.

And now apparently I was to have one. Earning twice my money, doing half the work, and the pleasure of bossing me about. I don't think so. If there is to be a Silk in this case I'm going to choose him, and I know exactly what I want. Oil Court Chambers can whistle. There's no such thing as a specialist in terrorism. I'm having someone I know. Someone, and there are a few, I respect. Somebody who actually does know the law, can understand the case, and yes, I have to admit it, is a better advocate and does a better job than myself.

I sat brooding as the train rattled along. Instead of claiming the fees of a leading junior - leading a junior less experienced than myself - my fees would be reduced to that of an ordinary junior being led. No matter. Look on the bright side. If I picked the right leader - and I wanted someone who did the work himself - I would have considerably less to do. Possibly nothing at all.

I could doze behind the ramparts of my lever arch files safe in the trenches far behind the front, stirring myself occasionally to pretend to take a note and amble off for lunch. So by the time the train pulled into Kings Cross Station, I felt reasonably mollified, if not satisfied, and had sketched in the names of one or two fellows I felt it might be prudent to approach.

A 'runner' met me on the platform. I saw him walking along the train gazing into first class. I'd finished off in the buffet and so was able to satisfy his expectations by sliding across and stepping down, as if surprised to see him, from the leading coach.

"Mr. Wallace, Mr. Wallace ..." all smiles as usual, "so glad you could come. I've arranged a video conference with the client in the morning, I expect we'll be in court until well into the afternoon, and then we can fit in another conference with his family - there are some you've not already met - and I've set aside this evening so that we can go through the details of the case. We have of course to draft a provisional defence statement and the family are anxious about your application for bail."

I put down my suitcase and juggled with a sheaf of papers. Hull seemed far away. Appointing a Silk didn't sound a bad idea after all.

Chapter 6

Giles called an Extraordinary Chambers Meeting in what had now become our rather tatty recreation room. I was tired of either leaning on, or sitting under, the pool table and McIntosh and I arrived early and pulled up two easy chairs, the only easy chairs, and set them ominously at the front.

Of course I had stepped aside gracefully to give McIntosh precedence and had abandoned my ambitions in order to satisfy his. We had discussed tactics in the Stag at Bay. I was to rise immediately and set out, with many an expression of regret, the impossibility of continuing under Giles.

I was to propose a vote of thanks to Giles, thanking him for his wise counsel, his tireless work, his inspirational guidance, and his selfless commitments on our behalf. Setting out a long and exaggerated list of his achievements. His ambitions for the future. Sadly now, by reason of matters beyond his control, regretfully postponed.

A hand-wringing, yet cut-throat, performance. I was to turn to the blushing McIntosh, his eyes modestly downcast and propose his nomination in ringing tones. The dawn of a new era. A fresh and vigorous hand upon the tiller. Distant horizons of excellence now within our grasp. We had decided I was to hint at the possibility of Giles' return once his little difficulty had been despatched. Fat chance. With McIntosh in, and me the power behind the throne, there was no way he was coming back.

My eloquent proposal ringing in their ears Humphrey was to rise as seconder to caution against unseemly opposition, wounds were to be healed, matters of difference confined forever to the past. Before anyone could move against us a vote would be called for and before any resistance could be marshalled, McIntosh would be in - and Giles, dear Giles, poor old Giles, would be out.

McIntosh would stride forward, a purposeful glint in his eye and take his rightful station by the sink brushing aside Giles' sodden papers he would address us as to the tragic circumstances of his unlooked for promotion and thank us for what he knew would be our unqualified support.

"Thank you all for coming ..." Giles was bumbling about near the sink, "... this is a sorry day for chambers. A tragic lamentable day. As you all know, I have been accused of criminal offences. It is insufferable. It is outrageous. It not only casts a wholly unjustified slur upon my good self, it also reflects upon these chambers ..."

"Hear. Hear." I tried to struggle from my armchair.

"I will not countenance any attempts to traduce either Whitebait Chambers' reputation or mine."

"Hear. Hear." I wasn't quite sure what we were cheering about.

"We are the victims of some foul calumny which I assure you will be exposed in all its falsehood and which, brandishing the sword of justice, I promise you I will, inevitably, vanquish and destroy. Have no fears, no doubts, no second thoughts, no moments of wavering in the blackest hours of the night, your leader I, Giles Baring, shall prevail."

"Hear. Hear."

He held up his hand to stay their enthusiasm.

"However. There are dangerous times ahead. Unforeseen challenges. I have, thanks to the intervention of Wallace, been virtually confined to house arrest. My liberty has been outrageously fettered. My freedom of movement insufferably constrained. My powers of concentration temporarily diverted to the conduct of my own defence ..."

"Hear. Hear." McIntosh tried to manhandle me to my feet.

"In these parlous times for chambers, is it time, perhaps, to 'drop the pilot'? I have decided to temporarily stand aside ..." McIntosh had me up at last. I raised my hand as if in protest.

"No, Henry ... my mind is made up ... I have thought long and hard ... chambers' welfare takes precedence over everything else ..."

"But Giles ... I ... er ..."

"No Henry. I thank you. But not now. It is too late. The die is cast. I am resolved. I have already made the appropriate appointment. The hour has brought forth the man ..."

As if on cue, Pickles, the man in the silver suit appeared from nowhere at his side. "Horace here has volunteered himself, after much persuasion, to take on the task. His shoulder henceforth shall be applied to the wheel. I cede my title, temporarily, to his care. He shall be referred to as acting temporary head of chambers. I have informed the staff. I have written to all our instructing solicitors. Horace henceforth shall, temporarily, assume my mantle. Might I, on behalf of all of you, wish him every success with his task."

McIntosh and I sat rooted in our isolated easy chairs as cheering broke out from the back.

"Thank you." Giles blinked around him. "Thank you."

"Horace will take over. For my part I wish him well. I extend my congratulations to Horace in whose experienced hands I feel confident your welfare is assured. I step down temporarily from a position of high office it has been my humble privilege to occupy through long and arduous years ..."

"For Christ's sake fuck off." McIntosh whispered to me under his breath. I wasn't sure whether he meant me or was referring to Giles.

"I stand aside now - temporarily - in order to concentrate on the rout of my accusers," he ran a hand through his tousled, yet thinning, hair, "... goodbye and farewell."

We heard him stumbling down the stairs as Horace, eschewing the draining board, spread his papers under our noses on the pool table and fixed us with a tight, sardonic smile.

"Come to order. There are matters of importance with which I have to deal. Do you two have to sit there in the front?"

Chapter 7

McIntosh withdrew from my case. Not my case exactly. The case of Fotheringham versus The Rest of the World. Things were growing very difficult. The garage in London where Clematis had made her original purchase of this obnoxious car, had unfortunately bought it from another garage, who in turn, you guessed it, had bought it from a third. Some of the transactions involved finance and the representations of third parties who, it was claimed by one or other of the defendants, were acting as unauthorised agents making misrepresentations for commission on their own behalf.

I sat at my desk, the floor littered with files in the terrorist case that I hadn't found time to read, and put my head in my hands. How many defendants in Fotheringham had we accumulated? Count Potolski, 1st defendant, the original garage, 2nd defendant, some finance company or other, 3rd defendant: then there was the second garage and another finance company, then some seedy individual from the East End, and then another garage and another finance company. I should have taken the easier, quicker route - but costs were mounting and it was too late to change.

I meandered down the corridor to consult McIntosh and found him sitting grimly alone, reading yet another notice from our temporary over-active deputising head.

"Dear Members,

Certain matters of a financial nature have come to light. Naturally I do not wish to bother Giles. Attend please, if you will be so kind, this Saturday morning at an Extraordinary Meeting of Chambers, 10 a.m. prompt at the Oddfellows Hall, rear of Fishmarket Road."

I lit a cigarette and McIntosh had a cigar.

"This has the marks of another rise in contributions," he snapped.

I couldn't understand it. We got rid of Jackson (actually he resigned), to cut our costs. Without him we were supposed to save his not insubstantial fees.

"Why are our contributions always going up?"

"Jackson ran a tight ship. Checked the bills. Had the wit to turn off the central heating in the summer. He knew how to charge and how to make them pay. But Giles. With all his honesty, accurate figures, and no petty cash. Well …" McIntosh shrugged and blew a plume of smoke at the ceiling, "… not surprised we're in a mess. And Horace is the man with not the slightest clue of how to put it right."

"About this case old chum."

"What case?"

"You know. The small matter of a car."

"Not so small now though is it? What have you got, seven defendants? Or is it eight?"

"Nine."

"Not to worry. You're bound to win against one of them. It can hardly be your client's fault. And when you do - get the unlucky bugger to pay the costs of all the rest."

You cannot imagine the relief I felt.

"Is it really that easy?"

"Of course it is. Somebody must be at fault. Stolen the car, or handled it, or negligently gave it a warranty of title it so obviously didn't deserve. It can't be your client. It must be somebody else. Who cares who it is so long as they can pay?"

He was right of course. I could see it immediately. I didn't really need him to explain. Sue the lot and let them sort it out amongst themselves. Claim substantial damages, loss of amenity, interest and costs. I really ought to do more of this work. An absolute piece of cake.

Bugger Giles and Horace and the rest of them. I was going to ring Robin. The time had come to give Mrs. Fotheringham a call. And I didn't need Robin getting in the way, oiling about between us, constantly interrupting my flow.

"No Robin" I told him, "couldn't possibly impose upon you. Leave it to me. No trouble. No trouble at all."

I went round that afternoon on the pretext that I had won against all odds an important case that morning and found myself suddenly and unexpectedly free.

"So this is the drive?"

"Yes."

I took in the curving row of limes leading from the huge gilded wrought iron gate, disappearing into a hollow which presumably sheltered the house. Mrs. Fotheringham had met me in the avenue and opened the gate by remote control.

"So where exactly was the car?"

"Is it important?"

"Vital."

She was wearing a simple cotton shift-dress in grey, matching mules, no stockings, a dab of lipstick, and that glorious scented swinging glossy hair hanging free.

"Somewhere along here ..." she scratched her head, "... obviously. Possibly nearer the house ..."

I walked behind her taking in the view. A glimpse of a close-cut lawn between the trees, a grove of rhododendron, a small lake with a fountain playing, a stone terrace, Virginia creeper edging up the wall.

She paused with her hand on her hip. "Somewhere round here. Sometimes I like to walk through the garden and leave it to the help to put away."

"Do you have many servants?"

"Nothing out the ordinary. Is it important? I gave them the afternoon off. Now ..." she gazed about her, "... somewhere round here. Maybe ... a little closer to the house ..."

"I need to see the letterbox."

"The letterbox? Why?"

I smiled reassuringly. "It's called the locus in quo."

"Is it really? And I suppose you'll need to see the carpet in the hall where it landed, and the table in the kitchen where I open my mail, my small study in the back where I filed it, and the room where I read it to Rodney upon his unexpected return."

I looked at her and smiled.

"Yes. Well ... we have to be thorough ... be prepared for all unforeseen eventualities, no stone carelessly left unturned."

"I agree."

We loitered in the porch way, the slanting sun reflected from the leaded windows, she bent over towards the heavy panelled door.

"Letterbox is at the bottom ... unfortunate really ..." her bottom brushed against my striped trousers, "... no wonder the postman has a problem with his back ... it takes a bit of forcing ... you have to push against the spring at the back of this flap." She tensed her legs with the effort. "There ... that's how I imagine he did it ... slid the letter inside ... just about right there ..."

"And, er ..." I breathlessly suggested, "... it must have gone right through ... finished up on the floor in the hall ..."

"Must have done, mustn't it? Would you like to see inside?"

What do you expect me to say? It's not necessary. Seen enough already. Feign a glance at my watch? Goodness me, is it really 3.30? How time has flown. Got to read some papers in a case about terrorism. Shake her hand and say 'goodbye'. Crunch off down the drive? Wave as I disappeared round the bend?

"Yes, that would be lovely ... essential actually ... follow the trail to its end."

She looked back at me and smiled, those tiny white teeth flashing, as she applied her shoulder to the stiff metal hinge.

"Here, let me help you." I leant across her and, as we pushed together, Rodney opened the door.

"Mr. Wallace." He held me in his handshake, his huge shoulders bulging, the sweat rising from his singlet which he no doubt wore to throw around his weights. "Fancy finding you here. Got home unexpectedly The early flight from Zurich. Thought I'd go for a run. Saw you from that hill. Seemed to be having trouble in the porch."

"It's the locus in quo."

"Is it really? Why is this important to our case?"

"McIntosh insisted on it. He's my assistant. Fine man. I respect his judgement, even if prone to the pop. Necessary to be prepared for any sudden unexpected turn of events." I wished he would let go of my hand.

"Come in. Come in..." he ordered, "...the least I can do is offer you a drink."

We stood there in the kitchen and as he turned to open a bottle, Clematis almost imperceptibly narrowed her eyes.

"Montrachet 98. Needs drinking now. What do you say?"

What do you say to that sort of thing? I'm sorry it's not good enough. I'm tired of Burgundy. Throw it down the sink.

"Fine. Fine. That will be lovely." I nervously patted my waistcoat and found my cigarettes.

"Sorry old chap..." he clapped me on the shoulder with that giant fucking fist, "...smoking's not allowed. Injurious to health. Clematis and I like to keep fit."

I bet you do. I looked at the oak stumps bursting out of his muddy shorts, the hairs growing on his shoulders, I thought of him in bed with Clematis. She was lucky to survive.

"Good God, is it 3.30 already." I found my watch where he'd pushed it up my arm. "Got to read some papers. Another very important case."

"Don't think of it dear chap. Have another glass. Stay to dinner. Chef's doing mountain goat."

I had to get out of this place. I thought of leaving by a window. Possibly a closed window. Rodney must have seen me looking about.

"Like the place do you? Too bloody big for us really. Just me and Clematis and the servants ..." he put his arm round her shoulders and affectionately crushed her to his chest "... I'm not here often enough ... always having to leave her ... always flying away ... aren't I darling? Not to worry, can't wait to get back."

I banged my glass down for the second time, and taking advantage of the distraction, got into the hall.

"Terribly sorry. Another time perhaps."

They followed me to the door where they watched me struggle to pull it open until Rodney curled his little finger round the latch.

"It's been lovely meeting you." Without thinking I held out my hand. "And thank you Clematis, if I may call you that, thank you for showing me around."

"It's a pleasure." She slid forward and took my other hand.

And whilst Rodney kneaded my knuckles, I felt a nail, the discreet polished nail of Clematis's index finger slowly cut across my other palm. It was there. Unmistakable. Our eyes met for a second. I love it. Come to daddy. Treachery. The warm earthy smell of deceit.

Chapter 8

Whilst I waited for my next cluster of cases to be listed together, and whilst I toyed with fantasies featuring Clematis, and tried to get Giles off the phone, and forget about fucking Horace and his memos, and watched the clock and thought of the Stag at Bay, I decided as a distraction to get down to work.

Moghul & Co. had been bothering me with questions. Had I decided on a Silk? Where was the draft defence statement? Had I framed a bail application yet? Might they have some advice? Did we need experts? Other defendants were collaring the best. Did we need our own fingerprint man? What about D.N.A? What about explosives? Did the alleged bombs, the improvised explosive devices, actually work? And what about telephones? There was evidence (was there?) of 'clustering' around significant events. And what about Pakistan and Saudi Arabia? There were travel documents, passports, excess baggage and unusual withdrawals from what was alleged to be an 'operational' account. Should they travel to Islamabad and check his destination out? And what about his relatives? He would have to account for his movements. Why was he there when other co-defendants were also hanging about? Had they gone to a training camp together? And if not, what was he up to? Who had he visited and when? What was the purpose of his trip? He said he had gone to get married, or was it just to interview a bride?

His friends and relatives must be seen and statements taken. Could I get them legal aid?

The prosecution alleged a conspiracy to murder by exploding miniature bombs in bottles held against the walls of pressurised cabins of transatlantic flights to America as they flew over cities beneath causing maximum loss of life and, of course, inevitable death to themselves.

Were they deadly professional killers or disillusioned impressionable young men living a fantasy, acting out, as Moghul & Co. would have it, a joke?

I started to read the Islamist literature recovered from his room.

The Islamic Ruling with regards to Killing Women Children and Elderly in a Situation of War. Abdullah Yusuf Azzam.

'Islam does not urge its followers to kill anyone amongst the Kufaar except the fighters and those who supply Mushrikeen and other enemies of Islam with money or advice. That is why there is no need to kill women because of their weakness unless they fight.   Children and monks are not to be killed intentionally unless they mix with the Mushrikeen in such a way as to make it impossible for the Muslims to fight without killing them. This is the opinion of the Shafi'ees and the Hanafis.

The scholars have unanimously agreed it is just to kill a Muslim woman if she is taken and used as a human shield by the Kufaar. So why forbid fighting the Kufaar because they have their women and children with them? Are they not shields too? More so because they are willingly there. They provide comfort and solace. Do they not deserve to suffer too?

Is the sanctity of Mushrik women greater than that of Muslims? No. They that share the company of the Kufaar also share his death.'

So that disposes of any innocent civilians then. I flicked several pages ahead.

'The objective of most people is to have gold and silver, the company of servants, a beautiful house in which to live. But what does a pile of dusty bones and decaying flesh do with a golden necklace? The martyr's wealth is more valuable and enduring. For martyrs will live in the Gardens of Eternity, beneath them rivers will flow, they will be adorned with bracelets of gold and wear green garments of fine silk and heavy brocade. They will recline on raised thrones.

For those who love women remember that even the most virtuous and beautiful woman of Adam urinates, menstruates and defecates from the part you most desire. She coughs, spits and vomits from the place you long to kiss.

They are but dust compared to the women prepared for martyrs. They breathe the breath of a thousand roses. Allah has promised there will be companions with beautiful big and lustrous eyes - like unto well-guarded pearls. A reward for the deeds of the past. The women of paradise. One who loves women must chase martyrdom like a cheetah chases prey. A suicide bomber commits an act of merit and such a person will be a Shaheed.'

Did he really believe this stuff? Obviously. Enough people had died.

I flicked open copies of another book.

Love of Life and Fear of Death. Shariffa Carlo.

'It is upon us to raise our daughters to love a Mujahid husband. It is upon us to have daughters who will raise sons for Jihad for the sake of Allah. To be mothers who will sacrifice their sons. We must raise our sons to be fathers who will fight for Allah.

Let us stop loving life and fearing death. O Allah return us to the honourable state of loving You and loving sacrifice for Your sake and treating this life as a stranger - fighting to keep strong while not fearing but welcoming death in doing so. Ameen.'

Scrawled at the side, presumably in what would turn out to be an identifiable hand, were the words, 'Subhavallah' and an encore 'Ameen'.

Possessing wasn't believing. He was entitled to be curious. He was at liberty to consider other ideas. This was a free country in which the freedom of speech was supposed to be protected. He could read all he wanted. I admired his tenacity as I gratefully closed the file. He could agree with none of it, some of it, all of it, and change his mind in the morning. Whatever was his pleasure - he was free. Or was he? The exercise of freedom is subject to restraint.

The prosecution could and would use it as evidence against him. That is why I had 432 pages of it in a file. I could see what was coming. Carefully chosen excerpts included in a jury bundle. Days and days of reading out the worst. And the questions when he finally, as the Americans say, took the stand.

Do you believe in this? Do you believe in that? Why did you keep it in your bedroom? What do you feel about the justification for killing children? Do you accept that Kufaar women have to die? And what does that say biro'd into the margin in what our expert is sure is your hand? Repeat it for the jury. Ameen is it? Sounds rather like Amen."

The exercise of freedom no doubt carries responsibility, does it carry punishment as well? The evidence a jury can take into account in deciding whether he was a terrorist or a curious, if somewhat silly, boy.

"Do you believe in martyrdom? The sort of thing this text seems to recommend. Do you or don't you? And what about the women of paradise? Apparently waiting to sit by your throne, feed you sweetmeats, do duty in your bed. Do you believe in them? What have you written in the margin. That same biro that we know belongs to you. How many do you get? The women without earthly biological function. Those women with the lustrous eyes and sweetest breath. A reward for blowing thousands of people to pieces. Do you think that's what you get?

Do you believe the Koran forbids the killing of women and children? Do you? So why have you underlined the advice of prophets who argue against it? Yes the same biro. Mushrik women deserving of death. And yes another, of course another, hold it up for the jury, another 'Amen.'

Pauline was on the telephone, and glad of the diversion. I took her call in my room.

"Is that you?"

"Yes."

"What are you doing?"

"Reading a case. Considering the complexities. Becoming depressed."

"Do you know what time it is? I rang the pub. They searched the premises. Of Wallace, not a trace. Thought you might be lost."

"No Pauline. Looking at a case. Thinking for a change. You know the game. Black guys kill for drugs; white guys because they're drunk; the Chinese kill for profit. These guys kill for faith."

"Who cares? The police came round to the house. Our house. Mine and Charles. Think about it. The first visitors to our new home - I showed you the photos, overlooking the Wolds. The first knock on the newly-wed's door turns out to be the fucking police. Thank you very much."

I couldn't work this out. Why was it my fault? Once again Charles the injured party. Charles slopes away scot free.

"Pauline. It had nothing to do with me."

"Didn't it? One of your friends. Some twat with a hunting horn got his cock out for a joke."

"What Giles. I don't believe it."

"No. Not Giles. I doubt he's got one. Some big bloke in your party. Caused a lot of offence, and I'm not surprised. Why didn't you stop him?"

"Because I wasn't anywhere near him. Remember the seating plan? The man in the last seat in the tent."

"Well Giles came across. I put it in my statement. Giles did his bit. Tried to stop them fighting. Got his body in between. Where were you? What were you doing? Never there when you're wanted. Hiding I supposed. Cowering under a table. Getting yourself fucking pissed. Why didn't you help him? He got himself arrested. Cuffed behind his back, dragged off to the nick."

What should I tell her? I'm not very big, I don't like violence, I'd just lit a cigarette, visiting the lavatory, looking for the waitress, ordering another drink. True or partly true? Totally false. I wanted it to last forever. I wanted Charles to get drawn in. Possibly Pauline. Down in the mud rolling about in her dress. The whole fucking lot of them. Parading in a country church, pretending piety they never had. Funny money and phoney food. A marquee and lanterns, the distinguished bloody guests. I loved it. A total disaster. Smashed chairs, the wedding cake knocked over, splintered glass, the screaming and shouting, I wished it would never end.

"Anyway. I wanted you to know since you're supposed to be representing him. I put it all in my statement - insisted I write it myself - Giles totally vindicated. Apart from Charles, the only gentleman there. And don't apologise. I'm not interested. Just so that you know. I won't be around for a while. We're leaving this afternoon. Taking our time, going round the world. Nile cruise, safari in Africa, Maldives, Hong Kong. Thanks for fucking nothing. Get a message to Giles."

It was hard to get back to fundamental Islam. I thought of them laying back on recliners round the pool, attending the captain's cocktail party, dancing under the moon. Charles with his slouch hat and binoculars surveying the Veldt, standing up in his jeep, Pauline urging him to be careful, sunglasses parked on top of her head.

The twinkling lights through the portholes of their stateroom, their casual indolent love. A breakfast tray in the morning sitting up in bed.

Dust compared to the women prepared for martyrs. Those tiny calculating eyes. The Star Ferry labouring through choppy water on its way to Kowloon. Lazy lunches with chopsticks; the ladies' market, the night market, the flower market, the bird market. Their liner easing away into the South China Sea. Well-guarded pearls. The breath of a thousand roses. A reward for the deeds of the past.

I looked at my ticking clock slightly askew where the cleaner had dusted it on the wall. They couldn't find me could they? Did they think I was lost? I was lost and I had lost, but now - I pulled on my jacket - I'd had enough.

I pushed aside my papers, enough of this, I was going 'looking for work'.

Chapter 9

It was time I rang Clematis. Got back to the basics of the case. Establish the fundamentals, explore the nuances, drive home the inevitable conclusion, bask in the satisfaction of a job well done.

"Hello. What took you so long?"

"I've been looking up the law. Checking out the authorities, making sure of the procedures, covering any weakness, trying to guarantee success."

"Perhaps you should have done that before we started? Anyway ..." she laughed that hesitant throaty chuckle, "... maybe it's time we had another look at the drive."

We met in a village pub overlooking a duck pond. The usual place adorned with ploughshares and rustic prints. Pretentious and twee with a smiling inhospitality and a strained hush in the dining room, where couples, on a rather different mission, ordered their organic bangers and mash.

"When do I get my car back?"

I loved the way she was forever moving her legs, fiddling with her hair, dabbing at her lips.

"Scratched the Lamborghini on the gatepost. Rodney's not exactly pleased."

"Well ... the car ..." it was hard to concentrate, "... as soon as we set the case down for trial. Unfortunately rather a lot of defendants to accommodate. Some travelling an awfully long way. Might need a special courtroom … some of them … cheeky bastards from London … have lodged a counterclaim."

I watched as she crossed and uncrossed her legs. "Apparently Rodney's stopped the payments. So now we're pleading 'set-off' according to my assistant. Never seen so much bloody law."

She knocked back her double gin and placed her empty glass under my nose.

"Some preliminary matters listed for argument … I have to draft the pleadings. Robin's got some enquiries to do."

"The car …" she leant forward and fiddled with the buttons on her blouse, "Rodney wants to know. Give me some idea when."

"When? Good question." I summoned the waiter and ordered another round. "Not long now. A couple of months should do it. How is Rodney by the way?"

"Charged off this morning. I heard him banging around downstairs. Dubai or somewhere. Back in a couple of days."

"Really?" Time for a bottle of wine. I never knew a case could be so interesting. I stressed our strong points, derided my opponents for their baseless optimism, explained how I would overcome their paltry arguments, squeezed her shoulder reassuringly, patted her knee in encouragement, was moved to comfortingly stroke her neck.

I scratched my car on the same gatepost carrying its yellow badge of honour from its brush with the Lamborghini the day before and pulled up with a flourish sending a spray of gravel into the stoop of the huge front door.

"Fancy another drink?"

Well what do you think? We tottered down the hall, her heels clicking against the flagstones, and fell into the warm kitchen, the heat rising from the vastness of the Aga and leant together against a long refectory table, her head lolling on my shoulder, her tongue nervously licking her lips. Lustrous and well-guarded pearls. A reward for the deeds of the future? We tentatively drew together.

I managed, at last, to forget the fucking car.

Chapter 10

It is a matter of common knowledge that the best, indeed the only way, to forget, a fickle woman is to replace her as soon as conveniently possible with someone else. What matter if she's slimmer or fatter, younger or older, funnier or richer, more refined or educated, obsessed with style or fashion, more interested in sex. For better or worse, she's different. Whatever her faults or virtues - she's somebody else.

I decided to concentrate on Clematis. She had beauty, style, money, smoked and drank, interested in law, civil law that is - more accurately the law of compensation as it affected her. More importantly, apparently interested in me. For how long? Who cares. She was available, immediate, belonged to the here and now. All I had to do was pick up the phone and suggest a conference, dab some 'egoiste' on my chin and I was off. A strong but thankfully absent husband, deaf, blind and loyal servants, we had the run of the house. The kitchen, the master bedroom, I know it well, the marble tiles of the bath. The sauna, the shower, Rodney's sturdy desk.

I forgot the terrorist, neglected my pigeonhole, stopped counting the defendants in our case, refused to speak to Giles, avoided chambers' meetings. Ignored the admonitions in the frequent notes of Horace Pickles. Forsook, is it possible, the attractions of the Stag?

More familiar now with the Halfway House - a modern pile of open plan, halfway on the road to nowhere - the Duck and Drake at Chipping Barrow, the Pestle and Mortar overlooking the green at Burton Cross, the home of the silent restaurant and nervously scraping plates, bowling along in the scratched and dented Lamborghini, the wind flying through our hair. Large eyes, soft lips, the pop of the stud on her cami-knickers, I thought I had it all.

But did I?

Even during our laughing conversation, as we raced along in the car, before breathlessly falling upstairs together, my mind strayed back to that dyed blonde head leaning over the front rail of some liner far away, as it ploughed across the sea. It disturbed my tranquillity, frayed my nerves, wormed into the apple of my happiness, worried away inside me. What was she doing? And even as I made love, beautiful tender poetic graceful love with Clematis, I wondered what she would say.

I saw her looking down at us, sardonic at the predictability, dismissive at feigned passion, indifferent to the result.

Not such a commonplace of knowledge then. I had a different woman haunted by the memory of the past.

And of course she sent me postcards. Why? Were they only for me? Or was I, as usual, part of some job lot. I read the dashed and cursory messages.

'Passing through the Suez Canal.'

'A beach hut just like ours.'

And enigmatically, why? A hidden message? 'Charles sends his kind regards.' Possess the body. Try and possess the mind. I tried to concentrate on Clematis. One has to be polite. Did she have children, now grown up and far away?

"No. We have no children. Neither Rodney nor I."

"Oh dear. Well not everyone wants a family …"

"But we did. We needed both the distraction and the sense of purpose they provide."

"Yes … well of course … that's right …"

"But none ever came along and Rodney grew impatient, I don't blame him, so of course we did the tests, and it turned out to be me."

"Well they can do anything these days."

"No they can't. A popular misconception. Certainly not for me. So we threw ourselves into business. Our separate businesses. And we both turned out a success. Perhaps it was inevitable, we had nothing else to do. Apart from jogging that is. And building this lovely home ..."

We subsided into the goose down and lit our cigarettes.

"Rodney doesn't like me smoking. But I had to start again - not that I didn't want to - to cover the smell of you."

Better change the subject. I guided her back to the home.

"The paintings? Yes they are original. Should be in the bank, but Rodney insists they stay on the walls. He's got a passion for it. That and the sculptures, his ceramics, his stamp collection and God knows what else. What a monument to futility ... you see the wardrobes? Full of clothes, my clothes, designer clothes; I've got a passion for clothes, and Rodney likes me to look my best ... the shoes ... have you seen my shoes? What a collection, mostly Jimmy Choo."

A passion for this, a passion for that. What an abuse of the English language. I've got a passion for passion. I ran the polished nail of my index finger slowly down her spine.

But she wanted to talk. Wanted to flesh out the partner of her fantasies, wanted to talk about me. What about Laura? Did it take long? Do I miss her? Always. Of course I do. A long and lonely journey without her - dogged by the desertion of another - I lay back on those fragrant silky sheets propped up on one elbow and tried to explain as I blew smoke rings at the sky.

Tell them only as much as they need to know. What they want to know. What they like to hear.

I invented a fiction which I began to believe was true. A deep and lasting love doomed to disappointment by the disparity of our interests, the diversions of our ambitions, the attraction of someone new.

"No, of course not." I parried her questions. "Nothing like us. Nothing like you and I. We're much more spiritual. Intellectual. Bound together by instinctive understanding the physicality ..." (almost bestiality) I scratched the flat and muscular stomach, "... the fundamental sexuality of our love." It seemed to placate her, but only for a while.

And my ambitions? She needed to plunge into the obscure, probably non-existent, reasons for my life.

"A judge? Is that next? Will you become a judge?"

What sort of judge I wondered. I let my hand wander.

A district judge sitting in some draughty chambers of a lonely provincial court sorting out the custody of children, the division of paltry possessions, the custody of small-time crooks.

A circuit judge? A man in a wig and blue uniform sitting up on the bench presiding over serious work, delivering judgment in civil cases - I thought of the car - summing-up before a jury. A man with paid holidays and a pension. A man no longer independent. A slave to targets, hours, and figures. A man told what to do. Did she mean that?

I heard her sigh and raise her body imperceptibly.

Or a high court judge? Wigged and robed in London sitting in the Strand. Ferried around the circuit by a chauffeur, attended by a butler, dining at his lodgings, My Lord to all he surveyed. My Lord Wallace, Wallace J., Wallace L.J. Baron Whitebait. Is that what she wanted, wanted for me? For her? For us? I knew what she wanted. She turned into me, eyes closed, lips parted, the breath of a thousand roses, I reached to touch a petal, and ambition, past fictions and future prospects quietly dissolved away.

Chapter 11

I read how to make a bomb. It was all on his computer, downloaded from the internet. The formula and where to get the ingredients, just like making a cake. How to bring the components together, how to set a primer, when to detonate the charge. Little diagrams. Warnings to be careful. Alternative sources of supply. Click on and find it. A short cut to paradise. Pavilions of splendour, sparkling fountains, splintered light. Breathe the breath of a thousand roses. Sink into those lustrous eyes.

Jas tapped me on the shoulder.

"Mr. Wallace. Mr. Wallace. I'm back."

"You look tired." He loomed over me and took me in his arms. "You've been working too hard …" he inspected the ashtray, "… smoking too much ... not eating enough …" we embraced each other, " … how are you dear old friend."

God I was glad to see him. Why had he taken so long?

"Mr. Pickles told me to share your room." He looked around him - Fotheringham strewn as ever on the floor; Iftiquar Khan, piled up in lever arch files taking up a wall.

"Great to see you Jas. Nice suit." I pinched the material of his waistcoat. Those ostentatious heavy chalk-stripe suits the younger bar seem to favour, tailor-made, with spare trousers and a waistcoat - it must have set him back two grand.

"You're looking good," I playfully punched his arm and nearly broke my wrist. Christ he was strong. He must have been in training, filled out by at least two stone. I looked up into his beaming face.

"What took you so long?"

"A few things needed sorting. Had to arrange some funds. Mr. Pickles tells me I'm your pupil. When do you want me to start?"

"Pull a desk in. Park yourself in the corner. Do you see this?" I nudged Fotheringham affectionately with my foot. "Put it all together. Get it in some sort of order. Read it through ...." Who needs McIntosh?

"Could take you forever. Spent hours on it, one way or another, myself. Let me know what you think."

God it was great to see him. His happy presence; that giant mind; his ready humour - all at my beck and call. A winning team reunited. Well, not exactly a winning team, but a team reunited nonetheless.

"Just check it out. I'm fairly satisfied I've covered everything. Let me know what you think." I reached for my jacket and clapped him on the shoulder.

"God it's good to see you."

"And you Henry."

We stood smiling at each other. I thought back to that meeting months ago when Giles was still in the chair. Why had I harboured misgivings? Would he bring us work? Would he fit in? Had he any special expertise? Of course he had. Being my assistant. Sorting out this mess. Giving me his unqualified support. I shrugged on my overcoat and tightened up my scarf.

"Make yourself at home. Got to nip out for a moment. Conference with a client." Ah, the warm inviting smell of freedom. "Study it carefully. Let me know what you think."

I clattered down the stairs and away into the fading sunlight torn between Clematis and a drink.

It's good to have a pupil. A recipient of my accumulated knowledge. A subject to tutor in the art of advocacy. Someone to carry my bag. I skipped across the cobbles. I might let him look at the terrorist case. Check the categories. Log the pages. Write the bail application. Settle the schedules Read the pages of dross.

I headed for the car park. What a lovely day. I could introduce him to Moghul & Co., take him to conferences with the client; a unique insight into what a terrorist stood for, whatever moved him, if it did, to cruel excess. Jas would know the secrets and pass them on to me. Jas would sort out all the mounting pages of statements, exhibits, surveillance logs, forensic reports and the rest. Jas would get it into order. Tell me the weaknesses and strengths. Did we need a Silk? I doubt it. I eased the car into the traffic and headed for the bridge.

Jas would give me his opinion. Give Fotheringham a look over. Arrange my other cases and tell me what they were.

A weight the size of a piano slid from my shoulders. I joined in a song on the radio. Wound the window down and breathed, it seemed like ages, the scent of the countryside air. That long slog in St. Albans had not been for nothing. It had brought Jas and I together in admittedly unfortunate circumstances. But now that little local difficulty had receded into the past. I raced the engine and lit another cigarette.

In my mind's eye I could see Jas rearranging the furniture, tidying up the bottles, decanting an ash tray out of the window, setting up his desk, laying out his no doubt impressive array of law books ... picking up Fotheringham and giving her his best.

Ah Fotheringham, Fotheringham, wherefore art thou Fotheringham?

I slewed the car into her drive and was greeted by Rodney in shorts and singlet who obligingly changed direction and, effortlessly keeping pace, jogged along beside.

Chapter 12

Pauline and Charles invited me to dinner at their lovely house in the Wolds. I was getting used to countryside driving and was able to find my way in the dark. I should have taken a taxi. Somehow I couldn't see Charles showing me into a guestroom and sending up a breakfast tray. I faced an evening's desperate drinking amongst strangers. But no matter, I could take a taxi home even though it would cost a fortune. On the other hand, I could always telephone Jas.

Converted stables, she'd told me. Some conversion. Towering stone, a clock tower over an arch, servants clustered under a lantern at the door ushering in the guests. Why was I here? To envy what they had?

"What are you doing here?" Pauline hissed at me as I was shown into the hall where a footman took my coat. I should have brought my invitation: 'Charles and Pauline request the pleasure of the presence of Mr Henry Wallace at a welcome home dinner following their happy return from a round the world honeymoon tour.'

"I thought you invited me. That's why you sent me a card."

"Well. Don't just stand there. There's drinks in the drawing room. Charles will have his little joke."

Did I know anybody? Not really. Not actually. And obviously none of them knew me. But they all knew each other. They always do. Boisterous booming voices of the landed middle-class. Talking about barley, the price of labour and the pleasures of the hunt. I sidled about on the periphery impersonating Banquo's ghost.

"Glad you could come." Charles pumped my hand enthusiastically resurrecting the damage done by Rodney and Jas. He looked around with satisfaction. "Know anybody? Let me introduce you around."

Desperately, that it should come to this, I searched for the Recorder of Hull.

We dined at a long oak table under a bright chandelier dripping glass. Silver cutlery set out in formidable rows foretold a night of many courses looming miserably ahead. But there was something about the room, its over-bearing panelling, the hardness of the chairs, the flitting silent servants, the scrape of cutlery upon china, the metallic bitterness of the wine. Conversation faltered as Pauline tried to put it right.

"Oh Rio. You should see it. Sugarloaf Mountain. The Statue of Jesus Christ. Have you been there? You should."

Not everyone could marry Charles.

"Not at all like Table Mountain. Charles and I, one morning we set out to walk to the top. Very bracing. You know how fit he is. Hours actually. Much further than it looks. Not much at the top. Scrub really. The view? Didn't see much of it. Seconds later down came the mist. And Mount Fuji …"

I was getting tired of this. We all were, but fascinated at the effort - mesmerised - I gazed at her with glassy eyes.

"Oh yes the west wing used to be stables. Original features. Preserved as much as we could."

Perhaps it was the ticking grandfather clock, the wind beginning to rattle the casement, the baying of distant dogs.

"What a shame. You've got to be going. Davies will get your coats. Two more courses. You really must try them. Figs in Greek yoghurt and honey. What's that? You don't like figs. Oh but these are different. Specially brought down from London. Totally different to those you get in a box. You don't like yoghurt either? Don't worry. There's always plenty of cream. What? Ten o'clock already. You've got to make an early start?"

The rain blew in gusts against the windows as the candles flickered and guttered on the table. A trolley was trundled across creaking boards to rest against the chair occupied by a silent Charles.

"Cheese, Sir? Which does Sir prefer? A carrot baton perhaps? Or a little celery and a grape?"

The trolley trundled onwards circling the remaining guests.

"Good Lord. 10.15 already. Afraid we've got to go."

Pauline sat at one end toying with the rings now cluttering her fingers, Charles at the other glowering into his glass. I remained somewhere in the middle separating Citizen Kane from his bride. The wind howled across the Wolds as the last car accelerated across the gravel and receded into the distance bouncing away to the gate.

"Bloody good party" I mumbled.

Pauline seemed to notice me for the first time.

"Thank you Henry. So glad you were able to come."

We drew up our chairs to the dying embers of the fire. There's nothing like travel for broadening the mind.

Chapter 13

"I'm not very happy with the way this Fotheringham business is going." Jas tapped the folder and frowned.

Nor frankly am I.

"What's wrong with it?"

"You'd better get hold of Mr. Parmenter. Check he's done the research. Make sure they're all in funds."

"Why shouldn't they be? Garages, hire purchase companies, the bastions of bloody British enterprise, some count who lives in Eaton Square. Why shouldn't they be?"

I don't like trouble.

"What's the matter with you? What's it got to do with us?"

"Somebody's got to lose. We know that better than most. And when they do, they pay the costs. It would be nice to know they can."

"Of course they can. What's the matter with you? All right. All right ..." I could do without this. "Tell Doreen to get him on the phone."

"It's funny" said Robin when she put him through, "Every time you call I was just about to ring you. Forget Fotheringham. More trouble than it's worth. I don't know what you've done to offend Rodney. The fool's been on from New York, complaining. About you. Every time he comes home he finds you skulking about in his drive. Wants to know what his drive's got to do with it. According to you it's central to his case. And his letterbox. And, apparently, the dimensions of his hall. Anyway, forget it. There's something better. Far more important.

"Fuck Fotheringay. I've got something right up your street. Wouldn't normally touch it. Probably legal aid ..."

Solicitors are always the same. A bit like builders. Once they've started a job they bugger off to look for something else.

"... I suggest we meet in the Stag. Let's say twelve o'clock." I went along early. Better continue the good impression I was no doubt making, and be ready with the drinks. Robin burst in out of breath.

"You'll never believe it ..." his eye caught the double gin and tonic and he dashed it down in a trice, "... be a good chap. Anyway as I was saying, I've been impressed with the way you handled Fotheringay - meticulous attention to detail, nothing too much trouble, researching the background, visiting the site ... thank you I don't mind if I do ... piling up the price. But this is something else. Not something we usually do. Happened to be looking after his conveyancing, upwardly mobile, moving from east Hull to west. Killed a man ..." he paused to polish off his drink, "... or so it is alleged. Just for fun - some tramp in a doorway. Sleeping rough in a blanket, you know the sort of thing. Stove his head in with a piece of wood. Blood everywhere. Got rid of the weapon in a skip. A bit of history unfortunately; one or two nasty assaults. In and out of mental hospitals - or whatever they call them if any exist these days - a psychopath, obsession with violence and fascination with death."

I felt like a drink myself. But Robin was right, I was easier, more comfortable with something I could understand - back in the world of crime.

"I'll send round the papers later. What precious few we've got. And I've arranged a conference ... I say do you mind? ... a bit of travel, hospital for the criminally insane. He's been there before. Probably the same room, the usual table for lunch. Going tomorrow. Pick me up in the car ..." he knocked it back and banged his glass on the bar, "... bright and early, meet me at eleven o'clock."

"Are you sure about Fotheringay?"

"Oh bugger Fotheringay." I looked at him again, as we rested our elbows on the low brass bar and drank a mutual toast.

"How's Giles going?"

"Who? Who's Giles?" He seemed to have forgotten how this all started. Everything leads to something. The case that brought us together.

The reason why we are here.

"Oh. That Giles. Papers coming in - not had time to read them …" he raised his glass as if to wave goodbye, "… bugger Giles as well."

It was late when I got back to chambers and unusually, I could see from the street, a small light burning in my room. He was sitting behind my desk, his jacket slung over my chair, my cigarette box open, one of my cigarettes in his mouth.

He closed the file he was reading.

"Just brushing up on our terrorist, getting it straight in my mind …"

"Forget the terrorist. We're going to Rampton tomorrow. You can pick me up in your car."

Chapter 14

I boned up on the papers in the back seat as we bounced along in Jas's sports car. The dead tramp had slept in his own particular doorway, the same doorway - it must have seemed like a home - night after night after night. He had been garrulous, if dirty, small and friendly, a professional man with marriage problems, something about dishonesty, a decent man temporarily fallen from grace. His easy manners had made him popular, a favourite at cinema queues begging or selling the Big Issue - probably both - adept at playing the burger bars, surviving on a bag of chips.

The murder weapon - a piece of scrap 2" by 4" - forensically examined at the police laboratories in Wetherby was stained with his blood and brains. But nothing from the defendant, who had been picked up - it took time to work it out - because he had been identified on the inner city CCTVs going into the doorway and walking past a skip.

I went on to his interviews and read the headline. Queens Gardens Police Station. Mr. Pendlebury Eaves represented by Mr. Robin Parmenter. In attendance Detective Sergeants Woodford and Stokes. The introduction, the explanation of his rights, the caution.

"You have been arrested for the murder of a tramp er ... domestically challenged male person ... living in the doorway of a shoe shop in Ferensway,

Hull on the evening of Friday the 20th of September. He had been beaten to death by repeated blows to the head using a heavy piece of scrap timber that caused his skull to fracture with severe trauma to the brain. Death probably fairly instantaneous. Would you like to give us your account?"

Robin told me he hadn't coughed and Robin was right. He admitted presence but denied the offence.

"I admit to being in the city centre that evening. I remember it well. I had intended to attend a concert at the City Hall. The London Philharmonic. An evening of Vivaldi and Liszt. But my mood had changed. I couldn't fancy the mixture of baroque and exhibitionism and turned to the cinema by way of light relief. But the queue had been rowdy; beset by beggars and drunks. I decided upon a relaxing drink, possibly some small talk with a stranger at the Station Bar nearby. I had to pass the shoe shop and became aware of someone calling out. I peered inside, perhaps I shouldn't have bothered; some creature with a blanket round his shoulders, beard and benny hat, asked me if I could spare him a cigarette. I shouldn't have gone inside. It's kind of a little passage between display windows leading to the door - but I felt sorry for him, God knows why. I gave him a couple of Marlboroughs and he might have touched my hand. Surprisingly polite. I might have stepped on his blanket which became entangled with my foot. I pulled away, I admit it might have been fairly roughly but, I think you might understand, I was anxious to be off.

Anyway I left him. He seemed contented enough; walked away along the pavement, didn't notice the skip and booked into a hotel. Nothing fancy. A place used by adulterers and contractors. Pat's Place I think it's called. Near the theatre in the square. Went to bed early, suddenly I felt exhausted; woke up this morning to find you two banging at the door. No I didn't kill him. No, I've no idea who did."

It seemed remarkable that there was no forensic to link him to the weapon. Perhaps he'd been wearing gloves. But then there was no forensic on his clothing, no fibres, no body tissue, no red stains left by droplets of flying blood. Impossible. Quite impossible. I looked at the photographs of the body spread-eagled on the floor. Blood everywhere. Perhaps leakage of spinal fluid. But then I examined the head. The work of a maniac. Head smashed on one side. Livid marks and bruises, the left temple quite crushed in. How could his clothing, if he had been responsible, have avoided any trace? His shoes, those shiny black court shoes, the bottoms of his trousers pressed to a rigid crease, remain remarkably unscathed. Impossible. There would be blood, skin, hair perhaps, brains, something, if only a microscopic piece.

68

Unless he'd changed. But how and where? In the station? In a lavatory? He might have been carrying a package, apparently the video wasn't clear. But his skin. He couldn't change that. But he could wash it, take a bath or a shower, shampoo his hair, pay particular attention to his nails. He must have been meticulous. And lucky. Not to bump into anyone. Not to attract the attention of the proprietor as he booked him in at the small hotel.

Had they checked the desk? The ledger? Perhaps the stair carpet as he made his way to his room. Which room? I wondered. I think I knew them all. Was there anything on the handle of the door? The sliding Perspex of the shower? The window? The remote that controlled the ancient TV?

He had been lucky or, more likely, the Humberside Police had been their usual selves. So what was the evidence? Precious little so far as I could see.

Robin must have been watching me in the rear-view mirror, tired of competing with Jas over their assorted accomplishments, his attention drawn to me. "Keep reading" he ordered, "additional evidence. Shortly prior to charging."

"Ah. Ah yes. As I suspected ..."

We parked up and made our way through the usual security and set off walking, the three of us in good spirits, across what seemed a carefully cultivated park.

"The inmates do the gardening" Jas informed us, "they let them out to do it. Part of the treatment. Good for morale."

I'm not so sure about this. Psychopaths and murderers freely wandering about.

"Over there ..." Robin whispered, "... a man with secateurs. Christ another one with a spade."

We quickened our pace. "Where did you say this block was? The interview block. What did the guard tell us? Did he say block D?"

We fell into a doorway and tried to catch our breath as crunching feet approached along the gravel and eventually someone peered inside.

"You chaps seem to be in something of a hurry" he beamed genially, "allow me to introduce myself. Doctor Shipley. Anything I can do to assist?"

Is he? I looked at Robin and Robin looked at me. Casual clothes - boots, checked shirt and jeans. Hair tied back in a grey ponytail, beckoning us out with a smile. And, of course, wouldn't you know it, leaning on a spade.

"Do you have identification?"

Jas took over and examined the proffered card. "Seems to be all right

... head of convulsive therapy ... letters as long as your arm."

"We're not checking his qualifications," I told him. "Where's his white fucking coat?"

"Shouldn't that be fucking white coat?" The purported doctor finally abandoned his spade. "We are anxious here to avoid elitism - a feeling of them and us - it diminishes self-confidence and undermines self-worth, and can lead to unnecessary offence. Here we dress the same. Good for morale. Good for parity of esteem. An expression of mutual respect. We encourage the society of equals. What am I but a doctor? A man of some qualifications, a few publications, the author of original research. And what are my patients? They are those who lend me inspiration. My companions on a journey to what I may perceive to be the truth."

"Have you heard of Mr. Eaves?"

"None other than one of my patients."

"Can you tell us where he is?"

"Does anyone know where they are? Really know. Does ..."

Jas put a friendly arm round his shoulder.

"Straight ahead and first left."

We were shown into a richly-carpeted room.

"Tea?" Mr. Eaves addressed us. "Would you like some tea?" I sized him up as we sat down in an alcove of a nicely furnished lounge. Immaculate. Short fingernails, slightly perfumed hair. Now under medication and back in control. Showered, clean-shaven and impeccable with slightly protuberant eyes.

"Allow me to get you some refreshment. It must have been the journey. You look rather out of breath."

Robin introduced us. "This is your counsel, junior counsel, Mr. Wallace and this is his pupil, assistant and sometimes chauffeur, Mr. Jas."

We shook hands all round and settled down to wait for the tea tray that Mr. Eaves had ordered from a hovering nurse.

"Rather a nasty murder." I sought to break the ice. "Serious brain injury. Surprisingly ..." time to assert my authority, "... caused to that part of the brain on the opposite side to the blows."

"Yes. Very interesting ..." Mr. Eaves made a pyramid with the points of those immaculate fingers, "... called 'contre coup' I believe. You will find Mr. Wallace not so surprising after all. The blow or blows however many there are, causes the brain to ricochet within the skull smashing against the opposite side of the vault. Hence damage to the other side."

The tray arrived. "Ah good, chocolate biscuits. Let me help. Milk and sugar gentlemen? Or, like me, do you prefer just milk?"

So what was the evidence? The evidence that had resulted in a charge of murder and brought us all together sipping our tea through a hesitant silence in a hospital for the criminally insane. It was the police. Someone had had a bright idea. Little actual evidence, no forensic as yet, and definitely no 'cough'. They had rang up his brother and sister. In east Hull. Long suffering and running out of patience - would you like to pay him a call? And while you do, and while you talk to him - a police officer just happens to be passing, keeping well out of sight and recording your conversation and making notes in his notebook of everything you say.

"Ask him if he did it. We'll be recording his reply."

So his brother had gone to see him clattering down the steps and craning forward into the doorway of his cell had whispered the usual encouragement and support and eventually, after reminding him of his dead father and invalid mother had put the question:

"Pendy did you do it? Was it you who killed him? You can tell me anything. Tell me, was it you?"

And his sister had sidled forward and after suitable, if brief, expressions of affection had done what she had been brought to do. "Pendy love, you know you can trust me."

So two admissions then. Unequivocal. Unfettered by reservation, unqualified by excuse. "Of course I did. He deserved it. Dirty begging dross. Deserved everything he got."

"Mr. Eaves ..." I addressed him tentatively, my nerves already on edge, "... we face two difficulties, rather large difficulties, perhaps ... who knows ... ultimately insurmountable difficulties ... you seem to have admitted it might be you."

"Surely not. Have another biscuit. Entrapment. Members of the family, my family, charged with inducing a confession which in the circumstances cannot be reliable. Obtained in breach of trust. I was at my wits end. Violence upon arrest. Bruises and a broken bone in my hand and still waiting for the Police Surgeon to prize himself away from a dinner dance. No medication. I need my prescription to control my impulsive behaviour. My apparently delusive desire to impress. No food or anything to drink. I assume you have read the Custody Record. No blanket and freezing cold. My brother and sister offering their help and pressing me to confess. Suggestibility. Have you heard of that? The work of Gudjohnsson. Interesting research in Iceland. Very

71

interesting. A confession made in circumstances of physical injury, mental disruption, denial of food and medication, and family pressure couched in terms of affection, begging, almost begging, no doubt you have read the transcript? Anything to make me confess. How can that be reliable Mr. Wallace? How can you leave that to a jury? How can a judge permit it to be adduced? How can anyone say it can be reliable? Tell me the law. How in God's name will any judge let the Crown rely on that?"

"Er ... I don't know if Robin has any suggestions ..." he shook his head, "... well ... of course you're right. Outrageous. Entrapment. Not perhaps specifically forbidden. Frowned upon ..." Mr. Eaves frowned upon me, "... more than that. Potentially inadmissible. A fast moving facet of law. The latest authorities. Almost at my fingertips. The requirement of a fair trial ... due process er ... the demands of justice, the provisions of the European Convention now incorporated into English law Mr. Eaves ..." I finished in what I hoped Robin would mistake for a flourish. "Have no doubts! Leave this to me."

"I hope so. But of course we will have a Silk."

Not another one!

"Yes of course." These days we always do. I looked again at Robin I daresay he had somebody in mind.

"Chevalier de St. Croix."

"What? Is that a place or a person?"

"The finest Silk in England."

I'd decided it was a holiday resort. Somewhere south of Mablethorpe. Possibly facing France.

"Good old Chevy ... extraordinarily busy ... agreed to come up north ... would only do it for me ..."

"Can't wait to meet him ..." I clapped Mr. Eaves across his shoulders, I trust not too hard, "... a specialist in entrapment, on the inadmissibility of confessions obtained by deceit ..." I'm not too sure about Robin. I don't want to be critical, after all he had the good sense to pick me - but someone calling himself Chevalier, a denizen no doubt of Oil Court Chambers, what sort of fellow is that?

"Mr. Chevalier de St. Croix," Robin introduced us outside the old Sheffield Crown Court. I eyed him up and down and wasn't much surprised. Shiny shoes, pin-striped trousers, gravy-stained waistcoat, half-moon glasses and flowing white hair. "And this..." Robin continued with a flourish, "... is Henry Wallace. One of the finest juniors on the North Eastern Circuit.

Fortunate, if I may say so, to have him in our case."

"What?" he had his hand to his ear.

"Delighted to meet you" I told him, "our case turns, as I'm sure you know, on purported confessions."

"Did you say confessions?"

"Which we must keep out."

"The confessions?"

"Yes the confessions." I looked at Robin but couldn't catch his eye.

"We say entrapment."

"Do we?" He walked away pulling his suitcase behind him. "Call it agent provocateur, myself."

Chapter 15

I went to the Extraordinary Meeting of Chambers. We seemed to have deserted Oddfellows Hall and had fetched up in the meeting room of the Salvation Army. I seemed to recognise one or two of the staff. Horace, of course, was in the chair flanked by Browne-Smythe and a young barrister Makepiece, ferret-faced and ambitious who had elbowed his way upwards, known, I ask you, as 'Macca' to his friends. There weren't too many of them.

"I am sorry to have called you here at such short notice. I hope you like the new venue. An unfortunate disagreement with the Oddfellows over their bill. You will see from your agendas, admirably prepared at short notice by young Makepiece, that there are but two items that require our attention. Item one. Financial. Browne-Smythe here will explain.

"It gives me no pleasure. On the contrary ..." Browne-Smythe picked distractedly at his balding head, "...our former head of chambers as you no doubt recollect, I have the minutes if anyone needs reminding, stepped down as a result of criminal charges for which he currently remains on bail. In the circumstances I thought it better, and advised him accordingly, that his presence be foregone ..." he peered around, "... advice it seems he was kind enough to take.

During the currency of his term of office I am afraid matters seem to have deteriorated. Financial matters as well. Of course Jackson had chosen to leave us. A replacement is being sought. Perhaps that should be item number three. Anyway, I was instructed, kindly deputed by Horace here to give the accounts the once over and I deeply regret that all is not well. Irregular would be a better word ..."

Horace folded his arms and glared around, "Fraudulent a better one."

"Well yes ... as Horace so perspicaciously remarks ... Some might say so ... Apparently it has emerged Giles had voted himself a fund that he describes as 'entertainment and hospitality'. Certainly not within the categories of expenditure recommended by the Bar Council. Certainly not a feature of their model 'Best Practice in Chambers' ... which reminds me ... yet another feature of Bar Mark which so far, unfortunately, we have yet to comply. Perhaps we should have that as item four.

Anyway, this fund set up for the exclusive use of Giles has incurred what in my view, on any view, are unwarranted and extortionate expenditures. Meals in restaurants, drinks in public houses, afternoons in a hotel. Trips to London. Attendance at meetings and courses up and down the circuit. Train fares, taxis, the membership of a health club, a sauna for two, and the inevitable dinner at night. Sometimes accompanied by Mrs. Baring. Sometimes not. Lately, if the entries are correct - starting with a Fire Marshall's course in Stevenage - accompanied by none other than our Doreen. For the life of me I cannot understand what might interest her in a conference on paedophilia in London, taken apparently the week before Giles' arrest."

"Oh for God's sake ..." McIntosh stretched his legs and reached for a cigar.

"Not in here please. Expressly forbidden."

McIntosh puffed away to set it alight. "Perk of the job. Used to be Jackson. And if I remember correctly - Doreen occasionally went with him. What does it matter? How much has it cost?"

"Cost! Cost! It's the principle."

"No it's not, it's the price. A few quid here and there divided, as Jackson used to say, by twenty four and deducted from tax amounts to less than a packet of fags. Who cares?" Apparently everybody else.

"Outrageous. Contemptible ..." Makepiece looked towards Horace and was rewarded with a smile, "... how does he justify that?"

"To get work." I'd had enough of this. "It's what we do. It's what every chambers does. Christmas parties. Bottles of wine sent out by the clerk. Mock seminars followed by a dinner and drinks. You name it, they do it. Not for future work of course. Perish the thought. A token of thanks for the past. That's how they dress it up.

It's what everybody does. It's what we should do. And if he hadn't and somebody charted a graph - work down, less briefs coming in - a change of direction to London and Leeds. What then? Giles sadly lacking in enterprise, social skills, inept in the world of commerce; time to look for someone else. Who said 'outrageous' and 'contemptible' I think it was? Somebody in the direct line of benefit. Some ungrateful tosser racking up the work."

Horace looked astounded. "Never heard of such a thing. In all my time at the Bar. My practice depends upon ability rather, if I take your meaning correctly, the contrary to yours."

I looked at their sententious faces. Who would admit that their practice depended on the assorted lies and backhanders of Jackson rather than the enduring talent of themselves?

It didn't take long to find out.

"I move we instruct accountants, reputable accountants, to perform a thorough audit of our books."

"Is there a seconder?" Horace looked around, "… all in favour? Even Humphrey had his hand in the air, "carried with the usual majority, the usual two against."

"I want this on the record" I demanded.

"As you know I represent Giles in his current, and might I tell you, transitory legal difficulty. I anticipate I might be asked to continue to represent his interests if there is any whiff of an allegation of fraud. This places me in some professional difficulty. Also McIntosh, who has been kind enough to advise me in matters of this kind. In future, if this issue finds itself on your agenda we shall be obliged to withdraw and wait outside."

"I agree," McIntosh ground out his cigar on the chewing gum decorating the floor, "but be reminded. The current officers are temporary only and Giles, upon his acquittal, might be eager to return."

"Not if facing further charges he wont."

So that's it then. That's what it's all about. To step down in good faith and be hijacked by ambition, Horace, who pretended to be a friend, finding how the chair at the head of the table so comfortably fits his arse. Trumped up charges. A few expenses. A bit of money spent on Doreen. Anything to see him off.

Horace looked around and gave his snake-eyed smile. "Item two. Continued Practice Development. A new idea from the Bar Council. One to which I wholeheartedly subscribe. Too many people have coasted along for far too long. Trading upon imaginary success ..." he looked at me, "... now we know why, depending on the salesmanship of their clerks. Knowing no law, no precedents, no authorities, ignorant of procedure, taking on cases that they are grossly unqualified to accept. Not any more. The Bar Council proposes that in future it be compulsory upon renewal of your annual practice certificate to attend appropriate lectures and seminars and to complete accredited course work to bring you up, all of us up, on developments in the law.

Each course or item of work to attract the appropriate number of points depending upon its content and duration. Every practitioner to obtain 12 such points a year. A rather unambitious target I would have thought - but best to start gradually I imagine their reasoning to be. They should like our initial response." Once more those little eyes flickered round the room to the background of some drunk's rejected application for a bed. I thought I heard a scuffle at the door, "... do we have a proposer?"

My God. The Bar Council. Treacherous incompetents with a knife. Whoever thought of such an idea? And what, as in all things, were they getting as a reward?

"Any other business?" Horace still squinting around. "A joint submission prepared by Browne-Smythe and Makepiece here. I want you to think about it. I shan't be taking a vote." He cleared his throat. "Number one. Appointment of new clerk. Salary suggestion £25,000 per annum with no percentage for success. Success is part of his job. Oh dear. Caught you out there ..." he wagged a finger in our faces, "... shouldn't that be his or her job? Anyway, £25,000 seems fair enough to me.

Number two. Time to move into the twenty-first century. New challenges lying ahead. Need to slough off the old. Henceforth he ... he? ..." he wagged a finger again, "you never know it might be she, ... shall be known as Practice Manager. He or she will be flanked by an Accounts Manager and a Director of Communications to be appropriately tasked. We envisage a Promotions Executive. In time, a Human Resources Director and possibly an Administrative Advisor. A Director of Corporate Governance wouldn't come amiss.

Three. This team to report to a Management Committee or Cabinet elected democratically by chambers for a period not to exceed five years and in their turn answerable to head of chambers who will deliver regular annual reports. Any questions?"

McIntosh ground out his cigar. "Very clever. Put that lot together and what do you get? Sounds like an old- fashioned clerk."

Horace ignored him. "And finally. It's not on the agenda but … you know … Waterside Mews … it's still rumbling on … we have yet to identify those responsible for the damage …"

McIntosh and I rose as if joined at the hip. Perhaps we were. Time to go looking for work. With or without Giles' secret account .

Chapter 16

"Jolly interesting case this ..." Jas fingered another file, "... been reading the justification. What do you make of this? Irhabeyon Ana ..."

I looked blank. Not so much baffled by the words but surprised he was reading them at all.

"It means 'I am a terrorist' gazing at the hills of Hitteen, I am a terrorist terrorizing the enemies of faith; with sword and fire we repel the cunning of the sinister; the Lord is mighty and grants victory to the dutiful soldiers. They killed him, they betrayed him, they oppressed him. Today woe unto the aggressors. Disgrace and shame on those who support the perfidious. The Lord is omnipotent, legislated the Jihad of the dissolute. Blow them up, blow them up wherever they are and slaughter them. Expel them all and defeat them. Displace them, subdue them, do not be merciful towards them. They are the people who have caused mischief on earth. They are the kin of pigs and monkeys. Get rid of them. Crush Zion the lords of disgrace. Do not observe any truce, do not seek for peacemaking. Destroy them."

"Where did you find that?"

"In the file. Thought you might have read it."

"Whose file? Which category? Is it Iftiqhar Khan?"

"Category Q. Another friend of his. On his computer. It's a song.

Presumably what they sing round the campfire when they're in Pakistan."

"I can't think an English jury will take to that."

"No…" Jas laughed, "… nor a Jewish judge."

"No. Not anybody with an ounce of compassion or kindness …" I was getting sick of sympathising with these people, "… is it all like that?"

Jas was watching me carefully. "Pretty much. The same sort of stuff in books and poems. Speeches, newspaper reports, religious tracts. All on their computers. Even texts on their mobile phones. And of course the suicide videos. Their last messages to the world."

"Jas it's hopeless. What sort of jury is going to take a chance with these defendants? Risk everything. Give them the benefit of the doubt?"

"I can tell you. None. They're finished. Their life is over. 40 years minimum inside. Minimum mind. Minimum. If they're not mad now they will be then. It's over. No paradise, no glory, no sitting by the hand of the prophet in gold pavilions, no virgins with lustrous eyes. Nothing. Shame and contempt on their families. Disgrace for ever for them."

"But what if he didn't do it? All right he knew the leaders, hung around on the fringe, fascinated by their fervour, disillusioned with the west. Embittered by Iraq, even Afghanistan, inflamed by radical Imams, hovering at the edge, maybe moved to applaud – but not part of it, not joining in buying materials, looking up bomb-making formulae, hiding money, doing what he could to assist. What if he did nothing?"

"He's going down with the rest."

I've got to get on with this case. Start reading some of the files. Get them in order, make notes on what is relevant. Cross check interviews. Find out what the others have said. Have a look at these telephone transcripts. Bang up some sort of schedule. Think about experts. As Laura would have said, 'get a fucking grip'.

"Jas. I know you're interested. I know you stay behind until late. Don't worry about the cigarettes. Smoke as much as you like. I want you to get this case in order. File it up. Cross reference the evidence. Schedules of surveillance. Schedules of contacts. Look up the unused material. Produce a list of the items potentially relevant. Advise Moghul & Co. Sort it out. Good points, bad points, flag them up, forget the rest. I want to see a summary. Some light at the end of the tunnel. I want to know where we're at. Can you do it?"

Jas reached into my cigarette box. "I thought you'd never ask."

"It's not as if it's the only case I'm doing," I told him, "Robin's got me for this murder and then there's the usual rubbish trickling in, not forgetting Fotheringay." How could I possibly forget that?

I went into the empty library to give her a call. Why do I always whisper even when I know I'm alone?

"How are you? How've you been? How's Rodney. What's the fixture? Is he home or away?"

"Away."

"How wonderful. Nothing too near I hope."

"New York. Should be a couple of days."

"Look, he's getting a little chary. On the phone complaining to Robin. What about a nice hotel?"

But not Pat's Place. Somehow I couldn't face Pat. Perhaps I was keeping it safe. Still hoping for a return bout with Pauline. Hope springs eternal. I remembered the brittle tensions of her little dinner party. You never know your luck. Not that Clematis would like it. Too Spartan, too cheap. Still - those familiar springs welcoming a novel body. A lighter burden but the same bumbling fool on top.

"No. I don't think so. There's something seedy about an afternoon in a hotel. I was thinking of something more adventurous. Something 'au natural'."

"What?" I didn't get the drift.

"Something a little 'al fresco' ..." I wished she'd speak English "... something perhaps 'dehors' ..."

"You want to go on a picnic?"

"Certainly not."

"A walk in the country. Work up an appetite for lunch in that bloody pub?"

"Don't be silly. Meet me by the duck pond. I think I can explain."

So, having waved goodbye to the beavering Jas, and patted Doreen on what was now her suspiciously well-groomed head, I rolled up at the duck pond, in something of a dither wondering, but really knowing, what she might have in mind.

Chapter 17

She popped a bottle in the car and we supped together from cut glass.

"Could be fun."

"I don't think so."

"Don't be silly you'll enjoy it."

"No I won't. It'll be cold and wet. And then there's grit and nettles. Bloody brambles. Wandering hikers, gawping yokels, truanting children, bastards with shotguns, huntsmen and hounds, escaped prisoners …" was I overdoing it? "… pensioners shuffling out of their coach, botanists, bird watchers, joggers (I thought of Rodney), why don't we go to a hotel?"

So we did. Clematis in a resigned and decidedly non-active mode. This was getting expensive. £200 on the marina with a perfectly-manicured dummy who barely consented to move.

We lay together afterwards.

"That was wonderful." More or less it was for me.

"Was it?" I never knew she could be so resentful. "I hope you haven't forgotten my case."

"I think of little else."

"So when is it?" A good question I'll have to get more organised. Have a word with Jas.

"Soon. Soon. Relax." I stroked that glistening helmet of dark and scented hair.

"It's very soon. Very very soon." She seemed to know more than I did. "Why not try next week?"

"Next week!" Now that was another surprise. "Next week! Why didn't Robin tell me? God. Why didn't my clerk tell me? Now I remember. I haven't got a clerk. I felt a touch of trembles. Surely not self-doubt?

"Next week. Jesus Christ. I hope everything is in order. I hope Robin's lodged the pleadings. I hope ..." She raised herself to lean on one elbow. I can do without distraction.

"Everything is in order." I smiled up at her reassuringly.

"I hope to God you're right."

Chapter 18

Judge Irvine. What a stroke of luck. That benign educated face beaming down upon me from the bench.

"Mr. Wallace. How nice to see you. Straying into new pastures are we?"

I turned to Clematis and Rodney and shrugged apologetically. "He will have his little joke."

"And ranged against you I see a formidable array. London counsel. Even, dare I say it, learned counsel from Leeds. So who's who? What's the representation? Help me Mr. Wallace. This could take some time."

"There are eleven defendants Your Honour."

"An extraordinary number. Now then. I welcome you all. Squeeze up if you can. Oh dear. I think we must make room for Mr. Wallace. Of course you must fight cases vigorously but not literally I think …"

"I represent the plaintiff Fotheringay, Your Honour."

"Claimant Mr. Wallace. That's what we call it now."

"What did you say? Claimant? Why do we call it that?"

"God knows Mr. Wallace. Some fool in the Home Office. Parliament as ever ready to oblige." Ah. Nothing changes. Some timeserver wanting to justify his salary and pension fiddling with a name.

"For the claimant, Your Honour, Mrs. Fotheringay, the lady who lost her car."

"Yes. I've read the papers. Admirably framed might I say. This lady of excellent repute bought a car in London in good faith only to find a few short months later that it had been seized back in the night and taken away. Lamentable business. How can she possibly be at fault?"

How could she? I was moved to turn again. "And what do you say Mr. Wallace? One of those multitude of defendants. One of them at least must be to blame."

"Precisely, Your Honour."

"Well they are all here. Save perhaps for one."

I jiffled up the bastard next to me. "Who, Your Honour? I wonder who that might be?"

"Count Potolski. I have a letter from his solicitors. They wish to go off the record. Not seen him for months. Apparently failed to attend appointments. Given no instructions. They have made enquiries of his address in Eaton Square. Difficulties with service charges. Non-payment of council tax. Substantial arrears of rent. For today's purposes at least he appears not to be represented ..." he leaned forward to the clerk, "... call him again."

"Count Potolski. Count Potolski. No reply, Your Honour."

"Ah well Mr. Wallace. We must proceed in his absence. Hard to see how he might advance a defence."

So we've won. Another victory. With no bloody Count Potolski, how can I possibly lose?

"Your Honour. Might I open the case?" I churned away with confidence. "Agreed documents. Bill of sale. Log book. Warranty. Service records. Note from the absent count himself. Pushed through the plaintiff's ... er ... claimant's letterbox. Car no longer present. Unlawfully, it is for you to decide, perhaps lawfully driven off. Money paid in good faith. Reliant upon the representations and terms of contract given and entered into by the vendor garage who, if I understand their defence (should I say defences?) purported to sell with warranty as to title and in good faith."

"Thank you Mr. Wallace. Concise, helpful, and accurate as ever. I am most obliged."

I turned again, my neck was beginning to ache, and chanced a smile at Clematis. She was holding hands with Rodney, and Rodney didn't smile back.

"The first defendant please. Is it Mr. Cattermole? You produce documents, not, I believe, in dispute. Yes. Bill of sale. Assorted warranties. Purchased, I believe, by hire purchase - no need to trouble the second defendant hire purchasers, thank you Mr. Grapeseed no need, on to the third defendant. Another garage I believe. Yes. I have it before me. Helpfully included by Mr. Wallace in his bundle, another bill of sale. No issue taken to that. And then the fourth defendant. Who are you? Yes. Very kind. No issue I believe as to this. Some freelance fellow or other who sold this somewhat elusive car on. Mr. Shearing for the fifth defendant, you wish to say something? I understand you've come a long way. Bristol Chambers? Pleased to meet you. Have you had a pleasant trip? And, as I understand it, the sixth defendant? Yes Mr. Fotheringay? No relation? Curious coincidence of name. From Oil Court Chambers you say? Very interesting. No need to detain you I assure you. You want to say something? What about? No .. no ... I've read the papers, please be seated ... there's no need."

"The seventh defendant ..." I leant back, my hands behind my head to watch the show unfold.

Judge Irvine smiled all round.

"Please take a note of my judgment. This case revolves around a car. A very expensive car bought, as I find, in good faith by the claimant and seized back by the original owner, one Count Potolski who was good enough to leave a note of his intentions during the night of the 6th September 2003.

Count Potolski, having composed and posted his letter, drove the car away. It was never seen again. Certainly not by the claimant. It occurs to me at this point that the missing Count Potolski - for he too has done a similar disappearing trick as the car - must have had the keys. Perhaps he retained them. Perhaps he was given them by one or other of the garages appearing before me. Perhaps he obtained them in some other fashion. As he has chosen not to attend this trial - and I pause here to say I am satisfied he was given notice of these proceedings by his former solicitors who assiduously attended at his former address - we shall never know. Perhaps it doesn't matter. He was able to take away the car.

Now the claimant Mrs. Fotheringay does not, indeed cannot, know where the fault lies.

Does it lie with the missing count? Or might it lie with the garage she bought it from? Or yet again might one of the many garages and their hire purchase companies be to blame? I pause again. Mr. Wallace has very properly brought in the hire purchase companies. I daresay had he had his way and been given some sort of choice he would have happily left them out. But once again the Government has intervened. By the terms of the Consumer Credit Act or possibly the Hire Purchase Act, the buying and selling of cars, are now governed by legislation and, using its terms, not mine, are now said to be 'linked'. So everybody is joined in and everybody comes along. Today I welcome eleven. So be it. It is not the fault of Mr. Wallace, on that point I want to be clear. So we wander down the chain until we come to what I regard as the crucial sale. I will call it the primary sale. The sale in which the errant count purported to sell his car to garage number one.

This is a garage with premises in the Roman Road. Somewhere I am told in the East End of London. A garage, according to the pleadings, with something of a chequered history but now happily trading again. For some reason they have provided accounts. But I am satisfied that they purchased this vehicle in good faith. I have seen a bill of sale and a receipt signed by the fugitive count in the sum of £145,000. Obviously he has been paid and taken the money. The bill of sale which he is not here to dispute, says as much. It tells me he surrendered the registration documents and service records and current insurance certificate and was reimbursed for the outstanding tax.

So garage one, please don't interrupt me Mr. Fotheringay, received what I find to be a good title and passed it on accordingly to all the rest until it finally reached Mrs. Fotheringay whom I take to be the lady sitting behind Mr. Wallace," he paused to smile. "She received, I find, a good title as did all the rest. The miscreant is the disappearing count. I have no hesitation in finding against him notwithstanding that enigmatic note. I pause again. Had he not left that note kindly identifying himself, I daresay Mrs. Fotheringay ..." he beamed down upon her from the bench underneath the lion and the unicorn laboriously carved into those ancient oak panels centuries before, "Mrs. Fotheringay would have been left none the wiser as to who had deprived her of her car. She would no doubt have informed the Humberside Constabulary who, after the passage of days, if not weeks, would have eventually turned up when the trail was cold. Nothing would have emerged from their subsequent enquiries - it hardly ever does - and Mrs. Fotheringay would have been compelled to revert to her insurance company and make a claim against them. And there the matter would have ended but for that mysterious note. No matter. Having recovered it from the doormat in the hall - Mr. Wallace has been most precise - the paper chase began.

And now I bring it, thankfully, to an end. It has been a pleasure seeing you all if not hearing from you. Oblige me by noting the following orders which, at the invitation of Mr. Wallace, I am more than happy to make:

Count Potolski, defendant one, return the car.

He pays £150,000 damages in lieu.

He pays interest thereon of £81,300 and rising at the rate of £47.50 per day until payment or return of the car, whichever is the sooner.

He pays court costs to be quantified.

He further pays the damages of Mrs. Fotheringay, the claimant, for loss of convenience caused by the wrongful removal of her car.

He pays for the property, now missing, which it formerly contained. Mr. Wallace has helpfully furnished a list. It amounts to another £32,343. The property returned therefore or damages and interest in lieu …"

I turned round and smiled at my little party and Robin enthusiastically smiled back. Rodney was kissing Clematis. His iron arms were bound around her shoulders, his head was buried in her face.

"Mr. Wallace. Is there anything I have missed?"

"Your Honour, the improvements made to the vehicle by he claimant's husband estimated at a minimum of £15,000."

"You have them."

"And the costs of a replacement car. A very modest Lamborghini at £300 per day."

"They are yours. Is there anything else? Oh yes. The other defendant's costs. Not counting the disappearing count, there are ten of them. They have been put to considerable expense. Solicitors to advise, prolific pleadings, statements and interviews, documents, attendance at preliminary hearings, counsel appearing before me today. I am content to proceed on detailed costings provided to me or adjourn for taxation, whichever you please …"

My learned friends, finally allowed to speak, were on their feet as one pressing forward their detailed, and in the absence of Potolski, uncontested accounts.

"Well, let me see …" Judge Irvine was working on his calculator, "… yes I think that's right. Yes … defendant seven … yes … good God, what's that? Oil Court Chambers comes expensive … ah well, never mind … have I got them all? Goodness me … a grand total of £370,000. The total sum of course to be paid over by the claimant but I award - as I know Mr. Wallace is about to ask - I award full reimbursement from the defendant Potolski to Mrs. Fotheringay. This sum to be added to the sums I have already awarded to Mrs. Fotheringay and ordered that he pay."

He rose and smiling at Mrs. Fotheringay turned to me. "I am obliged to you Mr. Wallace for the way you have presented this case." I turned to my grateful little party and shook their hands all round.

"Be with you as soon as I've changed. Wait for me outside."

They were clustered by the great main door of the Guildhall flushed and excited with success.

"We won. We won." I told them and took Clematis by the hand.

"Yes. Excellent. Thank you Robin. Thank you all of you. A wonderful result."

"When do I get my car?"

"Ah. A good question. As you know, it appears to have gone missing. It's possibly with the count."

"So when does she get her damages?"

"Ah. Another excellent question. As soon as we trace the count. Robin tells me he is on the trail."

"And what about my loss of use, and all the bloody things inside?"

"Of course. Of course. A very proper enquiry. As soon as Robin finds the count. I understand he may be overseas ..." I looked towards Robin, "... Warsaw was it? Or possibly Gdansk?"

"And what about the cost of running that bloody Lamborghini?" Rodney narrowed his eyes at myself and Clematis. "Running it into the ground?"

"The count. The count. He must pay everything."

"And what about my costs?" Rodney took my other hand.

"Of course. Of course. Perfectly natural you should want to know. The count is liable for the lot. Rightly so. As soon as he is traced."

"But what about the costs of the others in the meantime? Costs that, if I understand this correctly, I shall have to pay. The thick end of about 400 grand?"

"To be lodged with the court within fourteen days."

"So, let me get this straight." Rodney loomed forward not letting go of my hand. "No car, no damages, no property, no interest, and no costs but from somewhere I have to find £400,000?"

I looked at Robin and Robin looked at me. "Put that way ... er ... yes. Plus what you owe me and Robin of course."

He looked around - his blank stare not registering with the hurrying shoppers, the busy traffic, opposing counsel and their teams waving us goodbye. He sighed and held my hand even tighter.

"Thank God we didn't lose."

Chapter 19

Jas had done an excellent job. As bundles of papers arrived from Moghul & Co. lashed together with tape or sliding about in treasury tags or even rubber bands, he had carefully sorted them out into the correct order, page by page, punching holes when necessary, and filing them into lever arches with the correct category, page numbers and date, written along the spine in his immaculate hand, and had stacked them one upon the other against the wall.

He and I stood looking at them in awe.

"163 lever arches, 67 ring binder files, 127 DVDs and counting. The biggest case in the world."

"Certainly the biggest in England. Take a lifetime to read. But read it I must. And not only read it - understand it. Make notes of contacts - telephone, fax, e-mail, face to face. Prepare schedules of purported surveillance. Compile lists of items, incriminating items, recovered from his home and car. Advise experts. All sorts of experts. Amazing these days what there is to be expert about. Computers, obviously. Mobiles of course. Explosives inevitably. But radicalisation? What on earth is that? But Moghul & Co. had been on again of course - experts in irritation - they wanted an advice recommending we appoint and instruct one. Of course. As soon as possible. The usual panic; before everyone else 'snaps them up'.

And what about a Silk? Time apparently running out. When are we, if ever, getting one of those? Rather sooner than they think. And it won't be that lunatic Chevalier. I'd been putting out some enquiries. A man in Bradford. Academic, self-sufficient, a good rather than a great advocate, meticulous, generous and bright. A great luncher and, just for a change, a Silk prepared to put his hand in his pocket and buy a round of drinks. More than that. He respected the old traditions that Silks, being paid more, look after their juniors, who get paid less. They buy lunch and dinner. They put their hands up for the champagne, take care of the bill in the wine bar, and get on with the work. Not one of the usual overpaid and incompetent poseurs. I'd already told him he'd got it, and judging by his grateful response, it was something he was glad to get.

Let him take over. Do some of these schedules and advices. Talk to Moghul & Co. Meet the family. Have an away day at Belmarsh. How radical is that?

Giles walked in without knocking. "Glad to find you working on my case."

Do I need this? Do I need Giles? Not for too much longer. I explained the position.

"Giles. Try and concentrate. I have just completed a very important case of civil litigation involving about fifteen defendants. Successfully completed. Costs about half a million pounds ..."

"Not yours I hope?"

"Don't be ridiculous. The combined costs of the action. Mine and Robin's unfortunately yet to be paid. I have returned today to chambers to begin my preparation for this ..." I waved at the lever arches towering over his head, "... not exactly a punch up at a wedding party is it? No. An act of terrorism, an alleged act of terrorism, involving the potential loss of thousands of lives. And you want to know, no doubt, how I'm getting along with yours." I blew smoke in his face. We both did. Amazing how the pupil adopts the manners of his master.

"Let me tell you. Just fine. I have studied the papers that Robin has finally got round to sending me. The usual mess. Drunken witnesses - some, if not all of them, probably culprits themselves - blaming the other side. Misidentifying the players, the team, the goals they're kicking at or in, the date, the time, the place. But all of one view. Unfortunately for you. A belligerent fat man wearing striped trousers and an air of gratuitous interference throwing about his ample weight. A fat man insufferably rude to the police. A fat man dragged away through the mud in handcuffs. A fat man kicking the inside of a police van. A fat man that I strongly suspect is you."

"This is outrageous. A conspiracy of lies. What about Pauline? She told me she was giving a statement that totally exonerated me. What about the Recorder of Hull? And his lady wife? What about McIntosh? What about the rest of our table? Come to that, what about you?"

"Leave me out of this. I'm your counsel not your witness. I saw nothing. Next to nothing. I saw you, come to think of it, running towards a fight urging us to follow. I saw fists, feet, and bottles flying. I seem to remember seeing you."

"Doing what?"

"Giles. Let's have a drink." I pitied his wild-eyed desperation. "I'll pay. Jas can get on with this. Don't ask questions. "Trust me …""

I ushered him down the stairs, helped him on with his overcoat while Doreen stood and stared; took his arm across the street, and whispered some good advice in his ear.

"Whatever I am as a counsel, as a witness I'd be worse."

But he was right of course. It was time to knuckle down. He had been patient, the patience born of despair. Now his wife was getting fretful - no money coming in, no social invitations falling through the letterbox, contact with chambers' wives unaccountably drying up. She had heard whispers of what was being described as a 'slush fund'. Money Giles had been spending that allegedly wasn't his. And not just spending on himself. Of late, another companion in dishonour. Someone who was employed by chambers. Someone of the opposite sex.

"Look Harry. Let's get on with it. What I need is an early trial. Get Listing to bring the case forward. Have a word with the prosecutor. Some fellow from Leeds leading a higher court advocate in the pay of the Crown Prosecution Service. Probably still that bugger we turned down. Find out who they are. Suggest breaking the case up into more manageable trials. At the moment over a dozen have been charged. We can't wait for all those to get sorted. I'll be out of work forever. Talk to these people. Get them to bring on my case …"

I remembered the higher court advocate in question, Potter whatever he was called. Interviewed and rejected by Giles. Something of a resentful manner. Unlikely in the circumstances to be queuing up to help.

"And get my witnesses together. Have you spoken to Pauline yet? She told me she knows of others. Others who are favourable to our cause. Saw the same as her. Support everything she said."

"Giles. Robin is working on it."

"Is he? I rather doubt it. Saw him in the street. Seems to have forgotten my name. And then there's this other thing. Pickles seems to like being head of chambers. Should never have given him the chance. Apparently objecting to my entertainment account. The account, if I remember rightly, you and McIntosh were anxious that I set up, and let's not forget, were always pleased to share. What about that? My wife seems to think Horace has got his own accountant on the job. More bloody expense. Why don't they come to me? I never made it a secret. Didn't take handfuls out of petty cash. It's all documented. Doreen kept a record. Details of everything, or nearly everything, we spent."

I had to agree with him. Roped in with lots of different defendants his case could take forever to get on. And whilst he was swinging in limbo Horace used the time to build up another case in that precise meticulous way of his, not being one to leave a stone unturned. Driven by ambition and malice, guided by his suspicious nature, aided and abetted by his growing number of friends. Storm clouds were certainly gathering, and they were confining their attention to Giles. What could I do? The usual. I sought to mollify him by the pretence of action. I pretended to be getting on with the job.

"I'll speak to the prosecution. Get your case listed for mention. Preferably in front of Irvine. I've spoken to the Recorder of Hull. His heart, according to him, goes out to you. Unfortunately acquainted with too many of the parties and has been forced to disqualify himself. Anyway says he didn't see anything, happened to be looking the other way. Same with his good lady wife. She not only lost her shoes but her glasses. Seems to have lost her memory as well. They both send you their best wishes. Unfortunately unable to accept your wife's kind invitation to dinner. Away at a sentencing conference. One he's been called on to address … But Irvine wasn't invited to the wedding, or if he was, he certainly didn't accept. He's our man. Get it listed in front of him. Persuade him to sever your trial away from the rest. Get it listed and go and see him in his room. You know the form. The usual indication – a bit of probation, an iota of unpaid work. A couple of hours in the local Oxfam shop should do the trick. Kind words at the point of sentence – an understandable reaction in the circumstances, if something of an over-zealous response. Tired and emotional. A flash of adrenalin. A little 'over the top'."

Giles banged his pint down on the brass top of the bar. "Are you insane? Haven't you listened to a word I've said? I didn't do it. This is a 'not guilty', I know you're not used to it, a 'not guilty' all the way. No sidling down the corridors of power, no compromises, no deals, no offers of guilt. Any adverse verdict would ruin me. The Bar Council would step in. Disciplinary proceedings. It doesn't bear thinking about. Abigail would leave me. Take the children. And with the children goes the house. No income, no home, no job, no prospects and Horace beavering away with his pals in chambers, pals I had assumed were mine, to lay charges of fraud ..." he drained his nearly full glass and glared expectantly for another, "... much more of this I'm getting a counsel from Leeds."

Much more of this and I'll be offering to help.

Chapter 20

The murder case was easier. At least it was easier to get on. With only one defendant it wasn't a problem and in truth it wasn't a complicated case.

Mr. Chevalier de St Croix sat in number one court in the new ugly Sheffield Combined Court Centre trying to get used to his revolving mobile chair. His bottom reared on oak benches didn't easily adjust. His powdery white hair covered by a powdery white wig, his portly belly encased in a waistcoat held together by a silver watch and chain, he listened to his opponent open the case for the Crown.

The prosecution was straightforward.

"Look at the CCTV. There is the defendant, Mr. Pendlebury Eaves, does he seem a little agitated? Taking what he told the police was a bit of an evening stroll after changing his mind about going to a concert, and edging into that doorway. Did he furtively look over his shoulder first? And is he carrying something in his right hand pressed against his side? Hard to tell from the grainy texture of the video but it's a matter for you to decide. And here he is again, a matter of a minute later – a minute we say spent smashing in an unfortunate tramp's head – and carefully avoiding flying droplets of blood, the weapon, that timber, in the hands of what we say is a murderous expert – perhaps having paused to savour the dying man's death throes – makes his way, see here he comes, leaving rather faster than he went in. Still carrying something is he? We say the blood-spattered weapon held down but no longer touching his side and there he goes, why is he hurrying away? Past that skip, remember the skip where that weapon was found, is there a pause as he passes? It's difficult to see, but a pause nonetheless, long enough you might think to dispose of the weapon, and now walking a little slower, a little more naturally, it's a matter for you, relieved perhaps that he's got rid of the weapon and there he goes round the corner, no longer agitated, no longer hurrying, no longer tense, making his casual way off to book into a seedy hotel.

He was arrested next morning. Sufficient time we say to take a shower. To take several showers. To wash his hair and clean his nails. To maybe change his clothing. To somehow dispose of his suit and shoes. Maybe he had already purchased a duplicate outfit and left it waiting in that hotel. We cannot say because there was no record of his ever staying there. No entry in the hotel register. Apparently he paid the only person present, the receptionist, a witness who you will hear from, he was pleased to pay – and I daresay the receptionist happier to receive – settlement in cash. The receptionist has a hazy record of the time. So, it is a matter for you. Is it possible he had substitute clothing waiting? You might think he had ample time. And when the police got there, you might think with admirable speed, he was sponged and slicked-up to perfection and the clothing of the night before all now disappeared. That is what we say. A well-known tramp sleeping in his customary doorway became the object of a carefully-laid plan.

So what did he say when interviewed? A pack of lies. Admitted his presence. Obviously clever enough to know his whereabouts would be recorded. Admitted going inside the doorway. He would have you believe to proffer cigarettes. Admitted some exchange of words and possible touching admitted, it is part of his plan, roughly pulling away. Admitted, and you may think he had little choice, walking past the skip and arriving some time, he cannot be precise as to that, at a cash taking, non-registering, no questions asked, hotel."

And then the inevitable pause. "My Lord. I stop here. There is legal argument which need not concern the jury. I anticipate it will take the rest of the day. Perhaps the jury might be released until tomorrow?"

And the jury filing out. And Chevalier and his rather clever adversary rising to argue the law as to whether the confessions to his brother and sister go in or out. And if they go in the prosecutor can tell the jury all about it in the morning – but if they go out? As Chevalier is about to argue. Ah, a rather different story. This jury, nor any other jury, nor the press, nor anybody else will ever hear of them and we will be nicely placed, with a fair wind at our backs, to secure an important win. Is this justice? Of course – it is the law.

"I say agent provocateur, My Lord. The law is clear."

"Take me to it."

"Er ...Archbold, My Lord. It's in Archbold."

"Where?"

"Er ..." he turned to me, "...... mon vieux, where?"

"Try Section 78."

"Section 78, My Lord."

"Section 78 of what."

Chevalier turned again. An empty bucket to an empty well.

"Er ..." I turned to Robin. "Police and Criminal Evidence Act. Page 1267."

"My Lord, I have it at my fingertips. Page 1267 to be precise."

We read it together. Something about excluding evidence if it would be unfair to admit it. There were lots of examples. Several pages. We searched for agent provocateur, the clock ticking away, but in vain.

"Why not try Section 76?" The prosecution had already flagged it up. Kind of them to leave us to struggle so long.

"Ah yes. Of course. The law is even clearer, My Lord. A confession to be admissible must be reliable, notwithstanding it might be true. As to reliability ..." Chevalier spread his hands and smiled, "... Your Lordship knows the arguments. Sleep deprivation, violence, no access to medicine. Confused and emotional ... Perhaps, My Lord, we can proceed on the voir dire?"

It was always coming to this. A different oath and a different procedure. Witnesses called in the absence of the jury giving their evidence before the judge - setting out the circumstances, submitting to defence cross-examination, leaving His Lordship to decide.

"I call P.C. Worthington." Smart, short back and sides, a parting like an arrow, boots newly shined. "Tell us how you came to record the conversations between this accused and his siblings on the night of his arrest."

"Desk Sergeant and C.I.D. mentioned it might be an idea. Station myself with a notebook out of sight. Strictly no intervention. No words, no looks of encouragement, no shaking of the head. Eyes open, mouth shut, pencil at the ready. That's what they told me. That's what I did."

"You produce your notebook?"

"I do."

"Is the entry signed?"

"Signed and dated."

"Copies for Your Lordship. Copies already served upon the defence. Paginated with numbered paragraphs. Might I take Your Lordship through it? We say a confession; precise admissions freely made."

He read it out in all its gory detail.

"I hate street beggars littering up the place. Getting in the way, standing about with Big Issues and bottles of cider, whining and cadging, living off state benefits, rotting sleeping bags and blankets, spreading fucking disease. I'd seen him before and somehow he recognised me. Enough is enough. About time somebody did it. I thought about it. Decided that somebody should be me. So I got a piece of wood and hid it up my sleeve. Walked into that doorway. Slipped it out. A reassuring thwack across the palm of my hand. So easy. I nearly took his head off. You should have seen the look of surprise. Out cold twitching and jerking. A few more cracks and he's dead. He didn't scream or cry or even groan. He lay there while I hit him again and again. Stepped over the swelling trickle of blood, one last look and away. Slept like a log in a room already booked. Surprised they found me so soon. No need for them to be violent ... at this stage he laughed, My Lord ... said it didn't seem right to complain."

"Thank you P.C. Worthington. Please remain ... there may be some questions. Mr. Chevalier de St. Croix?"

"I put it to you that you knew full well that this defendant had been deprived of lawful medication."

"No, Sir."

"Of sleep?"

"No, Sir."

"Of the services of a solicitor?"

"I was told one was on the way."

"Had been subjected to a violent arrest."

"I understood he had resisted arrest."

"And was clearly emotionally disturbed."

"All I can say is he sounded all right to me."

"He was crying."

"He was laughing."

"He was begging his brother and sister not to go."

"No, Sir. I would have recorded it in my notebook. Once he told them, told them what I recorded, he asked them to leave him alone."

"Your record is wholly fictitious."

"Mr. Chevalier de St. Croix, pause a moment.   Perhaps I have misunderstood." His Lordship was still writing. "I had assumed you accepted the accuracy of the record but was seeking to undermine its reliability by reference to the circumstances in which it was obtained?"

Chevalier looked at me. I looked at Robin. Robin turned to Mr. Eaves.

"Do we now dispute what was said?"

"Your Lordship, might I have a short recess?"

"This is new" I told them. There is nothing in the police statement about laughing. About a general tenor of bravado. We had assumed, perhaps wrongly, that he was distressed. You must challenge this. This is new. An afterthought. An embellishment. Someone's put him up to it. Altogether different to what we imagined. Not a pathetic creature prevailed upon to confess - rather more a psychopath bragging about his success."

"I agree ..." Robin looked at Chevalier, "... we should have checked the notebook."

"I assumed it bore some resemblance to his statement. Apparently not."

"So ask him why ..." I pressed him, "... why this wasn't in his statement which he must have made while looking at his notebook. Why miss out something as important as this."

"Unless ..." Robin was ahead of us, "... it wasn't in it. This is not his notebook. This is another concocted afterwards in its place."

But no. They wouldn't take the risk. Not for the sake of some old tramp. Why bother? This is not the IRA or terrorists. A 'leg-up' the police call it. Fabricating evidence to give the prosecution a lift. And Mr. Eaves? Dangerous no doubt. But not more than many others. A lonely psychopath occasionally violent to people who don't matter very much if they matter at all.

"No Robin, they wouldn't do it. It wouldn't be worth their time." If he was laughing he was hysterical. If he was bragging he was trying to impress. If he was confessing he was looking for sympathy. If he said he was the murderer it was a deluded mistake."

We filed back into court and Chevalier went through the motions.

"Police constable, you're obviously not a doctor?"

"No."

"Nor a psychiatrist?"

"No."

"Didn't see his injuries? His condition? The look on his face?"

"No, Sir."

"Precisely. You were hiding round the corner. Keeping out of sight."

The best we could do in the circumstances. Cold calculating killer or unloved fantasist? I had a fair idea what his Lordship might decide.

"Call Mr. Artemus Eaves."

Chevalier seemed to have lost his enthusiasm. He turned and shook his silver head. "You can take him," he said.

Thank you very much Chevalier. Thank you very much for all the notice, thank you for ducking the fast ball, thank you for staying in the trench your bottom now fully accustomed to your chair, and sending me over the top.

I watched our opponent lead the witness in chief, as following the steps of his clever dance-master they waltzed around the floor.

"Mr. Chevalier de St. Croix." His Lordship looked up and nodded.

"No My Lord. My junior on this occasion."

"Really? Oh. I see. Very well."

No preparation. No careful consideration of his statement. No noting of inconsistencies. No planning of where to go, whether he answered 'no' or 'yes'. But I had to do it. Chevalier sat tight with his arms folded. Robin pretended to take a note.

"He was tired obviously?"

"A little."

"Yes he seemed to you a little tired. And he was dishevelled wasn't he?"

"Yes."

"Tired, a little tired as you would have it, and dishevelled. He had dried blood on his face didn't he?"

"Er …"

"Didn't he? Around the nose?"

"It was dark down there. I'm not sure."

"So there might have been?"

"Yes."

"Yes. So what have we got? Tired, a little tired, dishevelled and he might have shown traces of blood?"

"Yes."

"And he was surprised to see you, you and your sister, wasn't he?"

"I think so."

"Because he was expecting somebody else. He told you didn't he? He told you. Think about it. Take your time. He was expecting somebody else."

"Er … I think so."

"A doctor. Was it a doctor? The police surgeon. Or was it his solicitor? Somebody to give him legal advice."

"It was his solicitor. He mentioned a solicitor. I think he said he was waiting for his solicitor but that he might not come."

"Really. So I expect he was worried about that?"

"Well yes. I think so. That's the impression I got."

"Let me give you a name. The name of the absent solicitor your brother was in some anxiety to see, fearing he might never turn up. Robin. Robin Parmenter. Does that name ring any bells?"

"That's it. Robin. He was asking for Robin. What's the second name?"

"Parmenter."

"Yes Parmenter. That's the man."

"And he'd not seen a doctor had he?"

"No. I don't think he had."

"Because he wanted his medicine didn't he? He was asking about his pills."

"I'm not sure ..."

"Think about it. Your brother needs his medication doesn't he? Without it he becomes irrational and depressed."

"Yes."

"He becomes emotional doesn't he?"

"Yes."

"And violent?"

"Yes."

"Inclined to fly off the handle. Do anything. Say anything. Wholly unpredictable in what he says and does?"

"Yes."

"And he hadn't taken any medication had he? Pills, medicine, an injection, whatever it was, he hadn't had it, and he wanted you to know."

"Yes. He wanted my sister to ring his doctor. Now I remember. He wanted us to help him out."

"And I daresay you said you would do what you could do."

"Yes."

"But in reality you could do nothing could you?"

"No."

"But offer him some support?"

"Yes."

"But you thought that he'd done it didn't you? You thought he'd murdered a tramp?"

"Yes."

"Because of his past. And the way he behaves when he doesn't take his drugs?"

"Yes."

"And because that's what the police told you he had done."

Silence.

"In the police car when they picked you up?"

Silence.

"Come on Mr. Eaves. You didn't all travel all the way down to the station in that car saying nothing did you?"

"No."

"You must have been asking the police what it was all about. There you were, you and your sister, hoicked out of your respective houses and being given a lift by the police. What could be more natural. You wanted to know what it was all about?"

"Yes. We didn't want to go."

"Of course not. And you wanted to know why the police were insisting that you should."

"Yes."

"So they told you didn't they? They must have done. They told you he'd murdered a tramp?"

"Yes."

"Listen carefully Mr. Eaves. I suggest they also told you this. That they had evidence …"

"Yes."

"And they were certain it was him?"

"Yes."

"And of course it would be much better for him in the long run if he was prepared to admit his guilt?"

"Yes. They said they could get him treatment. That he might get a shorter sentence, perhaps in hospital. Serve less time in jail."

"So naturally you wanted to help him. Didn't you?"

"Yes."

"It would be for his benefit. To get him to confess?"

"Yes."

"And that's what you did wasn't it? Both you and your sister. You told him what you thought was the truth. What a brother and sister would do. Better to make a clean breast. You know the sort of thing. Better to own up and admit it because you thought it was true?

"Yes. And he did. He told us what he had done."

"We agree Mr. Eaves. Have no doubt about it. He made a full confession after you had told him, persuaded him really, that the evidence, as you had been told, was overwhelming and it would only be for the best."

"Yes. That's right. It's what we believed. It's what we told him. It could only be for the best."

"And he believed you? Obviously. After some hesitation he finally took your advice?"

"Yes."

I turned to Robin sitting upright in his chair.

"I don't think there's anything else."

His Lordship signalled the witness to wait.

"You do realise, don't you, what Mr. Wallace has suggested?"

"Yes."

"That the police told you what they thought he had done?"

"Yes."

"And that bearing in mind his history both you and your sister were convinced that the police had got it right?

"Yes."

"So in a spirit of trying to help your brother you thought it best if you got him to confess?"

"Yes."

"And you found him in something of a state?"

"Yes."

"Dirty, dishevelled, possibly bloodied?"

"Yes."

"Asking for his medicine?"

"Yes."

"Do you know. You might not know this. Had he been given food?"

"I don't think he had. Not even a cup of tea."

"Did he tell you that?"

"I think so. Yes."

"And, this is my final question. Did he appear to you distressed?"

"He was crying."

"Are you sure? If I suggested to you he might have been laughing what would you say to that?"

"No. He wasn't laughing. He was crying."

"Sure?"

"I'm sure."

"Thank you. Your evidence has been most helpful. You may go."

Chevalier wheeled round in the chair he was beginning to master. To his credit he showed neither envy nor regret.

"Very good. Well done. Take the sister as well."

So I did. If anything it was even easier. I was inspired by my luck. I went through the same routine. Not perhaps in the same order nor with the same emphasis, and, as might be expected, not with always the same response. But we got the gist of it. She corroborated her brother's account. Convinced - they had become convincing. That's really what it came down to. What this hearing without a jury was all about.

"I shall retire and give my judgment in the morning." His Lordship rose, bowed, and made his arthritic exit from the bench.

Chevalier, Robin and I made our way to Chevalier's humble hotel, dropped off his papers and walked across the road to the nearest pub for a drink.

Next morning we sat in our respective places, Robin and I making our respective careful notes.

"The defence submits that confessions made to his siblings and recorded by police should be excluded ..." He repeated our arguments. "I have heard evidence from those present. It is inconsistent so far as the police seem to have found him voluble and cheerful whilst his brother and sister remember him dishevelled and distressed.

I have not troubled myself unduly with this issue although, had all three agreed that he was in good spirits, I might have hesitated over its effect.

I find that he had not seen a doctor or solicitor and that he had not been given any of his prescribed medication and nor, for some reason, any food or facilities that might have allowed him to refresh. I further find that his brother and sister had been produced, indeed the police despatched a car to fetch them, to induce a confession and that the police had hidden one of their number to record all conversation and that this ploy, as it was, was rewarded

Paul Genney

with success. I make no criticism of this plan. It seems to me it was a perfectly proper exercise of their duty to thoroughly investigate this serious offence. What I must decide, according to statute, is that are his undoubted confessions admissible in evidence as reliable - notwithstanding whether or not they are true.

This is a serious offence. It is in the public interest that those responsible be convicted and punished. It is in the public interest that the jury be put in possession of all admissible evidence upon which they can eventually decide. Guilt or innocence. It is in the interests of justice that relevant evidence shall not be withheld.

And yet. The circumstances of this unequivocal admissions are so abnormal as to make me pause. Do they exceed the provisions of S.76(2) (b) and raise such a serious doubt as to their reliability that I am driven to withdraw this evidence from the jury?

I want you to know that I have thought about this long and hard. In effect, this was an interview. An informal interview, an unofficial interview. An interview performed by amateurs, his brother and sister, but amateurs he trusted most. They asked questions of him and he provided answers. That is what an interview is. Now had this been a police interview of a distressed individual deprived of legal assistance, food, rest, and medication, I would have no hesitation in excluding this evidence from going before a jury. Should I treat it differently because although the police organised it, and covertly attended at it, the questions didn't come from their lips?

Put this way the answer is obvious. In reality there is no difference. If anything, because of the trust he understandably reposed in his family, it is even more unreliable. I am driven to exclude it. A happy result for the defence perhaps, but I apply the law as it is."

He looked across at Mr. Eaves. The smiling Mr. Eaves.

"I hope you have understood. If not, your legal advisors will explain. This trial will proceed."

Well let's look at this for a moment. What have the prosecution got? An admitted contact, an admitted passing of a skip supported by a few vague stills from a run-down CCTV. It's over. I know it is. So does Robin. So does Mr. Eaves. Only Chevalier seems ready to keep plodding up and down the pitch ever ready to try and score a goal, but, having got his measure as I suspect I have, I suggest we are in danger of one of those spectacular overhead bicycle kicks going into the roof of his own net.

"Ask the judge to rise." I pull his gown knowing how irritating it is.

"Why? What for?"

"Stock take. Assess what's left."

We gathered round the table in the robing room and weighed it up.

No forensic, no blood, no D.N.A. Nothing on the weapon. Nothing on his clothes. No confessions to the police. And now, thanks to me, no admissions in his cell.

"You've done very well" I told him, "least said, soonest mended. Say nothing. Ask no questions. Let them call their evidence. Let their case stagger on to the end, and when it finally runs into the buffers at the end of the line, make a submission of 'no case'."

Why does the obvious always surprise?

"What do you think Robin? Perhaps I should see Mr. Eaves."

No need. He knows the form. He shook hands with Chevalier in his cell. No more cold beds and cold soup. No more long lost rambling trips with Global Solutions, as Group 4 now laughingly call themselves, wandering up and down England dropping off prisoners as they occasionally stumble across a court. No more intensive sessions with psychiatrists, men madder than himself, in high security hospitals. No more trays of tea with us.

"I agree. Say nothing. Anyway, what is there to challenge? Keep mum and I'm off."

Which is exactly what we did. A new role for Chevalier who could waffle with the best. For once he kept quiet until the jury filed out at the end of the prosecution case.

"My Lord. We move 'no case'. Insufficient evidence upon which a jury properly directed could possibly convict. What do we have? We have a cultural evening planned in Hull. We have …"

"Yes Mr. Chevalier I remember … it seems an unlikely prospect … I am familiar with all the evidence. What does the crown have to say?"

But what could he say? Make the most of what he had, what little now was left, make it look as significant as he could.

"Thank you. I will rise and consider this overnight. I shall give my ruling in the morning."

I booked into a cheap hotel, and lay in my shoes on the bed. Time to ring Clematis. A far more important case. Time to make some new arrangements. Time perhaps, and this might please her, time to try the great outdoors. But also time to tell her of my achievements, how I took over the case, fielded the baton from Chevalier's faltering hands, crossed the line in triumph. Time for a drink, a little love, a lot of passion, the hunter home from the hill.

I got reception to put me through.

"Hello. Hello." I cried in expectation.

A rough voice answered, Rodney obviously at home.

"Wallace. Is that you? What happened to my fucking money? Where's my fucking car?"

Chapter 21

We trooped back into court in the morning looking the worse for wear.

"I have considered this case carefully taking into full account the submissions made by counsel yesterday which I have found, in one instance at least, to have been most helpful.

There is no forensic evidence in this case and this troubles me. I have heard suggestions as to how this might have arisen and whilst I have sympathy with the argument in reality there is no evidence to assist. There are no admissions in interview. Thanks to my previous ruling there are no confessions in the hearing of the police. The evidence, such as it is, revolves around the admitted encounter and inferences the jury might be invited to draw from the inferior recording of the video cameras and the enhanced stills the police have obtained. I am hesitant as to this. I daresay during the course of that fateful evening other members of the public might have been tempted or persuaded into that doorway. Unfortunately the police have not kept the rest of the film. But this is a busy roadway in the centre of a city containing a tramp no doubt in the habit of asking passers-by for cash. Any number including the murderer might have been tempted to respond. So Mr. Eaves is one of their number. I accept he seemed agitated to a limited degree when he left. But what is that? It could be as he said in interview - a sudden determination to be away. And what if he passes a skip? There are enough of these in Hull. This one has been parked up, for some reason, in one of its major streets. How many other people that night might have hurried by? Again, the police in what I am assured is standard practice for Humberside, have thrown the rest of the video away. The prosecution say there is enough left upon which a properly directed jury might convict. The defence as might be expected, and if I understand Mr. Chevalier de St. Croix correctly, say otherwise. They say there is not enough. I have reminded myself of the leading cases of Galbraith and Shippey, to which I have not been referred. No matter. I find that following these authorities that the evidence, taken at its highest, is not enough upon which this jury might properly convict. Accordingly ..." he paused to gather up his papers, "... this case is dismissed."

Chevalier rose to detain him. "Yes Mr. Chevalier de St. Croix, the defendant is discharged - and costs from central funds."

The three of us ran over the road to the pub.

"Mine's a double gin and tonic."

"And mine's a double brandy and ginger, mon ami."

I shuffled off to the crowded bar, and reliant upon years of practice, slid my way to the front.

The victor in the case of Regina -v- Eaves.

"And mine's a small glass of wine."

Chapter 22

So I asked Doreen out for a drink. Why not? We're both single. Or I assume she is now that Giles is out of the picture concentrating on his case - which is more than I am. Anyway even if he's not out of the picture he's certainly out of funds. No work, no income and, thanks to Horace, no expense account to fall back on. So no little trips either. It seemed the perfect moment to intervene.

I was a little surprised at her reaction. "What do you want to take me out for?"

Well there's a question. Better to be careful with the truth.

"I think you'll find we have a lot of things to discuss."

"What things?" She looked at me over her glasses. "What have you got in mind?"

Now I wasn't expecting her to punch the air and break into song, but her suspicions were becoming disconcerting.

I tried to squeeze her hand as it rested on the phone but she quickly moved it away.

"Let's not go into that here …" I soldiered on, "…best left to when we're alone."

"All right. 5.30. After I get finished in here."

I was relieved at having got so far.

"Make it the Stag at Bay shall we?" and I nonchalantly strolled away.

Bloody women, I don't know why I bother. My first pint didn't touch the sides. Putting it out for Jackson. I could understand that. But succumbing to the slothful charm of Giles? I thought of them in London. Giles by day attending the Bar Conference, sweaty brow over his notebook, beetling back to the hotel to be by her side at night. Throwing open the bedroom door of their hotel, his belly poking through the straining buttons of his sodden shirt, and Doreen, with all day to get ready, lounging on the bed in her silk pyjamas propped up on one elbow balancing a glass of wine.

After him it should have been easy. Enter Wallace coming up on the inside at a canter flashing past the post in front of the goggle-eyed Giles.

"I'll have a gin and tonic thank you."

She was wearing a long green coat buttoned up to the neck against the cold. I noticed she had changed her shoes somewhere and was now tottering on unusually high heels.

"Slimline with ice and slice of lemon please."

We took our drinks into the plotting parlour and, pulling up our chairs in front of the fire, balanced our feet on the grate.

I offered her a cigarette and was surprised when she took one and expertly rolled it to the corner of her mouth

"Well Mr. Wallace, this is very cosy. What is it exactly that you have in mind?"

I gave her my reassuring smile. The one I use on punters. The one that succeeds every time. But it didn't. Somehow she was impervious. It wasn't what I wanted - what I wanted was her head back laughing, occasionally lowering her eyes. We talked seriously. About chambers, about Jackson, about the absent but somehow ever present Giles. But not in that silly flirtatious way I was expecting and that I was anxious to promote. She was genuinely concerned about our future and when, if ever, we were planning to appoint a new clerk. She had nothing but praise for Jackson. Not in an exaggerated way, or even a bitter way as one might adopt who had suffered at his hands, but in a matter of fact tone which genuinely assessed his worth.

"A great clerk. We're going to miss him. I doubt you understand the work he brought in. And good to you Mr. Wallace. He used to sing your praises. The times I've heard him persuading people to send stuff to you. To all of you really. Very even-handed. Even to Mr. Pickles. Always gave the young ones a chance." She sighed and assented to another gin.

"You'll find it difficult to replace him. A great shame he's gone."

And on to Giles. Again without prejudice or side. I found it impossible to descend into the playful - she passed through suggestion and innuendo with that same implacability of tone.

"And now Mr Baring, I can't believe it. To be charged by the police with grievous bodily harm. Whatever are they thinking of Mr. Wallace? It's incredible. You couldn't meet a nicer man. What about his wife and family? No longer our head of chambers, no work coming in, whatever is he going to do? I hear you're representing him. Overheard really, I couldn't, if I may say so, think of a better man."

Was she genuine? Genuinely concerned I mean, or was this a ploy to put me off my unwelcome stride?

"Thank you Doreen." I gravely told her, missing her hand yet again. "I'll try to justify your faith."

And so we chatted away for hours, drinking steadily growing in friendship, our feet glowing in front of the coals. She was decent, very serious, concerned and a little garrulous. But good company. We talked about things we knew, about a life we superficially shared. And I confess I enjoyed it. I ventured the odd joke, certainly not good ones, diluted as they were by the seriousness that somehow undermined the purpose of the occasion, but rendered it nonetheless enjoyable on its unexpected level instead.

"Baring and Jackson. You're right Doreen. Those were the days. Days of wine and roses. Whitebait Chambers. No doubt a little fish in the eyes of the Bar Council – half of them probably never heard of us. Probably just as well. But they did the job, they brought home the bacon, they meant a lot round here."

She suddenly seemed to notice the time and started to her feet. "Goodness me, I've kept you."

"No Doreen." I caught her hand at last. "It's been lovely. I've enjoyed it." And I meant it. It hadn't been what I expected but how nice to enjoy a simple pleasant chat. As always I thought of Laura. That was roses; that was wine.

"Let me walk you to the bus station. You never know in a city like this."

She protested, but I insisted. I wasn't going to let her go tottering off across town through the dark streets, past clubs and pubs when I had been plying her with drink. Certainly not. I escorted her to her stop and waited patiently until the bus, late as usual, stopped to pick her up.

"Goodnight" I told her, "I've enjoyed it."

"Yes" she said, "so have I. I've had a pleasant time."

I waved to her from the pavement as her bus finally pulled away into the rain and I caught a glimpse of her white face through the window, her coat still buttoned up as she waved, more animated than she'd been all evening, and mouthed a final goodbye.

Flying in the face of this decency my thoughts drifted to Clematis and Pauline, and the steadfast suffering of Laura. What am I doing here? What am I trying to achieve? I know what I'm trying to achieve, and it doesn't look like it's about to happen soon. But what of it? I missed those nights with Laura, buggering about in the kitchen while the potatoes boiled dry in the pan. Things you take for granted; things you miss the most.

I had enjoyed being with Doreen. Her pedestrian good nature, her optimism, her concern for others. Her resolute refusal to join me in deriding those I was anxious to traduce.

I walked away as the bus splashed around the corner. A decent girl, I'd got her wrong. Not that I hadn't tried. I'd had a good time in spite of myself. She was right, it had been pleasant. What was coming over me? I looked forward to doing it again. Does everything have to be physical? Isn't it possible to be friends?

I trod warily through the dark streets of central Hull, making way for a lurching figure stumbling towards me; hurriedly crossing the road to avoid three silent men in hoods. Cars stopped with a squeal of brakes and suddenly accelerated away, a dog's lonely barking echoed from an alley, I was startled by a distant shout. I was beginning to regret walking Doreen to her bus. But how would she have fared alone? Another drunk staggered away from a pool of urine trickling out of a shop door and belched as I made way for him to pass. I decided to nip into chambers, attracted by the lights still burning in my upstairs room.

Jas would accompany me to my car. I felt I had gone far enough.

But first the reflex trip to my pigeonhole; picking my way along the pitch black corridor, I finally found the light switch and was surprised to see another note from Horace which I nearly crumpled up.

'The Appointment of our new Senior Clerk.' I read it with some interest. 'Shall be decided by a full meeting of all members of chambers - as becomes the new spirit of transparency and openness - each member to have equal voting rights, the opportunity to ask questions and, if necessary, speak.'

'This meeting to be held at Oddfellows Hall.' We must have made it up with their committee. Perhaps we'd paid the bill. 'This coming Sunday

afternoon 2 p.m. prompt. The candidates have been short-listed as follows:-
Mr. Royston Stringfellow; Mrs. Pauline Tomkinson; Mr. Adolphus Bling. CVs
enclosed.

I ran upstairs to find Jas in his shirtsleeves, the ashtrays overflowing,
wading through a lever arch file making notes as he went. "Jesus Christ. What
do you think of this?"

Chapter 23

But I wasn't really interested in what he thought. Why should I be? He didn't know any of the candidates. He had no idea of the past. I wondered if 'in the spirit of openness' he'd be allowed to vote, and, as Horace so charmingly put in, 'if necessary' speak.

I helped myself to one of my own cigarettes. God Almighty. Where was this coming from? Why was she doing it? She's loaded with money, playing the pretty housewife, hostess at dinner parties, faithful companion on worldwide tours. Silent partner in repetitive sex. Why was she bothering? Did she really want it? I doubt it. Was she looking for some idle distraction? Something to pass the time. A reason to get out of bed.

I paced up and down the room while Jas put his files away, thinking aloud of the possibilities, debating what it might mean.

Did she want some excuse to get involved with me? Ridiculous. It was stupid to flatter myself. Anyway there were better ways of doing it. Tried and tested ways. Why not a telephone call to Pat?

Then what is it? Why a job like this? And what might it mean for Whitebait Chambers? I considered the bigger picture. Certainly we would pick up all the work from Cranmer Carter & Co. Of late a little had been trickling away. That little rivulet would rapidly dry up. On the other hand we don't just depend on Cranmer's for our work. By no means. There are other solicitors in Hull. Not so big and not so well disposed perhaps - Parmenters for example. Might they not suspect favouritism towards Tomkinson and take their work elsewhere? A nice balance. A difficult equation to resolve. Putting it brutally, all of Tomkinson's work set against the possible loss of others. A plus or a minus, it was difficult to know.

But why was I skirting round the periphery? There were more fundamental questions to decide. I told Jas to keep quiet. What was in it for me?

We sat on hard wooden chairs arranged in rows as if at a church service, wearing overcoats and scarves (McIntosh in a deerstalker) puffing out our cheeks against the cold.

We can't have been all that chummy with the committee - they'd not put on the heating, the bar was shuttered, the canteen firmly closed. Horace and Browne-Smythe were sitting on the stage alongside the three candidates who were waiting to address the hustings in an election that I assumed had already been rigged.

Tomkinson had reinforced it in one of his rare telephone calls to me.

"Listen Wallace. For some reason Pauline wants something to do. I would have thought she had enough on her hands looking after me. Apparently not. She wants a career. Misses the cut and thrust of court. Fancies a bash with you lot. God knows I've warned her. There must be better things to do. Anyway, her hat's in the ring and it had better stay there. I've spoken to Horace. Made him aware of the score. He's seen the force of my arguments. Understood how especially useful Pauline might be. And that goes for his chums in chambers which, as I understand it, is almost the lot. Just make sure you and that crowd of knobheads in the Stag don't rock the boat. Nice talking to you. Goodbye."

I don't think I'd said a word. After 'hello' that is. But I'd certainly got the message, and Humphrey and McIntosh got it too.

I had no idea what she'd be like. I could see her rolling in late and leaving early, spending precious time doing her nails. On the other hand, and one never knew with her, she might throw herself into it, even be good at it, something like Jackson; out for lunch with solicitors, joining me in looking for work.

I quite fancied that. Cruising round town with the lovely Pauline, my hands up to the elbows in chambers' entertainment account - no one would dare to query Pauline - my hands into piles of new instructions, my hands ...

well who knows where it might end.

"Might I introduce Mr. Stringfellow?" Horace was on his feet, wringing his hands, blinking through his glasses, reading from his notes. "A public relations adviser, as I believe, to a multinational company, copious references which I am sure you all have read. Wants to return to his roots. Wants to come back to Hull."

He smiled as Mr. Stringfellow nodded and got to his feet. "The procedure will be the same for all applicants. A short speech and an opportunity for questions, the candidates will retire whilst we take a vote."

And Stringfellow wasn't bad. He knew what to say, and said it with confidence. It was all about publicity apparently, putting your brand name about. The press, local radio, Classic FM, interviews on Look North.

"Publicity's the name of the game. Good, bad, or indifferent, get your name in lights. Look at the world outside - chambers moving into new and exciting fields, extending their premises, taking on new staff. Don't neglect the detail. A marriage, an engagement, the retirement of an old and faithful member of staff ...." What a chance we'd missed with Jackson. Whitebait Chambers settles out of court. Payment estimated at tens of thousands of pounds. Jackson moving to a villa in Barbados on the proceeds. Photographed saying goodbye to his friends, "...the recruitment of new members. I'm told you have a new pupil. Put it in the paper. Let the locals know what you're about. New and exciting cases. The results of those you've won. I hear one of your number has just secured a surprising acquittal in a murder ..." he paused to read from a postcard ... "Mr. Wallace I believe. Why not an interview with him? In your library. Mr. Wallace posing reading a book. And show your versatility. Mr. Wallace again, as it so happens, triumphing against several defendants in the recovery of a luxury car ... promote your leading members, put your best talent in the shop window," he was oblivious as to how popular this was making me, "... advertise your, dare I say it, our success. Get the word around. Everything leads to something. Always in the news. Always linked to success. Believe me, publicity is everything. It brings work rolling in.

Winning ways with Whitebait. People upon whom they can depend. With me you'll be a household name. With me we'll increase turnover, cut costs, maximise returns, and all be better off. I hope I get the opportunity to help you. To help you to help yourselves.

He should be a barrister himself.

Horace rose to his feet holding his hand up to stay the applause.

"Well. I must say. A very fine presentation. Hmm. Wallace the victor in two cases. I think that should be checked."

He looked around at the crowded pews. "Questions anyone?"

Somebody or other asked the inevitable. "What first attracted you to Whitebait Chambers? Why would you like to be our clerk?"

I stifled a groan. An underarm bowl to a professional batsman. I watched it whistle into the stands.

"Thank you. Thank you." Horace holding up his hands again. "What I think would be helpful, and again demonstrating that democracy is to be the future keynote of our deliberations, might I invite a question from our newest member? Over to you Jas."

Jas? Jas? What has he got to do with it? I'm all in favour of democracy. In principle that is. Practice is taking principle too far.

Jas got to his feet, that amiable smile playing inevitably on his lips.

"How very kind of you to ask me. I hesitate to presume. What do I really know of such a successful chambers? What do I know of Whitebait whom only Whitebait know? Anyway. Allow me to make a few small enquiries on your behalf."

He looked directly at Mr. Stringfellow who, all smiles himself, waited to put another slow ball into the crowd.

"Assume chambers' gross income at two million. Just for the sake of argument. What proportion do you propose be used in publicity?"

"Well, that ultimately is a matter for chambers, but as an initial investment to get the show on the road, something in the region of 10 percent."

"So two hundred thousand pounds. Is that what you're saying?"

Mr. Stringfellow straightened his bat.

"If that's the calculation. I suppose so. Yes."

"And how do you break that down? T.V., radio, the press, legal journals, interviews. How do you spend 10 percent of our income on that?"

Good question. Two hundred thousand pounds. Jackson did it for a round of drinks. We heard 'broad brush' 'enhanced market position' 'invest to accumulate' 'reverse gearing' what's that?

I think I'd heard enough. Two hundred thousand pounds. Time to bring back Giles.

Jas was still on his feet. Pretending to scratch his head.

"Sounds like chambers' contributions might be going up."

Next candidate. Mr. Stringfellow on his way back to the pavilion. Pauline had drawn second lot.

"Well" she said, "I agree with much of what Mr. Stringfellow has said. However, I think Cranmer Carter & Co. already know your worth. As some of you will be aware, I have very good connections with that firm. They are anxious to support you - being aware, without publicity might I say, of your value to them. I look forward to enhancing our special relationship. Building on it. Making it 100 percent. I don't see publicity could make it any better. With the greatest of respect to Mr. Stringfellow that is. I think it would be better to build on what we have rather than cast about, at what sounds enormous expense, to bring in others who have previously shown total lack of support. I know you. I know you all. I know what you can do. I know that I can help you do it. I rely on you, and I hope you can rely on me."

We don't need any questions from Jas. Pauline subsided into her seat. I examined, why do I bother, the quality of her shoes, her suit, her impeccable, what appeared to be starched, shirt, or is it a blouse? Sophisticated and smart. She rooted around in her handbag and produced her spectacles, adjusted them about half way down her nose and expectantly looked about.

"I think we all know Pauline. I don't think I'll trouble you for questions. Let's move on." So much for democracy. Horace signalled to the third member of this disparate triumvirate. A fat man. Worse than a fat man if that's possible. A fat man with ginger hair,

"… Mr. Adolphus Bling. The floor is yours."

"Well I must say. Very kind, very kind. A bit like Pauline here I also know who you are. Been trying to queer your pitch for years. Clerk at Pinnacle Chambers in Leeds. Not senior clerk unfortunately. That's what I'm looking for from you. Why I'm here. But let me tell you one or two secrets. Might find it interesting. As far as I'm able to go. I daresay you've been wondering how it is we pinch your work. I daresay there's been times you've talked about it. Wondered how it is so much stuff goes down the road and you the only outfit in town."

"We talk of little else." McIntosh sitting under a sign with a cigarette extinguished by a red skull and crossbones lit up a large cigar.

"I'll bet you do. First thing, number one, total contact. They may complain but they like it. They love it. Over and over again. Always, but always, as soon as you get a brief. What we do is that we write an advice. It doesn't matter if it's about nothing. Totally meaningless, who cares? It gives them security. Covers their collective arse. What's more, gives them something to do. Make enquiries, look for witnesses, bugger off and take photographs. Get the runners running. Then they bill for the work.

Number two. Keep them informed. They may complain you're always on the phone but they like that as well. Let them know how the case is going. Bring them up to speed. If possible, after mature reflection, give them something else to do. Bang out another advice. Get the runners out of the office. Allow them to charge more fees.

Thirdly, after the case is over. I know what you lot do. Or most of you. Bugger off for a drink. Perfectly natural. It's just what I would do. But before you raise the crooked elbow why not give them a call? Bask in their congratulations or, as is more likely, give them advice on appeal. Another contact. Something or other for which they can raise a bill.

Fourthly. Entertainment. Get to know the staff. That is everybody. Top man. Bottom man. Even the tea girl. Find out their birthdays. That's what we do. A nice card, bunch of flowers, maybe a case - a case not a bottle - of wine. And Christmas. You know the season of goodwill. Send them a seasonal greeting. Fuck it, another case of wine. £25 outlay and in a fortnight a brief worth more than five grand. Groom your clients gentleman, stroke them. Occasionally muss their hair. But look after them. Know them. Make them your friends, your chums, your acquaintances, but always, make them yours.

Number five. Continuing education. A load of crap but so what? We run seminars. Some nerd or other gives a presentation about the continuing changes to the law. That's all this government ever does. Good job. Don't complain. Turn it to your advantage. Tell them how it affects them. Tell them what it means, what it does, and how it reflects in fees. Then off to the restaurant. Very chummy. Starter, main, desserts. Bonds that are forged in steel. Toast another change in the law.

Sixth. Come to the football. Not Leeds United. Not any more. Manchester United instead. A corporate box and prawn sandwiches. And if you're desperate. Why not take them to Hull?

Corporate hospitality. The St. Ledger. Didn't know we did that did you? And always take them to York. And the rugby. Understand you boys play league. Down to Wembley then for the cup. Train fare, match, dinner, and clubbing. Everything arranged. Still wondering why we do so well? Another generation. Another story. I don't care how clever you are, what you're like in court. This is the way we do it. I'll not go into everything. But this is how we steal your work."

There was silence. It made you think. If we didn't take him it sounded like he'd steal some more. Browne-Smythe had his hand in the air. "Permission to speak?"

"Yes. Yes get on with it." Horace was deep in thought.

"Unfortunately work is contracting; crime figures are coming down …"

"So they are. But crime is going up. And do you know why?" he looked around, "because no one bothers to report it. What's the point? No insurance and fear of reprisals. But imagine this - and it'll take some imagination - by a miracle the police stumble across some culprits. Ah. Different story. Fully recorded. So detection rates are going up."

Well. Just imagine. Our work shrinking when there was even more about. And down to bastards like this.

"Thank you. Thank you. I think we'll take a vote." Horace turned to the candidates sitting beside him. "Would you mind for a moment waiting outside?"

"Well …" he looked around the meeting, "… three very effective presentations. Last chap seems to know a lot. On the other hand, Pauline knows a lot of people … questions anyone?"

Browne-Smythe had his hand in the air but Horace ignored him. "No one? Yes Browne-Smythe, pass around the ballots. Secret of course. Single transferable vote. 1st preference. 2nd preference. 3rd preference. Perhaps that won't be necessary. If no one candidate secures an immediate majority, the one with the least votes is eliminated and those voting for him simply substitute their second preferences in the second vote. I think I've got it right. Hurry up Browne-Smythe, let's get on."

He gave me the job of ringing Tomkinson.

"After all you know the family. Understand you're one of Pauline's oldest friends. Why not ring him tonight?"

I think I need a drink. Probably several. But what with meeting up with McIntosh and Humphrey to discuss the situation, naturally in the Stag at Bay, and then making my way slowly home down the back roads, putting the car away, feeding the animals, opening a bottle of wine, it was not till nearly midnight that I rang his number and listened to the ring tone chiming endlessly away.

I was about to put it down when he answered. "Tomkinson. This had better be important," he said.

"Wallace here. Horace asked me to ring. It's about the job Pauline applied for. No doubt she's home by now. You've had a little chat."

"Matter of fact she's not. Apparently gone to her mother's. Make this snappy. When does she start?"

"Ah … not home yet …"

"And how much have you decided to pay? She's not doing this for fucking nothing. And then there's holidays. I saw your stupid advertisement. Nowhere near enough. Next month we've booked a cruise."

"Well … certainly don't bother cancelling it …"

"And what about her percentage? For all the work I'm going to send you. In a way, the work she's bringing in."

"Yes. Her percentage … obviously you heard about Jackson?"

"Jackson told me himself. And I'm rather inclined to agree with him. She won't be coming for less."

"Well no. You're right in a manner of speaking …"

He grew impatient. I could sense him checking his watch. "Get Horace to ring her in the morning. Some time after ten."

"Charles. She didn't get it. I'm very sorry. Somehow she didn't get the job."

I thought he'd put the phone down. Rather hoped he had.

"You're telling me are you … are you Wallace? You're fucking telling me, at midnight, that Pauline, my wife Pauline, the wife of your biggest, perhaps only, supporter is somehow by your reckoning not good enough for your fucking job. Are you serious? Is this a joke? Are you trying to be funny? What are you? Some fucking late night prankster trying to pull my leg? If I thought you were serious, you deplorable little prick, I would take your head and boot it over the Pennines landing by the banks of the Mersey on a suitably positioned spike."

"Charles. I'm sorry. It wasn't me. I voted for her."

"Of course you did you lying little shit. What happened? Take your time, tell me about it. Tell me how you bunch of ignorant lemmings contrived to jump off the cliff."

"She was very good. Charles. Excellent. None better. Well perhaps one better. Democracy in action. Something went wrong with the vote. Won the first vote by a landslide. Unfortunately just short of a majority. Had to have another ballot. It's in Horace's new constitution. Second time round she came in… er … second. Terribly, terribly close. Some chap from Leeds won it. Absolute charlatan. Fat – and ginger to boot. You might know him. Looking forward to meeting you. Hoping to continue with our relationship. Happy to continue doing your work."

"Are you serious? Are you fucking drunk, stupid, or both?"

"I'm sure you'll like him ... tomorrow if you're available. He suggests a business lunch."

"Business. What business? Tell Horace. Tell the mad Scotsman. Tell the pomaded poofter. Tell Giles if you like. Tell anybody. Tell this cunt from Leeds. Get it through your head. That near perfect vacuum that you call a brain. There won't be any business. You might as well shut your fucking shop."

"No need to raise your voice."

"No business, none, fuck all, zilch. Especially for you, you oily little shit. Nothing. Absolutely nothing. What you already have - box it up and send it back."

"Charles you must be disturbing the neighbours ..."

"Turn down Pauline. I don't believe it. Turn down her - you turn down me. And without me you're finished. All of you. Every man jack of that tired fucking dishonest fucking incompetent band. Don't ring me. Any of you. Don't try and contact me. No notes, no letters, no messages, no e-mails, no fucking whinging calls. You're over. Fuck off the lot of you. I don't even know your names."

I rang Horace immediately apparently getting him out of bed.

"I'm afraid he didn't take it too well."

He listened in silence whilst I described Tomkinson's rather adverse reaction.

"Enough ... enough. I shouldn't have trusted you with the call."

Chapter 24

We sat opposite each other, our knees cramped under a Formica table. I captured her hand at last.

Doreen smiled from under her head scarf holding her mug with both hands.

"What are you doing about Giles? He's getting awfully low."

What am I doing? Nothing. Absolutely nothing. Of course I'm not. He's the man with time on his hands. A resident of sleepy hollow, the land where time stood still. Let him do it for himself.

"Everything possible is being done." I squeezed her flaccid knuckles reassuringly. "No stone unturned. Got an enquiry agent on the job. Casper Jones. Ex-detective inspector. You might know him. Taking statements from all those on the guest list, rooting round the hotel tapping up the staff; been to see the band, those idiots in blazers and straw boaters, remember them? Sorry forgot you weren't there …"

"I wasn't invited."

"Really? Anyway, interviewed the management, still trying to see the Recorder of Hull. Proving a bit elusive. In London with his lady wife. As soon as Caspar's got it all together he'll send me a dossier. I'll give it all I've got …" I kneaded the palm of her hand, "… weed out those who might be useful

- stuff the rubbish down the can. Unfortunately he seems to have lost Pauline. Withdrawn her statement. Tomkinson has let it be known that if we force her, you know issue a summons to make her come to court ... er ... well ... she might have a different story to tell."

"Mrs. Baring's been on the phone wanting to speak to you. Like to give you a statement herself."

I bet she would. But I doubt if it would be helpful. On the other hand. I thought about our fleeting meetings at chambers' dinners. Rich folds of yellow fat. A concertina about the waist. Lacquered hair you could see through. False breasts, false teeth and a false smile. Perhaps not. I concentrated on Doreen, that wistful upturned face. Why did we always talk about Giles?

"Giles would like the new clerk," she told me, disentangling her hand to pick up her mug, "seems to know what he's about."

"Does he? He'll have to, there's bugger all work in Hull."

"Yes I know. He's on the phone constantly. Ringing up his contacts in Leeds."

"Probably wants his old job back. Now that Whitebait Chambers has finally nosedived to oblivion. Wondering if they'll take him back."

I thought about it. Was it a cunning ploy? Slide the bastard into us. Defeat Pauline by lies and promises. Lose our work to them. Then pretend to grovel, false desperation and humility, begging them to take him back. A fat and ginger Trojan horse. Was he as clever as that?

No. We're talking about Leeds Chambers. I had to remind myself. If anything, dumber than ourselves. Anyway how would they know that Pauline was applying? Unless she'd told them herself.

I lit a cigarette to give this serious consideration.

"I'm sorry. Will you put that out?"

What? I should have realised. No ash trays. No customers either. A voice echoed out from behind the tea urn. Pious and insolent at once.

"This is a non-smoking café."

A non-smoking café. Can you believe it? No wonder it was empty. I could remember the welcome of its smoky steamy warmth. Shopping piled up in the corner. Happy faces shouting to each other through the noise. In a few weeks they'd be boarding up the windows, another friendly oasis forever lost.

I strung her out playing for time.

"When did this happen?"

"Last week. Legislation's coming. A healthy and smoke free environment. Why should workers be subjected to your foul and dangerous smoke?"

Because it's your job. Obviously. Why should smokers, incidentally the backbone of your trade, be forced to smoke outside? Another British institution lost to political correctness. If I wanted fresh air I'd take a flask to the park. Put on running shorts. Take a few laps round the green. Handstands in front of the bandstand. Why would these intolerant keep-fit fanatics want to sit in a café? Obviously they didn't. That's why it was empty, why they had nothing to do. Just like us they had cut off the source of their income. Just like us they were waiting for bills they couldn't pay.

I put my hand tentatively, as if by accident, upon what turned out to be Doreen's rather bony knee.

"Let's get out of here. Anywhere." I could see her hesitate. Doubtful of further intimacy, unsure of where it might lead. I had to do it. Lies triumphing over honesty. I had to do it. I knew what was good for her.

"So we can talk about Giles."

But it wasn't long before I had to talk to Giles himself. He was on the phone first thing in the morning, catching me coming out of the shower, I hopped about on cold lino with the cordless under my chin. I was hoping it was Clematis or Pauline or Doreen or anybody. Why did it have to be Giles?

"This is preposterous. Can you hear me? My trial's fixed before we're properly prepared."

Funny. I thought that's what he wanted

But fixed? How can it be? I hadn't been to court for a preliminary hearing. I hadn't discussed pleas with his co-defendants and the prosecution. We hadn't collectively decided which witnesses we wanted, or tried to find a date we were able to attend.

"It's been done administratively ..." he complained working up a head of steam, "... something to do with saving money."

Money. Money. Why is it always money? What happened to justice? What happened to fairness, the presumption of innocence? Whatever happened to that? Why does it always have to be cash? But the bastards were deaf to my remonstrations. Refused to take it out. I think it's something to do with the Recorder. Apparently now taking a cruise. Definitely not available. Has ordered it be listed immediately. According to him too important to wait.

"I know he couldn't come to dinner, but has he given us a statement?" Giles persisted. "I wrote begging him to reconsider. "He was on the top table as you might expect. Saw everything. He must have done."

"Apparently not." He had to know sooner or later. "Casper's been on to him on ship to shore. Locked in conversation, looking the other way. Wishes you the best of luck. His lady wife sends her regards."

"Jesus Christ. I can't believe it. He used to be a chum."

"So did a lot of people. They're not so chummy now."

"What about Horace? He was there. Told me before my last chambers meeting he'd do anything to help."

"Anything apparently but being a witness. He won't give us a statement. He can remember vaguely your charging off commanding us to follow; an order he regretfully declined. Thereafter all was chaos - but he seems to recollect seeing you in the middle of it, in a role he is unable to determine or describe."

"Fuck him. What about Browne-Smythe?"

"There again we seem to have a problem. He'd like to help of course. Nothing would suit him better. Nothing in the world could give him greater pleasure. But what he saw or what he thinks he saw might not be helpful and he is very sorry but feels - if he goes into the witness box - duty bound by his oath."

"Does he now? The first time in all the years I've known him; fettered by the truth."

"Anyway. Best to have a few good witnesses than a legion of bad ones. I know I can rely on McIntosh and Humphrey. I can can't I? I know we've had our differences in the past, the odd misunderstanding, but whatever else they have guts and independence or I thought they had. Tell them I'd do the same for them."

"Giles, it's not possible. I talked to them myself. They haven't got a clue. Too far away and too drunk to take it in. Remember our table was virtually in the street."

"Nobody saw anything. None of my friends, my colleagues, my chums. Nobody saw anything. Too drunk, too far, too busy, otherwise looking away. Pontius Pilate and the three blind mice. You couldn't make it up. Thank God I've got Pauline. Without her I'd be fucked."

How to tell him? "Giles unfortunately it's not that simple. A lot's happened since you've been away. I assumed that Doreen's told you." He caught his breath.

"No. Not exactly. I thought it better not to take her calls. In the circumstances. Mrs. Baring hovering in the background. Making sure I wasn't disturbed."

Ah well. Giles too. Another one looking away.

"Listen Giles. Horace called a meeting to elect a new clerk. Surprisingly Pauline turned out to be a candidate. It certainly surprised me. Tomkinson's reluctant backing. Anyway she lost. Might not be the best decision we ever made. No job for Pauline, no work for us, and no statement for you."

"Jesus Christ. Wallace, all I've got is you."

"I'm not too sure about that. Just checked my diary. It's not a date I can do."

Chapter 25

Clematis finally called. At last. I tried to sound a little less enthusiastic than I felt.

"How are you? Nice of you to call."

"When do I get my car?"

Why are some people obsessed with private transport? Does it matter what vehicle you happen to drive? As long as you get from A to B in relative comfort and safety, what sort of jerks are you trying to impress? Other jerks like you apparently, and Clematis wasn't impressed.

"Rodney's got a letter from Parmenters. That outfit according to him that saw fit to pick you. They want to send an enquiry agent to Poland. They want Rodney to guarantee the expense. Some chap called Jones. Apparently it could take several weeks and run into thousands, Rodney's not so sure, what do you think?"

I think it's hopeless. On the other hand Rodney's yet to pay my bill. If we don't find Potolski we won't find the car, and if we don't find the car, I rather fancy we won't be finding the cash to settle my account. Something of a long shot, but then if you don't buy a ticket you won't get your name in the hat.

"Well it's tricky, obviously. I don't know much about Poland. Even less about the count. How many Count Potolskis are there? Assuming that's his name. And even if we find him, will he have the car? Or will he have a bank account instead? And if he has, how do we get our hands on the money? Jones could be kicking around for years. On the other hand, what else is there? And then again does an English judgment have jurisdiction in Poland? Have we signed a reciprocal agreement? Does it help they've joined the E.U.?

"You're the lawyer. I've relied on you throughout."

So she has. And so has Rodney. And I've relied on McIntosh. I think I'll stroll down to his room and try and find out.

"Need a little time for research. In the meantime do you fancy another inspection of the drive?"

I waited through the pause. The tiny wheels in her mind racing through the risks.

"We'll have to be careful. Rodney's not so stupid as he looks."

I sensed her calculating the odds of detection or was this what her call was really about? I found to my surprise how much I wanted to see her, visions of the lovely Clematis came flooding into my mind.

"Well not at your place and it's far too risky at mine."

"Anywhere in Hull?"

Anywhere expensive I should have said.

"I'm not so sure. When Parmenters mentioned Jones, Rodney already knew his name."

Did he? Did he by God. Did he know his telephone number as well? And did he know his fees? How much to keep a beady eye on a wife. An errant wife. His own wife. How much did he know?

"You say Rodney's not so stupid?"

"Of course he's not. Just because he's big doesn't make him thick. He's perceptive. Very perceptive. And protective. Very protective. I thought I told you all about it. We couldn't have a family ..."

I wasn't going to blunder about in this maze again.

"You did. You did. I think you told me it was all your fault."

"What if it was? Rodney forgave me. He got used to the idea. It might have taken him some time. But that's natural. What you might expect. What I didn't expect ..."

"Clematis. It's getting late."

"... was his concern for me. He didn't want me to brood about it. He was worried I'd blame myself. So he tried to distract me in the only way he knew. Diversions. Trips. You know, holidays and pleasures. Little outings, but always by ourselves. The theatre and restaurants. He used to call them treats ..."

"Do you know, it's nearly half past three."

"... and we stopped sleeping together. Slept in separate rooms; eventually in separate sides of the house. In the early days he was all over me, but it gradually faded away. In the end I became his daughter, the one he couldn't have. He dotes on me ..."

"Clematis, this is all terribly, terribly interesting."

"Absolutely adores me. You've seen the house, probably every bloody room, and you've seen the furniture and the paintings and all my clothes in the wardrobes and the hundreds of pairs of shoes. But you haven't seen all the jewellery, the trust funds he's set up for me and the occasional - God help him - toy. Toy. Do you understand? I am his family; I am his children. Me. It's all he wants and it's all he's going to get. You're not playing with his wife - be careful - you'll be abusing his child."

"Jesus Christ. Well look ... let's forget ..."

"So it'll have to be outside."

"Well ... I don't know ..."

"So meet me by the duck pond. You know the one. I can't stand here talking all day."

God. What to do? There's a saying in Guatemala: a hot woman has more pull than a team of oxen. I can vouch that it's true.

I jumped into the shower, and into fresh underwear and, in a matter of minutes, into my car.

She was already there when I turned into the car park and wound down her window as I pulled alongside.

"What took you so long? Follow me."

What was I thinking of? An encounter in intermittent woodland with the day already dwindling away, my windscreen wipers squeaking against occasional drizzle, the rising wind beginning to stir the gently creaking tops of the ranks of darkening trees.

Where were we going? Where was she taking me? We shot through tiny villages down increasingly smaller roads like two demented rally drivers, we turned and twisted into the Wolds. I'll never find my way out of here. Is that what she intended? I knew she was angry about her car but was she planning to do me in? Intern me by an old stone wall locked in a shallow grave? A piece of rural England forever Wallace? Of course not. I knew what she wanted to do. What she'd been circling and hinting at for ages, I felt a primeval stir. We were climbing into foothills now; she seemed to know her way, passing the odd isolated cottage, rushing along beside a gurgling stream tumbling down the fell, she spun into a gravel track - I could see the lurch of her car as she changed down several gears - and with stones spinning under her wheels she slewed the car through a tumbledown gateway and along a forest track slowing to a stop by a pile of logs in what I assumed (and hoped) was an empty glade.

"Come on. Hurry up. Grab those blankets off the back seat. Don't forget to lock your car." Against whom I wondered. "This way. Don't hang about. We haven't got much time."

She plunged into the forest and in my shiny shoes I slid along behind.

"This'll do." She stopped in a stand of pines, hands on her hips, her chest heaving beneath her tracksuit, muddy trainers planted wide. She tossed that lovely raven hair and smiled. "What do you think?"

I really wasn't sure. As we lawyers say - on the one hand it was getting a bit nippy and night was closing in, on the other hand, those sparkling eyes, the flush of her cheeks, those small white teeth - reluctant to forego the preliminaries I gently unzipped her top.

"No time to fuck about."

How romantic is that? Not quite what I was expecting. Not quite a relaxed idyll in the woods. She slipped out of her tracksuit, pulled her sweater over her head, put both her hands behind her back and unhooked her bra, turning round she wriggled out of her knickers and leaning against a tree kicked off her trainers one by one.

"Come on. What are you waiting for?" She lay back on the blankets, eyes closed, lips half open, dew already pricking her hair, goose-pimples rising on her thighs. Well. The moment of truth. A gentleman couldn't leave a lady like this.

I laid my jacket carefully on a grassy mound and tried with numb fingers to undo my waistcoat buttons, as I hopped around trying to get my shoes through the legs of my trousers, which became entangled in some brambles which wouldn't set me free.

"For Christ's sake hurry up. How long do you think we've got?"

My God, it was cold. And wet. And prickly. Lots of sharp stones, hidden thorns, the odd nettle poking through the grass. Was it safe here? What if a deranged gamekeeper, an escaped lunatic, a crocodile of ramblers came sauntering through the trees? A mob of birds-egging schoolboys or an angry farmer set upon an evening stroll with his offended and goggle-eyed wife.

And there was another problem. One I hadn't envisaged. Clematis noticed it too. I daresay I'm pretty near the national average, whatever that might be. Is it weight, mass, length, circumference? My mind went back to the physics laboratory - elasticity, resistance, tensile strength? Clematis seemed to be getting impatient.

"What's the matter with you now?"

Nothing. Absolutely nothing. I hopped over towards her and fell into her comparative warmth. And it was nice. Odd and different. Intense, primeval, strangely moving and thankfully not prolonged. Clematis finished in some urgency for once ahead of me.

My God it was lovely. Panting and resplendent I lay back on the blankets, a cigarette clenched in my teeth blowing smoke at the stars.

"What was that noise?" Clematis was tying her shoe.

"What noise?"

"That noise. Can't you hear it? Christ I think it sounds like a car."

I marvelled how wonderfully she had attuned to nature. Lithe and graceful, her ears pricking up at the slightest noise - she cocked her head to listen to what I assumed was an imaginary sound.

"Hurry up. Get dressed. I don't like this, we've got to go."

"What a pity. I like to savour the moment, particularly after a performance like that. Interesting. Exciting even, but not something I was anxious to repeat. More an occasion to remember, something to savour in my dotage relaxing in a wicker basket chair.

"For God's sake Harry, get your clothes on. Don't you understand? We've got to go."

All right. All right. A gentleman will always humour a lady. I got dressed with the usual difficulty and arm in arm, oh happy days - I was moved to whistle a merry tune - we ambled back down a winding path - I hadn't realised we'd strayed so far - a lightness in my head, a spring in my step, an adventure over, we slowly approached our cars.

But now there were three.

As Clematis froze beside me, my merry whistling faded away.

"Who is it?" She was craning forward, the abandoned blankets dumped beside her feet.

"Do you recognise it? Do you recognise the car?"

I'm not very good at cars. Apart from the most expensive they all look the same to me.

"Can't see the number." She changed position, standing on the fallen blankets she put her hand to her eyes.

"My God."

"What is it?"

"Do you know who it is?"

"No. Of course I don't. My mind went back to an angry farmer. Obviously caught us trespassing on his land.

"It's Rodney."

"Rodney!"

Oh no. Anything but that. What to tell him? My mind was racing. Clematis, thankfully, more incisive than me.

"Run!"

"What?"

"Get running."

For a moment, in my panic, I asked to borrow her shoes.

"Harry. This is serious. Run as fast as you can."

So I did. What else could I do? I disappeared into the gloom crashing through the forest, jumping becks, fording rivers, scrambling up and down scree, cutting my fingers, scratching my face, grazing my knees, losing a shoe. I shot past the winking lights of distant farmhouses, floundered across ploughed fields, trudged through meadows past still and indifferent sheep. Where was I? And more importantly where was Rodney? Was he quietly stealing up behind me or had he somehow cut across and was waiting behind that distant rock? I thought of his great clenched fists possibly by now nursing a club. His taut metallic thighs bursting out of his running shorts - it all came back to me - those wild and staring eyes. I've never been one for jogging, now I wished I had. I collapsed against a gatepost. My legs ached, my head was bursting, I sensed an ominous pain in my chest. Shoes gone, clothes torn, spattered in mud, dressed in trailing thorns. Better get it over with. I had done my best. Exhaustion breeds defiance. The hunted animal turns to face its foe. I waited for Rodney to stroll up and finish me off. But he didn't. Perhaps I had outrun him, fear triumphing over strength and exercise. Perhaps he hadn't bothered. Perhaps he'd beat up Clematis instead. I tried to check the time but my watch was missing - how long had this been going on? I couldn't stay here. Not all night. The temperature was falling and frost was beginning to twinkle on the grass. I'd been looking for a memorable evening, well I'd remember this all right. The things you do for sex. Was this too high a price to pay? I was beginning to have my doubts. I stumbled about for hours until in the lightening eastern sky the landscape took on signs of mounting familiarity and with relief

I recognised the track those two racing cars had taken together, it seemed like a lifetime ago.

There was only one car waiting now. My car. I reached into my pocket and was amazed to find my keys. Thank God. Oh lucky man. I would rev up the engine, feel the warmth of the heater, make my way home at leisure, idling through those picturesque villages looking for some signs of movement, people coming out to their tasks, who knows? Setting out a table in front of a friendly café.

I didn't need my keys to unlock the door. Somebody had smashed in the windows, kicked in the headlights, bashed in the side panels with a heavy blunt object, it might have been an anvil, and then played mayhem inside. The steering wheel was twisted, wires had been pulled out under the ignition, seats ripped to shreds in a frenzy, fragments of my radio and CDs twinkled back at me and yes, of course, I hardly needed to look, all four tyres slashed.

Thank you Rodney. Very kind. I trudged away into the lightening dawn wondering if I had heard the last. Would he pursue me? Would Clematis call? Would I ever see her again? Would Rodney, knowing I was walking, be planning a violent return? I kept to the hedgerows and tried to cut across fields eventually approaching a stirring village, I was afforded some limited welcome by a terse woman in an apron who allowed me to use her phone.

Would I see her again? Deprived of the choice I wanted her even more. Would she manage to escape Rodney? Might she already be free or would she be on a life-support system and Rodney in the hands of the Humberside Police?

And how had he found us there? How had he known where to go? Had she been there before? Another occasion, another time. Another lover. Perhaps he'd seen us in our cars as he, driving hell-bent from the airport, passed us going the other way. Or perhaps he'd got home early, burst into his empty house crying out in pleasure at the thought of seeing her, shouting forlornly up the stairs.

An instinct. Some stirring of memory. He could recall an earlier time. Yes. That must be it. A memory of somebody else. No. That was wrong. It wasn't somebody else. I could see it now. Clearly. A vision unfolding in my mind. She had been there before. She'd been there with him.

I sat by the fire silently waiting for my cab. What a way, after such a triumph, to return. Would we one day be together? Or had I lost again? Clematis forever entangled with Rodney, after all he was her husband, or was it her father? God knows. Or would he, in the face of what was an obvious betrayal, ruthlessly cast her aside?

Had she finished with me? Come to that, had he finished with me? Or was he planning a further reckoning yet. I climbed into my taxi and took the long ride home. I sat and wondered as we crossed the Humber Bridge. One thing of which I was certain. We owed each other a car.

Chapter 26

They had moved Giles' case to York because of his local connection. Giles had wanted to object. In his mind it was to his advantage that people knew him, or at the least had heard of him, and knew the sort of chap he was. Precisely. I'd have been happier in Penzance.

We travelled by car - Jas behind the wheel sitting beside me in the front. Robin was wedged into the back with Giles in the direct line of fire - continually forbidden to smoke.

It's not many punters who enjoy the luxury of travel with their legal team and now I understood why.

"Harry, what questions have you prepared for the witnesses? I imagine your list is written down; and you Robin, what enquiries have you made of our supporters, and Harry are we challenging the medical evidence and I hope you've got argument ready to sever my trial off from the rest?"

I should have answered him with a note. A short note. It might have shut him up. As for me I have no questions rigidly fixed in my mind let alone set out on paper - it depends on what the witnesses might say; and no, you fool, we are not challenging medical evidence - we are not saying injuries were not sustained by victims - we are saying it wasn't us that put them there. And of course we don't want a separate trial, I want to cross examine the rest.'

Actually we were running a sort of sliding defence. It wasn't etched in stone.

First base obviously it wasn't us. How many fat men do you find at a party? And if it was us, on to second base. We didn't hit him. And if we did, we scramble for the third. If we did, it was an accident, and if it wasn't an accident, then hell-bent for home on self defence.

There must have been several cars that morning wending their way on the winding road from Hull. Six defendants for the home team, Tomkinson's side of the family. Six defendants, perfectly matched, representing the away team for the bride. And Giles somewhere in the middle for the supporters, coming off the subs' bench to paddle his own canoe.

But it didn't stay like that. It never does. Once we had the lawyers together in the robing room the trial started at last. There's always some 'wheeler-dealing' - people offering pleas to lesser offences, the CPS running around telephoning their superiors back in Hull.

"Will you take affray on the basis we deny kicking?"

"Surely you can't object to a common assault?"

"What about threatening behaviour on the basis we did nothing at all?"

It occupied all of the morning but by lunch it was a job well done, and we lined the defendants up in the dock. A mixed and motley bunch. All male - but young and old, rich and poor, fearful yet resentful, glaring at the other side. Whose fault was it they were there? Anybody's but their own.

Guilty to this and guilty to that. They shuffled off for the probation service to prepare the usual reports. All granted bail in the meantime, all promised non-custodial sentences behind the scenes by the visiting judge.

He looked at me with some perplexity. "Mr. Wallace, you haven't asked for the indictment to be put to Giles er … Mr. Baring … the man I believe you represent."

"Your Honour no. I have express instructions. Mr. Baring pleads not guilty. He says he's done nothing wrong."

"Does he now? How very interesting. No doubt you have pointed out the evidence against him. Identification. A fat man with a comb-over; an unusually red and aggressive face. And then there's his police interviews where he admits presence, even involvement, running accidental self defence. An intriguing prospect. No doubt you have advised him. I would have thought he might have known himself. The risks of a trial and, if found guilty, no credit for a guilty plea. He must know the score. All or nothing. If convicted, without committing myself, a strong possibility I might send him to jail."

He knows. Of course he knows. We'd stood outside the pillared portico of York Crown Court gazing at Clifford's Tower and Robin, Jas and I constantly passing the baton, had given it to him straight. He had puffed himself up and wagged that irritating finger.

"I'm not pleading guilty to something I haven't done."

They all say that. I must have heard it a million times. Giles is no different to any other punter. Gloriously optimistic, blind to any fault. That is until I get working on them. Subtly of course. Hinting at the dangers, pointing out the obvious weaknesses in the case, nudging them like an old sheepdog with a fretful stupid sheep until, safely in the pen, I can slam the gate on their bleating and watch the lorry take him away. Not that he will be 'going away' of course. The judge has already told us, made it abundantly clear. A fine and a little compensation - possibly the ordering of some costs. Why risk it? Giles was being more obdurate than usual. The perversity of the human mind.

"Christ Wallace. Can't you see it? If I plead guilty to some trifling offence or other and I'm grateful for what you've wrung out of the CPS, it won't make any difference. My case will be referred to the Bar Council - oh, those stupid money-grabbing bastards in London that purport to represent us and always sell us down the line. They will call for an investigation into my conduct, bringing the profession into disrepute, the profession I have practised for a lifetime - doyen of the criminal courts, a respected part-time judge, and the head of Whitebait Chambers - all this counts for nothing - they will drag me in front of some disciplinary proceedings in London represented by an incompetent buffoon before some pious, sanctimonious lay assessors and I will surely, inevitably, be struck off. Struck off, me Giles Baring and all I represent. By those time-serving politically correct suckers-up. No thank you. I'll take my chance before an English jury rather than grovel to cunts."

I could see his point. We all could. But what if we lost? And it wasn't going to be easy.

He could expect no quarter, no easing off the accelerator by the prosecution, no sympathy from the judge lest he be accused of prejudice, of being easier on our own. They would hold his feet to the fire. No latitude, no indulgence, no slack metered out to him.

I did my best. We all did. Asking the usual questions of the prosecution witnesses - how much had you had to drink? How could you possibly see from that table? How could you make out any detail through the crowd? And of course you had no idea who started it did you? How could you? All you saw were people involved in a scuffle, but how could you know who started it, who was the aggressor, who was defending himself? Impossible. Admit it. You have no idea who, amongst all those people, was the first to strike a blow.

I thought I did well. So did Robin. So, inevitably, did Jas. Always encouraging he urged me to greater efforts and by his support made me believe in myself. Three days of unremitting cross examination I was exhausted but exhilarated when the prosecution, that meticulous relentless, almost pitiless, prosecution finally ground to a halt.

"I think you've done it." Robin, maybe for the first time, actually buying a drink.

"Not enough to argue 'no case' like we did at Sheffield - that there isn't sufficient evidence to go before a jury - but enough to raise considerable doubt. I think so. Enough doubt Harry …" he clapped me on the shoulder, "… enough doubt that Giles here will surely be acquitted. Call no evidence. Rest where we are. Make a good speech. A little evidence, a lot of derision and we're off."

Shades of Mr. Eaves.

"Yeah" said Jas, "I agree. Stick don't twist. We're ahead. Miles ahead. Call no evidence. A grand gesture, shows contempt for the prosecution. Don't risk it all by stooping to put up some paltry defence."

I like the sound of this. There is one great advantage to which it would be cruel to allude. This way the jury don't get to hear from Giles.

"Call no defence? Are you serious?" that damn finger under my nose, "rest our case? No evidence? When they've not heard from me?"

Oh God. I sighed. If I don't call him and we lose I'll never hear the end of it. The man who lost another unloseable case. The man who got Giles, by his negligence, convicted and sent to jail. The man who went down to London, no doubt without a fee, to help him get struck off. The man who reduced him to penury, without liberty or profession, the inevitable loss of his wife. And his children. And with the children went the house. So another tramp in the making. Mr. Eaves again. Another lonely doorway singled out for Giles.

"All right. You've convinced me. I'll call you. And Giles …"
"Yes?"

"Try to keep it simple, try to tell it straight. Try to answer the question. Manage an occasional smile. Remember, this is a beauty contest. Try and look your best."

And did he? Did he follow my instructions, the same instructions he'd no doubt issued himself to other stupid punters more concerned with pitting their imaginary wits against the prosecution, exercising their injured pride. Trials aren't an intelligence test, they're a story you tell. The good impression you give. Look pathetic, put-upon, sorry, decent, pretend to be crushed down. Innocence cannot be demanded as a reward for cleverness, it's born out of sympathy by the jury for people like themselves.

And did he do it? Did he fall back upon his acting genius? A gentleman defending a lady. Portray a fat man doing his best? Of course he fucking didn't. He was Giles the man with the rapier wit. Giles the man with the affronted dignity. Giles of the giant ego. Giles the irritating, pompous, clever bugger who wouldn't answer a question. Giles the self-righteous, indifferent to the injuries to others - full of pity for himself.

"How did I do?"

Jas, Robin and I sat in the snug of a fake Tudor pub where nobody shuts the door, and looked at each other. What's the point?

"You were fine," I told him.

"Fine? Fine? Bloody magnificent. Superb. That prick who was supposed to be prosecuting never laid a glove on me and all you can say is fine."

"Not bad," said Robin.

"Have you all gone mad? Not bad? Not bad? I ran rings round him. Did you see the jury? They loved me. Every one of them. Their eyes never left my face. They were engrossed. Enraptured by my performance. Every man jack of them. There's only one verdict now."

I'd had enough. Christ will someone shut that door.

"Yes there is. And it's not the verdict you think. You were crap. Bombastic and argumentative. Thought you were engaged in some intellectual exercise. Rude and arrogant. How many times did you say 'preposterous' or 'grotesque' or any of the other prissy self-satisfied long, above all long, words that it seems to be your pleasure to use? They hated you. The judge hates you. You were rubbish. I hate you. Robin hates you. Even Jas hates you. Some beauty contest. You managed a spectacular last. Why didn't you do what we told you? Be pleasant, be polite. Don't get involved in arguments. Don't lose your temper. Above all, be nice. Yes there's only one verdict now. A verdict that requires you not to forget your toothbrush. Bring a small valise. Soap, flannel, and towel. Something to shave your stupid face. And some books. Preferably long books. Books that go on forever with a sad and miserable end."

It is a defence lawyer's most truly held belief that the defence is at its highest at the close of the prosecution case. Once you call the punter the defence begins to go downhill. Most witnesses are even worse and the more you call the worse it gets. Call your mother to give you an alibi? Call another criminal to support your self-defence? It's hopeless and you might think Giles would know it. But no, we're all the same. Fancy waistcoat and striped trousers – but a punter under the skin.

"Cheer up it's not over …" Robin put a hand on my knee, "… you can still do it. Finish with a rousing speech."

A rousing speech. It will have to be something special. Henry V at Agincourt. Shakespeare at his best. I'm good at speeches. I know I am. I talk the language of the man in the street. I skirt over the evidence; rest on an emotional appeal. Make the jury like the defendant, see his foibles, the little human errors that occasionally come creeping in. Make them sympathise, see the other side. None of us are perfect. Bind them to the defendant with the common chains of our human failings. Give him the benefit of the doubt. But Giles. Giles. Who could feel sorry for Giles?

"Yes you can. I've seen you do it. Nearly did it for me." Jas put down his orange juice. He must be a Muslim again. "Come on Harry, give it one of your best."

"After that I'll have to." I was tired sitting in front of this miserable fluttering gas fire, a steady draught down the back of my neck.

"Let's go. Wonderful." I looked across at Giles with a rare hatred. "After all we've done this last few days - it feels like weeks - and you with a spectacular bicycle kick put the ball in your own fucking net."

We drove back in silence and eventually Giles nodded off. I felt sorry for him really. A creature borne of habit bound by his own affectations, the way he prosecuted others, the same way he defended himself.

I worked hard on my speech that night, sitting alone at my empty kitchen table, the dog at my feet, a bottle at my elbow, a pen, always a pen, scratching across my legal notebook occasionally pausing whilst I found the right word to twist an unfortunate fact. Spin they call it now. It used to be persuasion. Perhaps it's really both. It took me hours and eventually I finished both speech and bottle and took myself, with faithful Sandy, finally and slowly to bed.

Giles was more chastened in the morning. Perhaps he'd used the same effort reflecting over reality as I'd expended distorting it the night before.

"Sorry about that. Got carried away. I don't know, that bastard got me going. You're right I was rubbish. I'm depending on you now. Make it one of your best."

I didn't have to. We pushed open the swing doors, were rubbed down by security and bumped into Pauline waiting outside the court. Giles, for some reason, didn't seem surprised to see her. He held out his hand; she took it and looked him straight in the eye.

"Sorry Giles. Heard about yesterday. Everybody thinks you were dross. Charles was laughing when he told me. Thinks it's hilarious, so do all his pals. Hope I can be of some help."

"Pauline. Dear Pauline. How kind of you to come. The only one. Others conspicuous by their absence I'm afraid."

"Really. No one from chambers? None of your so-called friends?"

"None."

Their absence was conspicuous all right. Absent to a man. 'What we have to say may be adverse.' I don't think so. Adverse to their careers maybe. Adverse to convenience. Interrupting a holiday, getting in the way of another case. A witness receives a standard fee for expenses, currently about £25. Not enough to try and save Giles.

"Don't worry." She reassured him. "I've re-read my statement. I know what I'm going to say."

And did she? Did she know what to say? Softly and with that affected modesty she'd practised as a bride, she told the jury what she had witnessed sitting on the top table looking out from that exalted position, struck suddenly sober as her wedding breakfast disintegrated before her eyes.

"A bad atmosphere. It was obvious right from the start. Even in church. My guests and Charles's guests didn't seem to mix. And the alcohol. All that champagne. I said we'd ordered too much. Hanging around at the reception drinking Guinness and wine. Lots of trays of fancy nothings. Hours to kill before they finally sat down. What was it about? What started it? God knows. I didn't see it. Only what I've been told. Some fool from the other side seeing fit to lower his trousers. It didn't take very much. Once it started, quickly out of hand. I saw Mr. Baring run across to try and stop it. The only one from his table. Others chose to look away. A lady had been hit with a bottle. One of my bridesmaids. There's no need to tell you her name. I assume you know it. Taken to hospital; suspected fractured skull. Mr. Baring tried to protect her. I could hear him shouting out. Asking people to stop fighting; telling them to get back. The only one? Where were the others? The other barristers I mean. Those who pretend to uphold law and order. I saw them skulking away. Not Mr. Baring, he stepped in between. Did he throw punches.? Did he connect? I should jolly well think he did. Holding my bridesmaid in one arm, blood running down his jacket, trying to keep them back. I should hope he did. What would you do? What would anyone with an atom of courage and justice do? Defend a lady. Defend himself. Try and prevent injury and damage. I wish there were more like him. Obviously there were not. I'm sorry did you say police? What are the police for? I'm sorry I don't know. They seemed to be waiting until it was over. Oh yes, and then of course they suddenly appeared.

Did they arrest Mr. Baring? Yes they did. Those responsible had mostly run away. He was supporting my friend, when they grabbed him. For the life of me I can't think why. My husband Charles had pulled me away by this time, but I stopped at the entrance to the tent. Yes I saw him protesting. Yes he did struggle. I wanted to go back and help him but my husband stopped me going back. No. I have no doubt. None. Absolutely none. Mr. Baring intervened to stop it. To rescue a victim. A lady. And what was his reward? The police arrested him and threw him into their van."

"Thank you Mrs. Tomkinson," the judge smiled down from the bench, "would you like a glass of water? No?" He turned to face the prosecution. "I don't suppose there's much you want to ask?"

What could he ask? It would only make it worse. He did the best he could, what the prosecution always do, he attacked her credibility, suggesting she'd made a mistake.

"Mrs. Tomkinson if you please. Just one or two questions. I needn't detain you long. When were you first asked to make a statement?"

"I wasn't."

"Really? You weren't asked to make a statement?"

"No. I volunteered."

"Er .. yes. And might I ask you to whom?"

"Parmenters I think they call them. For some reason Mr. Baring had decided to go there."

"And when was this, do you remember?"

"Not immediately. My arrangements were thrown into chaos. I had to visit the hospital; visit my relations in jail. And there was the honeymoon. We went away for a while."

"How long?"

"Three months. It might have been more."

"Three months?"

"Yes my husband insisted. He took me around the world."

"Did he really. Was that a sudden decision on his part?"

"No. Not really. I think he planned it long before. It was meant as a surprise."

"Yes. Yes. And when you eventually returned I daresay you were busy setting up in your new home?"

"I still am."

"So when did you get round to making a statement? Putting down on paper your recollection of what you believed you had seen?"

"A few weeks later."

"And of course that would have been several months after the event?"

"I could have written it down years after the event and it still would have been crystal clear in my mind. This was my wedding. Supposed to be a special day. Well, it was certainly special. Who could forget anything like that? No, before you ask me, I haven't got it wrong and no, I haven't made a mistake. I shall carry the memory to my grave."

"So did you give a statement to the police?"

"No."

"Why not might I ask?"

"They never came round to ask."

"So why not contact them? Why not as you would put it, 'volunteer' to them?"

"I did ..." she didn't skip a beat, "I left messages at the police station. Every time I rang I spoke to somebody different. Never the officer supposed to be in charge of the investigation. Always somebody else. Somebody who assured me he would pass on my message. Somebody who promised they would be ringing back. Only they didn't. And if you knew Humberside Police like I do you'd know they never will."

He had to do it. There was nowhere else to go.

Keeping one eye on the judge he went for the jugular instead.

"You've come here to lie for Mr. Baring haven't you?"

"Why in God's name should I want to do that?"

"Because he's a friend of yours. A long-standing friend. Someone you used to run for when you worked at court."

"I saw him. I know him. But the firm I worked for, my husband's firm, hardly used him. Apart from Mr. Wallace he was the last man on our list."

"But you invited him to your wedding."

"We invited lots of people. We had three hundred sitting down for dinner. I couldn't say many were friends."

"But Mr. Baring was an exception."

"Nothing special. I don't want to hurt his feelings, particularly after all he's done, but we invited the whole of Whitebait Chambers. Whether or not they came I frankly couldn't care less."

She left the witness box and walked out impassively not deigning to acknowledge me with a nod. Perfect. But as she passed counsels' bench I saw her glance up at the beaming Giles and with her back to both judge and jury, I saw it, I swear I did; for an imperceptible fraction of a second the slightest flick of an eyelid I saw her give him a wink.

I made my speech of course. The one I'd spent hours preparing and, as I tumbled into my bed the night before, thought might swing the case for the defence. Perhaps it did. Who knows what juries think about? Assuming of course that they think.

'Not Guilty' in twenty-five minutes. Pauline had disappeared and I couldn't find her to invite her to the pub with the flapping door where we went to celebrate our success. I couldn't find Jas either. He hadn't told me he was going. I was disappointed and a little surprised. We raised our glasses together.

"Well done Giles. You can't have been so bad after all."

"Well done Henry. A truly magnificent speech."

"Well done Robin. Thank you for your preparation. And for all the work you put in."

But where was Pauline? The star of the show. It would have been nice to have her with us. And there was something I needed to ask. My mind drifted back to happier times. The heat of a long fine summer afternoon. She was probably passing the hotel by now, on her way back to Hull.

This time travelling alone.

Chapter 27

I telephoned Clematis on her mobile and whispered down the phone. I couldn't stop worrying about Rodney. I'd seen what he'd done to my car - written it off without the benefit of a collision - and I wondered what he might do to me.

"Nothing. Don't be silly, he's fine. Much better now he's let off steam. No I didn't see it. I couldn't be bothered to look."

"I had to get it towed to the garage. They'd never seen anything like it. It's a total loss."

"Don't worry. You haven't lost much. Anyway Rodney has agreed to pay. Says he'll replace it. I'll send him round with the dough."

This was more like it. More than I ever expected. I wished I'd rang her before. I rather fancied a new model, something to impress my enemies, arouse the envy of my friends.

"Ah. Very nice of him. Do you know when that might be?"

"Yes. When you get back mine."

No time soon then. I'd have to claim on my own insurance. Get a police crime number. Fill in a million forms, deduct the excess - God knows what that might be - explain why I'd forgotten to mention the odd endorsement for speeding, argue the toss over the value, draw a few diagrams of where I'd left the car and, ah yes, I'd forgotten - tell them what it was doing unoccupied on a lonely fell. I tried to change the subject.

"What did you tell him we were doing. I imagine he wanted to know?"

"I said you rang me. Wanted to discuss the case. Thinking of lodging an appeal. I was going for a walk anyway. It's something Rodney and I often do. Far from the madding crowd, a love of the great outdoors. I asked you to tag along. Explain your latest ridiculous scheme."

"And he believed you? A bloody good job he didn't stumble over us in the wood."

"How do you know he didn't?"

I wasn't following this.

"Because then he'd know you were lying."

"You don't get it do you. It's not just me. Rodney's become a child himself. It's what he wanted to hear."

I didn't know what to think. I was trying to work it out.

"Anyway …" Clematis continued, "… what about my …"

I was getting sick of Clematis 'Where's-my-fucking-car' Fotheringay.

Erstwhile bride and adored child of Rodney the avenging cuckold hot on the trail, I still believed it, of what had become the invisible man. I was getting sick of Giles. I was getting sick of Jas forever disappearing off to London pretending to be on the terrorist case. I was getting sick, more than sick, of the ginger-haired whizz kid in chambers telling me I'd got no work.

I cut her short and put the phone down. Rodney may or may not be over it, he might have forgiven her, on the other hand he may not have forgiven me, he may or may not be ready to replace my car. He may or may not be ready to believe what he wanted to hear. I was sick of the lot of them.

But I was growing fond of Doreen. Her simplicity and sincerity, her concern for others, the sly beauty I was getting curious to know. Nothing to do with the absent Pauline, or the irritating Clematis, or the paucity of other contenders. I valued Doreen for herself.

I sat in the Bistro Beach Bar waiting for her to show.

Hardly a bistro, hardly a bar, not really a beach. I looked out at the wind whipping over the shingle raising white horses on the Humber as it rolled under the endless span of the bridge.

And they couldn't spell beech. Who spells beech with an 'a'? Beach is a tree. Everyone knows that. I read the sign contemptuously. If I could be bothered I might point it out. Confidentially of course as I leant against the bar ordering another drink.

148

But just a minute. Was I right? Perhaps you did spell that strand of pebbles and grey flotsam with an 'a'. Perhaps it was the tree that had two 'e's' No. It was the other way round. Or was it? I'd never had this trouble before. All my life I'd known the difference, and now I couldn't remember which. Better not go sauntering into the bar, or whatever it was, to point out their error. I'd look pretty stupid if it was me who was in the wrong.

Why couldn't I remember? What was happening to me? Only the other week I'd forgotten my pin number and nearly lost my card. I had a perfect memory. Impeccable. The gift of total recall. But I was always losing my keys. Putting them down and forgetting them, searching through my coat pockets, getting down on my knees and peering beneath my desk. And the other night, was it last night? I couldn't remember. I'd left them in the door. On the outside and gone to a blissful sleep with the house wide open and insecure, oblivious to the danger with only Sandy standing guard at the gate.

Is this how it gets you? The beginning of Alzheimer's? The very tip of the slippery slope that leads you spiralling down into nappies - sitting in a nursing home gazing in bewilderment at a son or a daughter that you've never met before. Is this how it starts? Forgetting how you spell a fucking beech.

Doreen came walking down the track in her headscarf and squinted around looking for me as I sat frozen in an introspective panic beneath the sign, I hated it, a word of one syllable that I'd forgotten how to spell.

"Over here." I waved to her. "How do you spell beach?"

Not a good beginning. I pointed to the sign.

"Don't worry about it. It's not important. Thanks for saving Giles."

"Giles? Who's Giles?" I know it wasn't very funny but for the moment at least (and how long might that be?) it gave me some relief.

"It was nothing really. Pulled it off with my speech."

We trudged away into the wind across the beach, shingle, mudflat whatever it was and however you spell it, and after a while she linked her arm into mine.

"I suppose he'll be coming back to chambers ..." she was watching my reaction, "... taking over again .. going back to where we were."

"Where's that?"

"You know. Mr. Baring, head of chambers. Mr. Pickles stepping down."

"Look Doreen ..." I stopped, put my hands on the shoulder-padding of her coat and, looking over my glasses, stared directly into her eyes, "... it's not as simple as that. Surely you must have heard? You take telephone calls,

149

pass them on, but when you think it's interesting listen in, you know what's been going on."

I might as well be brutal. "It's his expenses and not just his lunchtime expenses although Horace says they were bad enough It's his trips away …" now I was watching her reaction, "… not entirely alone."

"I always paid my way. Train fare, evening meal, we slept in separate rooms."

No attempt at denial. Didn't ask me how I knew.

"He used to tot it up when we got back to chambers and I would pay him back in cash."

"Well that's not what he claimed for. His accounts, or whatever he calls them, stipulated two. Put you down as his wife."

How very interesting. Not only attending wholly unnecessary meetings organised by the Bar Council - conferences on chambers' management ('Meeting new Challenges' and the 'Opportunities for Excellence') or going on some purported continuing education course or other rubbish, addressed by a visiting con-man calling himself a professor who charged the highest figure he could get away with and who we collectively paid. No not just that exercise in incompetence and political correctness during which he blissfully slept off his lunch - he was also taking a cut. Paying for one and charging for two. And poor little Doreen, I was moved to embrace her, bravely brassing up.

We clung together leaning into the wind, it seemed to be rising, and pressing my cheek against hers under her fluttering headscarf tentatively moved for her lips.

"Not yet. Not yet. It wouldn't be right."

"Why not?" I was getting impatient. Drinks after work, meals, well - bar meals, the occasional trip to the pictures, dragging along this forlorn estuary under lowering black clouds. The things you do for love. The things you do for sex.

"Why not?" I slipped my hands under her coat and could feel her jumping heart.

"I have to tell Mr. Baring first."

"All right, all right but when?"

"When you get back from London. I know you're going tomorrow. I'll tell him over the weekend. Monday come round to mine."

Savouring a promised pleasure is better than the pleasure itself. We clung together, my hand stroking her body over her skirt, as we felt the first drops of rain.

"So that was it. A new beginning. New horizons opening up before me, excitement ahead enhanced by the slight delay. I dropped her off home in my car, my practised eye recording, and hopefully remembering, the route.

"Until Monday," I whispered.

"Until Monday." She leant back into the car and we embraced again.

"You're sure you want to do it?" I felt confident enough to ask.

"Oh yes." She looked at me with a challenging intensity.

"I've thought about it. Thought about it a lot. Don't think I do this with everyone in chambers. I really, really care."

I drove away, a song in my heart. And so did I. I really really cared. Well not exactly. I liked her, I was fond of her, I fancied her. The whiff of excitement, the smell of a new body, the theft of a girlfriend from Giles. It's like scrumping. Stealing possessions belonging to someone else. The old story. Stolen fruit tastes the sweetest. In my mind's eye I planned the things I was going to do and - even better - after Giles I couldn't go wrong. I could imagine his pedestrian lovemaking, the pitiful attempts at foreplay, his hairy chest, that swinging pendulous paunch, great chieftain of the stomach race, blocking out the light as he lowered himself between her cringing thighs.

Well, welcome to a thin man. The master of the novel technique. It's not absence, it's imagination that makes the heart grow fonder.

And even better. I needn't worry about Giles. I hadn't told her. Perhaps I didn't want to spoil the moment, or was I saving my little revelation for post-coital conversation, carefully harbouring my store of interesting tales, or was it just my natural deception at play?

I needn't bother about Giles. Not for the moment anyway. We won't be seeing his shadow cross the threshold for a while. He'd telephoned me that very morning, beside himself with rage.

A letter from the Bar Council, had they nothing better to do? A little bombshell dropping through his letter box and bursting in his face.

They were pleased to hear about his acquittal. However, as he was no doubt aware, the standard of proof required in criminal proceedings was not so low as theirs. They were duty bound, in the public interest, to proceed upon the balance of probabilities - a much easier standard to establish his guilt. Accordingly it was with regret that they must inform him disciplinary proceedings were to be arranged shortly in London according to the new protocol (agreed between the Ethics and Rules Committee and the Home Office) that a tribunal comprising lay assessors and presided over by a retired judge - who no doubt both hated the Bar and loved throwing his weight about

- would determine, after hearing evidence, whether, notwithstanding his acquittal, he had brought the profession into disrepute.

Oh dear. Poor old Giles. Another hearing after all. Still dependent on me then, and probably Pauline as well. Yet another trip to London. This time at his own expense.

No room for tantrums and recriminations over Doreen. He was over the proverbial barrel, his striped arse in the air.

The good old Bar Council - for once I could fairly praise them - hounding the innocent Giles, whilst I skipped off with his girl.

Chapter 28

I got Jas to drive me down to London. Was he going anyway? But he was a better driver and I was the only one who could drink.

"How do you think the police, MI5 or MI6, the anti-terrorist squad, COBRA, whatever they call themselves, got on to them? Come on Harry, what do you think?"

"Information. Has to be. Shooting their mouths off at the mosque."

"Do you think so? Maybe you're right. There's plenty of informants who sympathise with the Kuffar ..." I looked across at his face set in concentration as he drove at speed on the A1. 'Kuffar'? It seemed a funny word to use, "... or who need the money. I assume they sold their friends for cash, or maybe favours. Promises that nobody keeps."

"And when they get names they start surveillance. Believe me Jas this anti-terrorist mob is good. Bloody good. The best equipment, the best men, all the time they need."

"Not in this case. They left it bloody late. Another few days ..." He was looking straight ahead. We reached the motorway section north of Stamford and he took us up to over hundred. The car began to shake.

"And of course they made mistakes," I told him.

"Did they?"

"You know they did. You've read the brief. Read more than I have. First of all they chose to play tennis."

He said nothing.

"How ridiculous is that? Trying to cut down on telephone calls, and I'll come back to that, they wanted to talk face to face. So they bought tennis racquets, nice new yellow balls, one of them wore whites, I ask you, and then they hired a court in the park. All of a sudden out of the blue they became tennis stars and always played in the same place - believe it or not even when it was raining. You've seen the photographs. Doubles usually, never mixed, once even triples pratting about trying to hit the ball from anywhere, even when it's out, forever conferring at the net. Not for seconds like players waiting to get on with the game, but serious bloody intervals after a random number of balls. And they couldn't even score. It was obvious. Have you watched the video? Taking it in turns to serve by whoever brought it back. Pathetic. They had a probe in the net. Have you listened to the tape? Not much about tennis there. Read the transcript. It's all about transatlantic flights in some silly childish code. And their passports. Remind me to tell you about that. Why didn't they play something they knew about? What about cricket instead?"

"Not enough for a team."

"Who needs a team? Why not practise in the nets? And what's wrong with jogging? Running in twos and threes. Any fool can do that. Enough of them do. Round and round the park, how can they bug that? What's the matter with these people? Tennis. Tennis. I ask you. Better feeding the ducks."

"What's this about passports?"

We were doing 130 overtaking everything - flying past in the outside lane. Jas seemed to be angry, but still, thank God, grimly staring ahead.

"You've read it. You know. All those previous visits to Pakistan. Some to Saudi. One or two to Yemen. The leadership must have thought this would be prejudicial. Arouse the suspicions of passport control at the airport, or the idiots on security, the resentful recipients of the minimum wage. So they decided to change them. Report them lost, stolen or otherwise missing. Fill in the forms, pay the fees, and there suddenly on the doormat is a bright new replacement devoid of any stamps. Brilliant. All of a sudden ten passports lost in Luton by a group of friends in the same age bracket, many of them living in the same street. What did the computer make of that? Exactly what it was programmed for. A bunch of pals with the same idea. All wanting clean passports. Now I wonder why?"

"Yeah ..." Jas slowed down as we left the motorway near the

Peterborough turn-off, but not by much, "… I get you. Not a great idea."

"And the phone calls. Not content with tennis they rang each other afterwards as well. No doubt to discuss the match. Have you seen the charts, the one with colours. Showing traffic, frequency and dates? And clustering? You know what clustering is. Bouts of hyperactivity related to significant events."

"What events?"

"Oh come on. I thought you were supposed to be helping. When they hired the premises for example. Two of them signed a tenancy agreement for a flat. An unfurnished flat. And did anyone move furniture in? No they did not. But the residents had plenty of visitors. Have you seen the photographs of them going in and out? At all hours. Sometimes in twos and threes. What did they think their neighbours were doing? I can tell you. Ringing the fucking police. So a probe went in. Of course it did. Don't ask me how they do it. With that crowd in and out it's impossible to tell. But they did. Of course they did. Maybe cleared the street on the pretence of a gas leak - maybe they're so quick it was worth the risk without. In and out and no trace of damage, and now they can listen to them in the comfort of the station. You can see it. Sitting about laughing, having a smoke, ordering bacon sandwiches, recording everything these fools were having to say. Then playing it back and another laugh. Sending copies off to the experts who can analyse bits of conversations, talking across the room, cut out background noise like flushing lavatories, or television, or music and produce an accurate, believe me accurate, record of everything they say. You've seen this stuff in the exhibits. All that shit about Jihad and martyrdom and Kuffars. How they were going to blow us up. And keeping it secret and the chemicals they were going to use. Hydrogen peroxide and the concentrations you need. Buying bottles of Lucozade or Fanta and sucking out the contents with a syringe so as not to break the seal. And in goes coloured sugar solution through a tiny hole in the base. And the detonators, stripped filaments of a bulb or a flash camera, hidden in a suitcase of junk. Talking about it, discussing what they were going to do, laughing all the way to martyrdom. Idiots. They had no chance. And you think the anti-terrorist squad may have left it too late. Never. They could take them at any time. They knew the flights, the personnel, how they proposed getting to the airport even, and how they planned the job. It was easy. They took them when they were ready. When they were sure they'd got the lot."

Jas slowed down for the speed traps at Sandy. The perfect motorist posing for the cameras, and once past - rapidly taking off.

"But if they'd got through. Two of them on the same flight. Mix the gear, flash the light and boom."

"Yeah Jas. Precisely. That's why they'll be doing life."

"So how much time is that?"

"Forever. They'll learn the meaning of eternity in practical terms. Forty years minimum after a trial. They can't get it through their heads, minimum means minimum. Before you can apply for parole. By then they'll be crazy, if they're not crazy now. They'll never be free. Never. All right, maybe when they're ninety and dying. None of the timeservers on the Parole Board will take the risk of letting them out. Oh yes …" I laughed, "… pavilions of splendour. Lustrous eyes and the smell of roses. They'll never touch another woman again. They might as well be dead."

We travelled on in silence until we reached the tunnel at Hatfield.

"So how would you do it Harry? There's got to be a way."

Well, maybe there has. And maybe one day they will. As the IRA used to say: 'Every day you lot have got to be lucky. We need to get lucky once'.

"I'd keep it simple," I told him, "go for an easy target. Forget about the planes."

Chapter 29

I took the usual pains with my toilet. Nothing less than immaculate grooming for the first serious bout. Gentlemen expect their partners to be fragrant (as Mr. Justice Caulfield once put it), why should ladies settle for less? I'm not into stubble, hairy chests, or animal odours. I look like a lady myself. Shiny shoes, a crease in my trousers, a shot of perfume down my pants. Teeth brushed, hair trimmed, nails filed, I sailed over the Humber Bridge in a cloud of scent, onwards into the back streets of the North Hull Estate.

One of many. There were several monuments to Stalin in Hull, constructed in breeze block and concrete, mould erupting round the steel frames of their windows, broken fences leading to burnt out garages at the back. That Doreen lived here. No. 29, 7th Avenue off 21st Avenue, off the Cloisters or something or other. What were we paying her? Obviously not enough.

I drove past a bunch of kids hanging about on the pavement in the light of a takeaway and took what I remembered to be a left turn at the next corner.

What a place. No one cut the grass in their gardens, the remains of a rusting bicycle in the gutter, a trampoline spattered with mud. I passed a triangle of green where someone had left the scorched embers of a fire; saplings with their tops snapped off. Two fat women in jeans stood chatting on the corner casually watching their children dismantle a fence.

19th Avenue, 24th Avenue, 37th Avenue, and onwards round the block. What mad socialist planners were responsible for a dump like this? No amenities, no playing fields, metal shutters protecting precious little shops. I found it in the end and pulled up outside a block comprising what I took to be four flats. Up the communal staircase to bang on the door, press the bell that didn't work, or alternatively rattle the grille.

It was turning dusk by now and the odd street light intermittently flickered on. But where was Doreen? In my mind's eye I had expected a small but carefully trimmed lawn, possibly hanging baskets, the twinkling light of a table lamp glimpsed through the curtains and the door thrown open impatiently and, producing a bottle from the inside pocket of my overcoat, a soft, and yes fragrant, reception inside. No answer. I reached over and thumped the rattling window. Nothing. I craned over and peered under the curtains. No lights and no music, no life from a silent television, no sign of Doreen and no response at the door.

I couldn't believe it. She had been so receptive, compliant, enthusiastic even. Why the sudden change of mind? She could have sent me a message, made a telephone call, pinned a note to the door. This was not her way. A person of candour and honesty. Who had I to thank for this duplicity? I suspected the absent Giles.

I thought about it dithering at the doorway at the top of her concrete steps. Perhaps I had got the day wrong? Or the time? The fault of my perfect memory letting me down again.

I had driven up from London, or Jas had, got changed and come straight here. Why didn't I ring chambers to check the arrangement? I can tell you. I had grown less confident over the weekend and didn't want her backing out.

But I couldn't stand there banging on the door like the rent man. A thought came to me. Was she cowering under the kitchen table waiting for me to go away?

I whispered through the letter-box. I shouted through the letter-box forlornly calling her name. No answer. Was she already in the bedroom immersed in the blubber of Giles?

I decided to look for a local pub, have a drink and come back later. It was obvious. I'd got the time wrong. She'd probably nipped out to the shops for a special bottle of wine.

I came back an hour later more sober than I'd left. A miserable hour sitting in a distant, no smoking, and thankfully empty pub turning our arrangements over and over in my mind. But as I climbed the flight of steps I knew it was hopeless. Still no lights and no music, no sign of Doreen, no sign of life.

Bugger it, treacherous bastard, falsely raising my hopes. I threaded my way out of the derelict maze and drove home over the bridge back to my lonely kitchen, the object of deception and derision, I pictured her laughing somewhere with Giles.

I don't want to be alone. I'm tired of being alone. It's not that I can't tell the difference between being alone and being lonely. Being lonely is when you don't want to be alone. That's me. It never used to be like this when I had Laura. When I had plenty of company - people forever hanging around dropping in and out - then I used to welcome a little respite. I used to relish those moments alone. Was it their rarity? An opportunity to consider what all this enforced society caused and implied. Or was it the contrast? A break from the endless gossip and chatter, the peace that silence can bring. An evening alone might be exciting. Stretch out on the bed and play a little music. Read the papers, watch a bit of football on T.V. The leisure to engage the brain. I think therefore I am. But it's not like that now. Not at all what I envisaged. I sit staring into the bottom of a glass, my mind a total blank, occasionally moved to stagger from my seat to visit the lavatory or let Sandy in or out. I itch therefore I am. I hate my own company; it only works, comes alive when it resonates against someone else. Someone like Doreen. Well it was her loss not mine.

I decided to throw myself into the terrorist case, do some real work - as Laura used to say, 'get a grip'. But I couldn't understand it. It was so unlike Doreen. If there was bad news, a change of heart, some rekindled affection for Giles, she would have stayed in and told me. It wouldn't have been easy but then it never is. She would have done it. To simply not be there. For some reason desert her home with no message. How strange and difficult women are. Just when you think you know them, have beguiled your way into their hearts, about to land a plump and submissive fish - that's when they wriggle off the hook and, in a swirl of water, dive and disappear.

Chapter 30

They found her partly-clothed body on the beach - an out-thrown arm occasionally lifted by the tide.

She was still wearing her coat, headscarf and sweater, but nothing below the waist, her legs spread in cruel indignity, blood coagulated on her face and neck, and only 50 yards from the Bistro Beach Bar where we'd made our tentative arrangements a matter of days before.

It was in all the papers. Front page of course.

'Barristers' clerk found murdered under the bridge. Partly-clothed body possibly washed up by the tide. The police are anxious to hear from anybody familiar with her last movements. Apparently she left her work at Whitebait Chambers early, saying she had an important appointment. Barristers to be interviewed by detectives investigating the case. According to a waiter employed in a beach-side bar she met a man (described as middle-aged and fat) and they shared a drink together. There seems to have been an argument. The deceased is described as 'storming off'.

Humberside Police have issued the following statement.

'We are anxious to contact this gentleman and invite him to come forward. Anyone knowing his identity or whereabouts can telephone the following number in confidence. He was probably the last person to see her alive.'

Shall I turn Giles in? Shall I ring the police on their confidential number? Will it be in confidence? I doubt it. Anyway I'm supposed to be his lawyer, represent his interests, appear for him in court. Would it be a breach of privilege or professional duty to turn him in to the police?

What would the Bar Council make of that?

I thought of Doreen. Instead of in bed with me in the warmth and comfort of her flat, playing our lovers' games, sharing a bottle of wine, falling back onto the pillows exhausted, marvelling at the novelty of a mundane act, listening to music, exchanging confidences, feeling a second stirring, entwined together, skin on skin, falling into repleted sleep.

She was dead. Cold white and silent, never to be opened to me, now open to the world.

Should I do it? Should I tell them? Give a false name perhaps, affect a different accent, whisper the name of Giles? There was no need. Robin rang me with that breathless voice of greed and incredulity.

"They've arrested Giles. Can you believe it? Somebody must have seen them together and recognised him and tipped off the police. Probably one of your lot from chambers. Anyway I'm wanted. Going to interview him tonight."

He rang me back later. "There isn't much evidence. Advised him to go 'no comment' but typical Giles, he wouldn't listen to my advice. Caught him on a video camera, closed-circuit television, shows him as clear as day. Couldn't be anyone else. Red face, hulking body, that fucking wagging finger and poor bloody little Doreen huddled up sitting opposite cradling a cup of coffee trying to get a word in as he was obviously telling her off. It's all there. She tries to get up and he catches her coat and pulls her back and then stands up and there's a struggle that rocks the table and she eventually pulls away. You see her running down the steps - this dismal café place - and he pulls out some money from his pocket and you can see him looking around and shouting and flinging it down on the counter and, a matter of seconds behind her, furiously striding out."

"Is that it? Doesn't the camera track him? Was he following her? Does he catch her up on the beach?"

"No. They go off picture. Out of range or something. That's the last thing you see."

The papers had a field day. 'Judge arrested in Humber Bridge murder mystery'. He's only a recorder, a sort of trainee judge. But when there's trouble it's instant promotion all round.

"Judge Giles Baring, Head of Whitebait Chambers, the foremost chambers in Hull, arrested and helping police in their enquiries into the brutal murder of his clerk, whose semi-naked body was found on the beach not yards away from a bar where witnesses described Mr. Baring and his former clerk as having a furious row.

He will appear before Hull Magistrates tomorrow. His solicitor Robin Parmenter issued a statement this morning. 'My client will vehemently deny any suggestion that he was involved in any way in the tragic and untimely death of a colleague of long-standing with whom he had enjoyed an entirely professional relationship over many years'.

Doreen Boggis aged 37 years had been employed by Whitebait Chambers in Hull since leaving school. A spokesman for Whitebait Chambers who didn't want to be identified but whom we can reveal is called Horace Pickles, said today, "We in these chambers have a long history in seeking out truth and justice. In the detection and prosecution of her killer we will fully co-operate with the authorities and assist in any way we can. Miss Boggis was greatly valued, much respected, and will be sorely missed."

Sorely missed? Will I miss her? Will Giles? Will anyone? Of course they will. She must have relatives. Mother, father, sister, brother, who knows? I didn't know. I daresay I would have done. Lying together talking as people do. But we'd not got that far, and now we never will. For all I knew she might have had a husband, possibly even children - she was certainly old enough - but we had never talked about her during our circling conversations. Only about chambers, only about Giles.

I thought about the post mortem, to most people only a word. But I knew the procedure, had flicked through the photographs depicting the opening of bodies many times. How old and unattractive they look lying on the slab waiting to receive the knife. Every organ one by one exhumed from the wreckage and examined, the skin peeled back from the face. Why was it necessary to examine her liver, the heart, the lungs and the spleen? And to photograph them. What was the point of that? Brain normal. Lungs slightly congested otherwise normal. Kidneys normal. Reproductive organs of a mature pre-menopausal female, normal.

Except she was pregnant. Foetal age approximately ten weeks. Robin told me almost breathless with excitement.

"There'll be forensic. D.N.A. could link it to Giles."

"What was it? A girl or a boy?"

Paul Genney

Why did I want to know?

"I think it's a little girl."

So where would that have taken us? Embarking on an affair with a new lover already pregnant by the last. If it was Giles. Might it be another? I realised how little I knew of her, how impossible for me to tell. And did she know she was pregnant? Of course she must have done. Women always know. Any test is a confirmation not a question. She must have known before she started an affair with me. Was I lined up to be the father? It's not the first time. Pretending the baby arrived early, denying intercourse with anyone else. What was in her mind when she agreed to meet me? And it wasn't just meet. We were going to start it. Make love, share secrets, pretend there was no one else.

"What does Giles say?" I asked Robin. "Does he admit that it's his?"

"Says it's the first he's heard of it. She never told him apparently. Of course he doesn't deny they were lovers. There's lots of evidence of that. Weekends away, neighbours seeing his car parked outside her flat. Apparently lives somewhere on the North Hull Estate. Or used to. Giles had his car broken into several times. Fool reported it to the police. No, there's no doubt they were lovers, he's admitted as much to me."

"So the baby proves nothing. One of them's been careless that's all."

"Afraid it goes further than that."

I wasn't following, but I wasn't going to ask.

"Assume Giles did know about it. That's what the police think and he's lying when he says he doesn't. He would be the first person she would tell. And he didn't like it. Almost certainly his wife would leave him. If you ask me she's been looking for an excuse. Assume he didn't want that. He would lose his children and his house. So he wanted her to have an abortion but at her age she refused. That's what they were arguing about. Say he didn't intend to kill her but they got into a frenzied row, he lost his temper, and she's dead. I liked the sound of this. It cut out another motive. That they'd been arguing about another lover. Another person that might happen to be me.

"You're right" I told Robin, "that must be it. Giles lost his temper, put his hands around her throat to stop her screaming not intending to hurt her, but doesn't know his own strength. Next thing her head goes back and she's dead. What does he say? With his baby inside her - and it will be - he'll have to admit it. What does he say?"

"Denies it. Denies everything. Never knew about any baby. Admits

163

they were rowing, shouting at each other, even admits grabbing her coat. It's on the video so he had little choice. But he denies catching up with her. Says she'd already gone. He stormed up and down the beach but couldn't find her so went back home to his wife.

"So what were they arguing about?"

"He won't tell me. Says he needs a conference with you."

"Why me?"

"Wants you to represent him. I told him about old Chevalier and he's quite content with that. But at this stage, before the next interview, his insists on seeing you."

Chapter 31

It's no good. I can't think about the terrorist case. I've given it back to Jas. Not that he ever let go of it. These days it's all he ever does. He spends more time in London than he does in Hull, visiting Belmarsh, having conferences with Moghul & Co., interviewing (according to him) potential witnesses, talking to the relatives and their relatives, attending on the Imams and the community leaders, meeting up with barristers representing the co-defendants, comparing experts, getting what he describes as the 'feel of the case'.

Well he can feel it all he likes. I've got other things on my mind.

And anyway, I'm getting tired of the general undercurrent of criticism and dissatisfaction. Mr. Iftiquar Khan is not very happy about this. And the solicitors are not very happy about that. And the relatives are not very happy about anything. They have heard about the reputation of barristers who claim to be experts on terrorism. No doubt deeply impressed by those bastards, the denizens of Oil Court Chambers. When was the last time Mr. Wallace went to Belmarsh? When was his last advice? What does he think about radicalisation? When are we going to have a bomb expert of our own?

We don't need one. We've already got one. He's called Mr. Iftiquar Khan.

I asked Jas if he realised the evidence was overwhelming and why, if he really wanted his thirty-five virgins in the pavilions of splendour he was doing the equivalent of denying Jesus Christ.

I was tired of tiptoeing around his sensibilities. "If he believes all this bullshit about the rewards he's reaping in paradise, why does he insist in denying the plot that might get him there?"

"He doesn't deserve to."

"Why on earth not?" I was growing exasperated with the lot of them - I was even getting irritated with Jas.

"Because he failed."

"But he tried."

"Yes. Sort of. In a fashion he tried. But he didn't do it did he? He didn't succeed. This is not banking, this is not some job in the city. We don't reward failure. This is serious. Literally life and death. Islam warns that upon his head shall be heaped everlasting derision and contempt."

"This isn't Islam. I've been on holiday to Morocco. I know what Islam is!"

"Do you Harry?"

I could sense his change of mood.

"Islam is deserving of the highest respect. This isn't Islam. This is politics. I know what Islam is. It's tolerance and respect for others. Islam teaches love."

"Islam teaches truth."

"Maybe it does. Maybe it doesn't. But its got nothing to do with killing innocent people. These murdering bastards use it as an excuse."

Jas smiled his slow and steady smile.

"You just want him to plead guilty. Give me time. He will."

"It's a pity we don't use torture."

"Don't worry Harry. We do."

"And rightly fucking so. I'm not interested in principles. I'm interested in saving lives. If torturing a terrorist makes him divulge a plan to kill people I'm all for it. Kindly count me in. With or without the Americans. Using rendition or not. If it saves innocent people I hope to God we do it. I don't care if the government admits to it or not."

Jas stared down at me with those dark and fathomless eyes.

"And what is torture Harry? How are you defining that?"

"Not by pulling out tongues or putting an electric drill through your eyes like they do. Not by cutting fucking heads off on a video. I'm not even thinking about that. What do they call it? Cruel and degrading treatment? Sleep deprivation. Waterboarding. Loud and incessant noise. Pretty unpleasant but it doesn't maim or kill."

"Ah but does it work? Is it reliable? If I waterboard you Harry you'll tell me anything you think I want to know."

Perhaps he's right. I'd admit to anything. But what if what I confess is true?

"I don't know if it works" I admitted, "I'm not an expert. I'm not in a position to check the truth."

"But if it works, even if only occasionally, you would do it?" He waited for my answer.

"You bet your fucking life I would."

He laughed to relieve the tension. "Very interesting Harry" he put his arm, as he used to, round my shoulders, "I'll try and remember that."

But I had no time for this. Not anymore. Yet another appointment with another demanding, not so very happy, client. The angry, the reproachful, another occupier of the higher moral ground, the insufferable ubiquitous Giles.

I went to see him with Robin down the Hedon Road and into a Victorian fortress; wallet, cigarettes, lighter, cash, car keys, into a locker - jacket off, waistcoat off, through a metal detector, back again and take off my braces, through again and back again and take some aspirin in metal foil from the back pocket of my trousers, through again to be patted down, and then waiting down a corridor pushed up against a door, waiting for a warden to fetch us and then across the prison yard looking up at the toilet paper stuffed into grilles over the windows, through another security door, keys jangling and into another corridor, waiting for more keys to jangle as another guard stirs himself to open up from the inside and into a cubicle and there pressed up behind a tiny desk was the impatient, fuming Giles.

"You bastard. How could you?"

I reassured Robin. "I think he means me."

"Of course I do you bastard. It was you who got her killed."

"No I didn't" I hesitated, I didn't like to be the first to say it, "Giles admit it. It's the better way. Your child inside her, all right you didn't know, but a furious argument over something or other ..."

"Over you."

"Giles I've done nothing. Never even touched her. Never been inside her house."

"No. But you were going to. Weren't you? Oiling round whilst I was preoccupied with my trial. Greasing up to her. Inveigling your way into her affections. Pretending to be working for me. She told me. Told me everything … tea and fucking sympathy … concerned about chambers … Jesus Christ … defending me … sucking up to her. All right we had a row about it. Yes I lost my temper. I know I tried to stop her walking way. But you. Don't you know what you are?"

"And don't you know what you are? Just the same as me. Just the same as all of us. A bit of fun with a willing female who unfortunately, as it happens, you thought belonged to you. But she didn't did she? Not your property after all. Bad enough I suppose that she was going. What you couldn't take, what your insufferable pride, your fucking arrogance, that self-centred obsession with yourself couldn't accept was that she was ready, was about to, Christ we had it planned, was to have an affair with me."

We sat in silence whilst Robin, head down, I hope as only a distraction, sat quietly scribbling notes.

"I loved her. You fancied her. Is no one sacred? The girl on reception. Your friend's girlfriend. The friend whom you represent. Whom you know has a wife and family and a million fucking distractions, Pickles and his committee inspecting every bill, the Bar Council, lowest of the low, wanting to haul me to London and ultimately, while I hang about waiting for their findings, strike me off. No job, no money, no family, no girlfriend. Thanks Wallace. Thanks for everything you insufferable little shit. You think I'm like you do you? Well occasionally look at yourself. You have nothing. No principles, no values, nobody you can call a friend. All right ponce about preying on women, kidding yourself you're an advocate, pretending you enjoy people's respect. What are you without Jackson? Look at your pigeonholes. What are you without Laura? Look at your empty house. What are you without chambers? A drunk on the fucking dole."

"And what about Doreen? Doesn't she come into it?" I shouted. "Hasn't she got any choice? She's not stupid. She knows, or knew, what she wanted and she'd rather be with me." But I was beginning to doubt it. Unnerved by the business of the child.

"So why did you assume she was yours? Look at you. Fat, pompous and filthy. Taking her away for weekends. Pretending to go to a conference. Charging chambers for a double and then taking cash from her. There's nothing worse than mean. I can't believe the goodness of some women, paying for fucking you."

"Come on. Come on." Robin got between us. "This isn't helping. Pull yourselves together. Think about the case. If Giles admits that he did it, and I know he says he didn't ..." he pushed Giles back in his chair, "... but if he did, and of course admits he did - couldn't we argue provocation? You know 'crime passionel' - restraint displaced in a jealous spasm - not unreasonable, bearing in mind the circumstances, the sort of thing that might easily happen; the reaction of a normal man.

Reduces murder to manslaughter, I'll have to ask Chevalier, but I rather think it might.

Think about it Giles ..." he motioned me to the door and rose to go, "... think about it. Instead of life you might be doing five."

Chapter 32

"He won't take it Robin."

"No …" he sipped his Chardonnay and sighed, "you're right. He won't. Hasn't got the sense."

"He hasn't got the offer."

"No."

He waved the barmaid over. Funny, they never come for me.

"Same again. But I'll have to check with Chevalier. Get him to come down. Try and make Giles do the decent thing."

"You know I can't represent Giles don't you? After this afternoon. Probably couldn't anyway. Now that this …" I wasn't sure how to describe it, "… other business seems to be coming out."

"Not sure he wants you."

"No. Didn't seem too keen."

Robin's mobile rang and he flapped around in his overcoat where he'd hung it over the back of the chair.

"Parmenter speaking" he covered it with his hand, "officer in the case …" he whispered, "what's he wanting now? Yes officer he was talking loudly for my benefit over the noise in the pub. Yes. Yes. What? When? Good God. Really. Really? What now? Yes. Yes. I'm on my way."

He jumped up and struggled with his coat. "Got to go. New evidence. Could be decisive. Going to interview him again."

He pushed passed the barmaid on her way with the drinks. "Sort it will you Henry?" He patted her bottom in passing, "You can drink them both."

So I paid up again. One of these days he'll buy me another drink. But what was it? What could be so urgent, decisive in Robin's words, they were going back to the prison no doubt to challenge Giles again.

I polished off his acidic Chardonnay and wandered back to chambers hoping for a message so that I'd know what was going on. I introduced myself to the new girl behind reception. Pretty and pleasant enough. I'm not going there again. I'm not going to my room either. I couldn't face the terrorist case at any price. It's funny how it always goes. A new case comes in and you're interested. Untie the ribbon, read the instructions, look at the statements. A feeling of excitement, guessing how the case might go. But then the usual anti-climax. Talking to the optimistic solicitor, a conference with the bored runner, the daft girlfriend hanging round, meeting the sullen punter, reading additional evidence, sorting out a mountain of paperwork, having to stand up in court. Golden cases that decay to dust. I never wanted to see the terrorist case again. So what if they sacked me? I'd be bloody glad to go.

I went home and sat in my kitchen and opened a bottle of wine. A fraction of the pub price for the same near tasteless junk. But it's not the flavour you drink for it's that sweet inevitable effect. It never palls; it never deserts you, my one reliable friend.

Robin rang hours later when I was thinking of rolling off to bed.

"You'll never believe it. Down to a man with a dog. Further up the beach up against the tree-line almost under the bridge. The dog found it. Excited yapping - running to his master and forever running back. I've read the statement. Fascinating. Eventually this oaf bumbles over and what do you think he found?"

"A premature baby in swaddling clothes?"

"A fucking great pool of blood. No doubt Doreen's blood. Must have been where he killed her, then carried her away and across the shingle intending to chuck her in the tide. Wash away the body, wash away all trace of forensics, probably fetch up in Bridlington or Withernsea, days later bleached, bloated and clean. Good idea. But must have been disturbed. Left her where they found her and immediately buggered off. No time to kick sand over the blood. No time to remove the weapon."

"What weapon?"

"Ah. Get's interesting. A bottle, a bottle covered in blood. Obviously smashed the bottom against a tree. Sharp edges. Ran it across her throat."

"Doesn't sound like Giles."

"Doesn't it?"

"Of course it doesn't. He's more likely to bore you to death. Ask any jury that's squirmed through an hour of his submissions. He is not violent. Ask that jury in York … just a minute …"

"He was indicted for violence wasn't he?"

"And …"

I looked at Robin, the light began to dawn.

"And?" Robin was there before me.

"He was supposed to have used a bottle."

"And?"

"Allegedly smashed it over …"

Robin finished it off, "… a helpless woman's head. Could have killed her couldn't he? He's got history for it. Recent history. Can't control his temper. Resorts to weapons. What's the matter with the man?"

"Fucking hell he's finished."

"Yes. And listen to this. At first he refused to let them take his fingerprints. Put up no end of a fuss. Said it infringed his human rights - forgetting they'd already got them. They've got his D.N.A. as well. And his photograph. Idiot. Kept them from the previous case."

"If he's innocent, what has he got to lose?"

But once again Robin was there before me. "Which rather makes me think."

"Bloody hell Robin, it's over."

"Yes. Simply a matter of time. You know the form in Humberside. They'll take the prints from the bottle and eventually get round to sending them off to the laboratory for the fingerprint expert to examine …"

"And compare them to those of Giles."

"And of course the blood stains on the bottle will match with Doreen's D.N.A, and there we have it – at the other end, the neck that he used for a handle, we find the prints of Giles."

"Robin, I need to think about this. Whatever Giles is he's not a fool. He must know there's no defence. This is damage limitation. He's not only murdered Doreen, he's killed his unborn child."

"Must be in denial."

"Yeah. Seen it before. Lots of times. A blind refusal to accept the inevitable. Obviously he cannot cope with what he's done."

"He's going to have to."

"Yeah. Sooner or later he will."

We wished each other goodnight and I set off up the stairs in a sober mood. Giles a man with everything - wife; family; a lovely home; social position and status; a somewhat pedestrian career but one, now that he had become a recorder, would inevitably end in his appointment as a judge. All gone. He'd be an old man before he saw the light of day again. If he ever did. All lost because of a personality defect - one that had not emerged until faced with raw emotion. He had succumbed to the primitive reactions of the cave, the slash of a primeval claw.

A tragedy for Giles and for his family. For his mother and father if they were alive. But above all a tragedy for Doreen. Unassuming Doreen who had paid him such respect and eventually would bear him a child. In a way she had loved him. Her fear and horror were unimaginable as in the night and by the river in his blind and selfish rage he had pitilessly cut her throat.

I tossed and turned between the cold sheets. Count your blessings. Whatever in life may befall us, nothing could be as terrible as that.

Chapter 33

I opened a bottle early next morning. I had no work in either court or chambers. There was nothing else to do. That's not true. I had plenty to do. To survive a widower must become a housewife. In a matter of weeks learn a trade that it takes a lifetime's training for a woman to become.

Hoovering is easy, I had to learn how to polish furniture, clean the shower, sink and lavatory, mop floors, wipe tops and dust shelves. Then there's the laundry department. It's hard to master the controls of the washing machine and drier and learn by bitter experience the difference between whites and coloureds, woollens and synthetics and not to leave the iron resting on a garment while you take a drag. And the bed. I was amazed to learn it didn't make itself. Nor did it brush the crumbs from between the sheets, nor did the pillows plump themselves. I could go on. There are thousands of things to do. Very difficult things. Things that if I applied my mind to it would take all day. But I didn't. It's not that I couldn't. Of course I could. I just shied away from the work. So the pots grew steadily in the sink and threatened to overbalance onto the floor, and the refrigerator slowly filled with food and the remnants of meals stacked one upon the other so that I could hardly shut the door. And then there's the shopping. And that's not simply remembering from time to time to buy fresh milk and bread. There's all sorts of things that have to be brought in – preferably before, at precisely the most inconvenient moment, you find you've got none left. What about baked beans for instance? Whenever you need them you always find the cupboard bare. It's exactly the same for gravy powder, curry powder, salt and vinegar and HP sauce. Where does it go when you're not looking at it? It somehow disappears in the night. I had loads to do and the more I thought about doing it the more complicated it became. And then there's the brass. I'd forgotten about that. Doing all the brass. No. That doesn't clean itself either. Nor does what little silver we have.

My God. I need another drink. And the more I drank the more difficult it became so that washing up and changing the bed fell out of the equation as the hours slipped away.

I opened another bottle and was delighted to be distracted by the phone.

"Clematis, how are you?"

But this time she whispered to me. "I thought I'd warn you."

"Warn me?"

"The least I could do."

"Warn me about Rodney?"

"Who else."

"How long have I got?" Long enough to raise the bottle and pour another drink. The bottle rattled on the glass.

"Is that your teeth chattering?"

"Just tell me where he is."

"I haven't the slightest idea."

"Clematis, this is serious."

Remember he'd found me with his bride or child or whatever she is, roaming in the gloaming looking flushed and out of breath.

"Christ what is he going to do?"

"Well. You remember when we went to court. When I used to own a Ferrari, before I was introduced to you. Which reminds me …"

"Clematis. For Christ's sake …"

"Well you might remember. There was a nice chap called Fotheringay. Bit of a coincidence. He had the same name as me. Thought nothing of it. It happens. Not all the time. Come to think of it never happened before. Not in court that is but then I've never been to court before. Apart from that time. Before that nice judge whats-his-name?"

"Clematis for Christ's sake please."

"Yes. As I was saying. Forgot all about him really. As you know I had other things on my mind. But Rodney didn't. Kept remarking about it over dinner and when we jogged along side by side. Funny that he kept saying. Chap with the same name as me. I wonder if we're related? So that eventually, and Henry I only learned about this the other day, he finally rang him up."

"So something good came of it after all. You traced a long lost son."

"No. Not a bit like that. And that's not funny. We're not related at all. Rodney went right into it in that irritating way he has. Wants to know all the detail. Up hill and down dale. This Fotheringay, this barrister chap, seems a bit of the same. They were on the phone for hours. Apparently became good chums."

"Glad Rodney's found a friend at last. For God's sake how long have I got?"

"Not much longer apparently. This Fotheringay chap told Rodney that you cocked it up."

"He did what?" I was astounded. One never criticises another player. Not to a punter that is.

"Yes. A complete balls-up according to Mr. Fotheringay. Rodney went down to London to meet him. Had a conference in his chambers."

"But this is totally out of order. Having a conference with another counsel's client. Going behind his back. Sowing seeds of dissension. Criticising another's conduct of his case. It's against the rules. About everything. Wait until I get on to the Bar Council. I'm sure they'll sort him out."

"Not before he sorts you out."

"What? You mean Rodney?"

"No. This Mr. Fotheringay. Apparently he says we've got a case. A case against you. And that oily Robin Parmenter. For gross incompetence. Negligence I think he called it. In the conduct of our case."

"Me? Negligent? Are you crazy? Has Rodney taken leave of his senses? Don't you remember what Judge Irvine said?"

"According to Mr. Fotheringay nothing to do with it. Apparently that judge is a pal of yours. We're looking into it. Fell over backwards on your side."

"Fell over backwards!" I poured another drink. "He awarded costs to every single defendant. Apart from that fucking count. In whatever amount they asked."

"Yes. And Rodney can get it back. He can get it back from you. And the car. And the contents. And the cost of the Lamborghini. And, according to Mr. Fotheringay, interest on the lot."

What had McIntosh been telling me? I'd followed every word he'd said. And what about Robin? Where had he gone wrong? But Clematis hadn't finished. She seemed to be enjoying herself. Was Rodney sitting beside her? Once again that odd inseparable duo, once again relishing another exhibition, once again at my expense.

"And Mr. Fotheringay took the trouble to look you up."

"He did what?" I needed topping up.

"Asked around. Made a few enquiries of his pals at the Bar Council. Nobody's ever heard of you ..." I swear I heard chortling in the background, "... not in civil that is. All right you do criminal from time to time. We're looking into that as well. But you've never done civil, what apparently our case is called, you've never done a civil case before. And no wonder. Do you realise what you've cost us? Do you realise ..."

I'd had enough of this. I used my most reasonable voice. It occurred to me this call might be recorded for security and training purposes so that, I'm no fool, I wanted to come out of it at my best.

"Clematis. Mrs. Fotheringay. And if he happens to be there which, in his somewhat furtive way, I rather suspect he is, Mr. Fotheringay as well. Might I remind you both - we won."

"Oh yes. By your lights. That's a victory according to your standards. Not according to the advice that we're being given. So you can look forward to receiving another writ. A writ from Rodney and I. This case I have to inform you is by no means ..." I was sure I heard laughing now. Possibly corks popping in the background, "... this case is by no means closed."

"But Clematis. Clematis my dear ... er ... Ms. Fotheringay."

"So you will be seeing me again Mr. Wallace. You'll be seeing me in court."

You can see why I never get round to housework. I sat and looked at the wall. Not for long. Never a dull moment. It was Jas, dear old Jas, Jas now on the phone.

"Christ. I've been trying to get through for hours. Never off the phone."

"Yes. Well. You remember that famous car case?"

"The one our clerk uses to advertise chambers?"

"Does he? Remind me to have a word. Anyway, some bastard in London has been seeing my clients behind my back."

"That's why I've been ringing ..." Jas cut me off, "... been seeing a lot of our Mr. Iftiquar Khan, going to Belmarsh is getting like going home ..."

"… and you'll never believe it. This bugger's got it into their heads that I've been negligent … and listen to this …"

Jas cut in again, "You'll never believe this either …"

"That barmy Clematis, the woman I thought was a friend, and that exercise machine in running shorts that for some unknown reason seems to have taken against me …"

"Can you hear me? Can you hear what I'm trying to say? There's been a change."

"Jas are you listening? Will you fucking shut up. They're going to sue me …"

"There's been a change of heart. I've been talking to the Imams, several important people. People behind the scenes …"

"For a million fucking pounds."

"Forget it."

"Forget it! Are you serious?"

"Forget it. The terrorist case is over. At least it's over for us."

"Over for us. What are you talking about? It's certainly over for me. Where am I going to find a million fucking pounds?"

"Try looking in Poland. Anyway. Will you concentrate? We're out of it."

"Out of it. Out of what? I'm certainly out of it. I'm out of everything. Out of money. Out of chambers. Out of work …"

"And out of this fucking case."

"What?" It was beginning to dawn on me what he was trying to say. "What? Another fucking traitor! Dispensing with the services of Wallace is he? Ducking off to some other bastard in London. Not by any chance called Fotheringay? A denizen of …"

"What are you talking about? What's the matter with you today? Just fucking listen."

Is this the way for a pupil to address his master? It's about time I sorted him out.

"Henry. He's never getting rid of me. Us I mean. And our bloody Silk. He's pleading guilty. Have you got it? He's putting in his pleas. Taken good advice. I've already told the clerk, and he's getting it listed in the Bailey. I assume you can come to London for that?"

I really will have to have a word with him. Maybe not right now.

"He's pleading guilty?" I was astounded. "Why's he doing that?"

"Because he is. Because he wants some credit. Get knocked back for parole in thirty years instead of waiting for thirty five. Because we've got the information and read the case. Because he does as he's told. Because he wants his virgins …"

"He won't find too many in Belmarsh. Female ones that is."

"In paradise. Pavilions of splendour, soft lips and lustrous eyes."

"Jesus Christ. He still believes in that shit does he?"

"Henry. Some of us do. Rather be dead myself. Live your life in Belmarsh? I don't think so. There's a better place to be."

Yeah. And it's in London. When he enters his plea. I had to get on to the clerk. "Remind me when you're not so busy to mention the name of Fotheringay."

"Henry. Check. You might be insured."

Why hadn't I thought of this? Of course I was. It was part of chambers' policy. Part of the stupid Bar Mark. Part of 'best practice' that the Bar Council was keen to impose. I really must get on to my clerk. About time he earned his money. Let him sort it out.

"On the other hand …" Jas put his mind in gear. Figures at his fingertips. A master at the ands, and ifs, and buts. "Assume you are insured. And then assume for some reason it includes civil. And then assume it is not limited to a figure rather smaller than a million pounds. Assume there is no express or implied condition that you only undertake work in which you have some modicum of expertise."

"That's a lot of assumptions."

"Allow me to make just one. You're not."

They raise you up and bring you down. At the mercy of the family Fotheringay. Back where I started. The ripples on the great lake of litigation spread to the most distant bank where I sit pissed and relaxing in my deckchair about to be engulfed. I really must talk to my clerk.

"Jas?" I said, but he'd already gone. I thoughtfully put the phone carefully into its receiver and was startled when it immediately rang again.

"Christ Clematis …" I may have been a little terse, "… what do you want now?"

"Forgot to tell you. Something else happened. Only the other night. Got invited to a dinner party. Some people called Tomkinson, got a huge place on the Wolds. Must be looking for friends. Dull as ditchwater, a bit like jogging sitting down. Got talking afterwards to the host, Charles I think he's called. Rodney was looking for excuses to go when somebody mentioned you. That got him going. Apparently he knows you well. Too well. Said you fucked up one of his cases. It got him in all the papers. An investigation into his firm by the Law Society, apparently still going on. Rodney took a note, wanted to know all the details. Then he told him about our case. This Tomkinson chap said he wasn't surprised. We were lucky to get out at under a million. Offered to do anything to help. Most obliging. His wife didn't say much though.. Bit of a boring blonde. Claims to know you as well. Said you were accident prone ..."

"Well really. This is insufferable ..." I was beginning to sound like Giles "... the gratitude of some people. After all you do for them."

"Don't worry. He said you won't be doing any more."

"No. And I wouldn't want to. You do a million wonderful cases and nobody gives a fuck. One mistake and you never hear the end of it. And it wasn't my mistake. It was some smart-arsed runner called Freddy who fancies himself. Got involved with a punter's wife and the punter ended up topping himself in jail. On top of that it came out that Tomkinson had lost his papers after I'd drafted a perfect appeal. Of course it got in all the papers. The punter left a note saying he thought they'd fitted him up. I'm surprised you didn't read about it. Coroner gave me a clean bill of health. Nothing but praise, not a word of reproach."

"Yes. Charles mentioned that. Couldn't understand it. Said you were absolute crap."

What is it about these people? I swear I could hear the stifled chortling of Rodney in the background, his ham-fist stuffed in his mouth.

"That bloody Tomkinson, or Charles as you prefer to call him, has only himself to blame." I'd better be professional. "Clematis, er ... Mrs. Fotheringay, I'm afraid you've been misled. This case that Mr. Tomkinson has unfortunately, in drink, referred to has got nothing to do with you. It is irrelevant. My advice is to forget it, and if you're still talking to your husband tell him to forget it too. And while we're on the subject. Your case has yet to be concluded. Remember we succeeded against the count. My suggestion is you direct your time and resources towards bringing him to book."

"Oh yes. That's what Charles said you might say. But you're adamant aren't you dear? We're coming looking for you."

Chapter 34

I finally got through to my clerk. The marketing wizard from Leeds.

"Bling here Mr. Wallace. What can I do for you?"

"You can tell me when this terrorist case is listed I daresay it's on the same day as everything else."

"Sorry, Sir. Couldn't avoid it. You know what it's like in the Bailey. Takes precedence over everything else."

What I would do for Jackson. He wouldn't take any messing about. He would have fixed a date that suited my diary, joined me on the train, and booked us in at a posh hotel. An evening out on the town with a show, dinner, a club. A leisurely breakfast and a stroll down The Strand. Pick up the money in the Bailey and wave the punter goodbye; sympathise with the relatives and leave the solicitors my card. And off to El Vino's to celebrate a case well done; a taxi ordered to take us to Kings Cross and into our first class compartment and order a bottle or two to see us as far as Doncaster where another taxi waited to waft us home. Oh happy days, why did he have to go? I hope he's happy on his allotment, or cooped up in Spain in a boiling hot apartment wishing he'd never gone.

I would have got Jas to drive me but he'd decided to wait in town, so I caught the early train on my own. In a way I was glad it was over even though I couldn't understand why it had suddenly fizzled out. This sort of trial lasts for ages as the overwhelming mass of evidence slowly weighs you down. And there were too many defendants. Packed together in the dock bored and fidgeting behind the security glass separated by guards and interpreters – what did they do? These punters were born in England, had they forgotten their native tongue?

I was going to miss it. Into court, out of court, round the corner for a sandwich for lunch and back for the slow grind of an afternoon session, the sun slanting through the windows at the back and finally, oh blessed relief, the hands of the clock crawling towards five o'clock and into the crushing tube and home to a cheap hotel.

I could do without it. I should be grateful to Jas.

He was waiting for me on the steps of the Bailey in intense conversation with a group of unknown men. He broke off when he saw me tottering up and gave me his usual grin.

"Henry. Mr. Wallace. You made it. Delighted you could come."

"Who are these people?"

"Onlookers. Supporters. Well wishers. Leaders of the community. The solicitors are with the relatives inside. And there's been a development."

"Oh God. Don't tell me he's changed his mind."

"No. The others have. Everybody pleading guilty. No reports, and no adjournments. Done and dusted today."

Well. This is good news. I didn't want to be the only one pleading guilty and then, the others - after weeks of buggering about in a trial - gloriously acquitted of every charge.

"Good. Good. Just the usual mitigation then. Credit for a guilty plea. Influenced by others more cruel and sophisticated than himself. A mere pizza delivery boy, and don't forget his age."

"No. He doesn't want it. None of them do. No mitigation. No appeals for mercy. No apologies and no remorse. These men are soldiers, mujahideen, they want to go with honour, falling on their swords. I have drafted a statement which he wants you to read."

Jesus Christ. I can hardly wait to see it. Is he trying to make things worse?

"Jas. This is England. We are officers of the court. We owe a duty to the court. Not to be gratuitously offensive, nor inflammatory, not to stir up hatred and dissent. Oh, give it to me. What does he want to say?"

I read the pages of long-hand rubbish interspersed with clumsy crossings-out. The greedy Kuffar invading the sacred lands of Afghanistan and Iraq. Raping their women and children, looting their treasure, siphoning off their oil. The terror and the torture; the horrors of Abu Ghraib. The glorious Mujahideen, the martyrs who destroyed the twin towers, those heroes who cut off your head.

"I'm not reading this." I handed it back to the frowning Jas. "He can read the fucking thing himself."

So. No affable evening out with either my clerk or my pupil, just the lonely train back home. And of course the judge refused to hear it. Why should he? If their master plan had been to go out in a blaze of publicity, it sadly came to nought.

"I understand the defendants have prepared statements?"

"My Lord, yes."

"All of them?"

"My Lord, yes."

"Hand them up. I'll read them in my rooms."

"And they refuse any mitigation?"

"My Lord, yes."

"Very well. I will rise."

He returned an hour later.

"I have read all the defendants' statements. They are remarkably alike. Nonetheless, I have found them helpful. Stand up please."

The defendants stood up one by one and by arrangement collectively turned their backs. The judge was unperturbed.

"I do not differentiate between one or another in the degree of your involvement in this calculated and unspeakably cruel plot. This was a joint enterprise in which each and every one of you had a decisive part to play.

And you were eager to play. And ready to die. And to take with you hundreds, possibly thousands of others. Innocent people. Women and children. I have read the flight lists. Businessmen going about their business. Families going on holiday together. Couples on their honeymoon. People from all walks of life. All races and religions. Old and young. Babies in arms. It mattered not to you.

And you came close. A matter of a few days away. But for the vigilance of security and the contribution made by observant and courageous members of the public who, unfortunately, I cannot name, you would have succeeded.

But you have failed. God willing you and others like you always will.

Life imprisonment. A minimum of thirty years. Take them away."

So it was all over, in a blaze of anti-climax with a whimper not a bang. Thirty years. I thought about it. Before you could apply for parole. Thirty years minimum. They were never coming out.

So I was now an expert in terrorism. But what did I really know?

I got back to Hull and went looking for McIntosh. I needed a distraction, and I also needed his help. We wound up as usual, it was reassuring to be back in familiar surroundings, in the arms of the Stag at Bay.

"Sounds pretty depressing," he told me.

"Yeah. Young lives wasted. Terrifying what they might have done. And it's all on the internet. That's the amazing thing …" I couldn't get over it, "…full of propaganda and bullshit. Technical advice on how to make a bomb."

He tried to cheer me up by diverting me to more mundane, but nevertheless pressing, concerns.

"Bad luck about Fotheringay."

Somebody suing me for the best part of a million and it worked, it actually bucked me up.

"Christ." I ordered a couple of pints of Fosters - anything for a change. "What can I do? I don't even know if they ever had a car. You know, I don't trust those bastards. They're closer than they seem. What if it never was stolen, whisked away by the phantom count? The more I think about it the more suspicious I get."

McIntosh listened in silence occasionally taking a deep pull at his rapidly emptying glass. I carried on excitedly.

"Did Rodney arrange to have it nicked? I can see it now. On the back of some low-loader with Clematis in the know. Down the M62 at two o'clock in the morning and into some old barn or dodgy garage under a railway arch, into the arms of some back-street bloody expert, a fresh spray of paint, new number plates and away. Thank you very much. Fifty grand for Rodney and twenty grand for him. Not forgetting Lady Macbeth. The one with all the extras and the fancy clothes allegedly in the back. I'll bet there never was a count … I'll bet they stole it themselves. And then off to Robin complaining, and Robin, for whatever reason, deciding to come to me."

"Perhaps that's the real mystery." McIntosh murmured to himself. "Anyway …" he banged his empty glass on the bar, "… not your fault. Did everything by the book. No need, perhaps, to employ every fucking page. But no one can accuse you of not being thorough. No. After all, you won."

"Thank God we didn't lose." But he'd heard the joke before.

"Very amusing. But the real fault's Robin's. He should have checked that bogus count. Made sure he'd got the money. Asked his solicitor. Had he been put in funds?"

"But he owned a flat in Eaton Square."

"No he didn't. He rented in Eaton Square. Did anybody ask his landlord or the agents? Did Robin enquire about bank accounts and deposits? Did he ask for security for costs? No he didn't. He dashed off a brief about a car. Bound it in pretty pink ribbon and, God knows why, sent it off to you. That's all he did. And when the inevitable happened and you won against the count - he looked around to find him and, surprise surprise – he'd gone!"

"There was no Ferrari either."

"Yes, another no doubt surprise for Robin. He'd fucked off with the car."

McIntosh beckoned to the barmaid. He always stood his round.

"No. You drafted the pleadings and had conduct of the case in court. And I know for certain - because that is what I told you - make sure that count had money. Alert your new pal Robin. Make sure he'd got the funds."

I must say I enjoy having a drink with McIntosh. The terrorist began to recede.

"Anyway. Even if the worst comes to the worst, I assume chambers is insured?"

"It is. You're not. Not for civil. I've already had a look. And even if you are sued. If this rat Fotheringay issues proceedings - what you do is join in Robin, the illustrious firm of Parmenters, pass the parcel to the second defendant and Robin can join in his insurers as the third."

Oh Christ. Not this again. A thought came to me.

"I don't think I've got the funds."

Chapter 35

I wasn't very keen to get in touch with Robin. Not in the circumstances. I don't know how he'd react to being joined into a case defending a million, and my eventually giving evidence against his firm. But I needn't have bothered, he got in touch with me.

"God you're elusive. Worse than old Chevalier. Been trying to get you for days. Got the forensics." He was shouting down the phone. What was he talking about? It didn't register. I couldn't equate it with a car. What had forensics got to do with it? "In case you might have forgotten in the case of our mutual acquaintance, and your long lost buddy, Giles."

"Giles. Giles." He had drifted to the back of my mind. Did he drift or was he pushed? No matter. He was centre stage now.

"Giles. You mean Giles." Someone with a rather more pressing piece of litigation than my own. "And er ... what does it show? Is it how we suspected ... you know ... er ..."

"Yes and no. You won't believe it. You'll never fucking Adam and Eve it. Brace yourself. There are fingerprints. Oh yes. All over the fucking neck of that rather damming broken bottle. But they're not Giles's. Oh dear me no. They belong, unfortunately, to another old friend. The enigmatic Mr. Eaves."

Paul Genney

"Mr. Eaves. What? Our Mr. Eaves." I kept repeating names.

"Yes. Of course. Is there any other? The guy Chevalier saved at Sheffield. Do you remember? We're back in business. The old triumvirate me, Chevalier and you - defending Mr. Eaves."

"What's his defence?" I asked Robin. "Has he got one?"

"Yes. With a little bit of help from me. Says he might have been on the beach the day before. Likes the view, interested in shipping, drank a bottle of lager and it was wrong of him he agrees, rather anti-environment, carelessly threw it away."

Unfortunate carbon footprint. Left it on Doreen's face.

"Anyway, the real murderer must have found it. Obviously somebody wearing gloves, or using a handkerchief. Somebody with a motive must have used it. And here's my little problem. Somebody very like Giles. One minute we're representing Baring saying he hasn't done it, next minute - here we are representing Mr. Eaves saying he probably has. Interesting isn't it? You can see the difficulty. On the other hand dear boy, one has to consider the fees."

"Ah yes, it's a tricky situation. Let me think ..." I paused while I pretended, "... how can we desert Mr. Eaves?"

I hung up leaving Robin smiling at our conclusion, and made my way to Oddfellows Hall to attend another meeting. Why do I bother? Called, according to the note in my pigeonhole, as an extraordinary general meeting to discuss the 'position' of Giles.

Heating off or on? Bar open or closed? Doors unlocked or bolted? It depended if we'd paid the bill. I made may way inside and found a chair next to McIntosh.

Horace was on the platform alongside our under-worked overpaid clerk.

"I'm going to propose a motion - Browne-Smythe will pass typed copies around - I want you to read it and consider it carefully, it is not something I take any pleasure in, it is not something, might I assure you, that I have not agonised over; I have canvassed the widest possible advice but, after detailed consultation, it is something I feel driven to support."

I read the single piece of paper, bowed heads all around. But they were pretending to read it. I know. They'd discussed it all beforehand.

'It is proposed that, in view of Mr. Giles Baring's involvement in (1) a criminal trial alleging public violence; (2) arrest for murder of our receptionist; (3) pending disciplinary proceedings before the Bar Council, (4) gross irregularities concerning chambers' monies - to be the subject in due course of a separate accountants' report, his membership of Whitebait Chambers be terminated herewith.'

"Does anyone have anything to say?"

Yes. And it looks like it's going to be me.

"He was acquitted by a jury of any violence - on the evidence of the only credible witness - the wife of a solicitor that used to send us work. The Bar Council have yet to consider his case and when they do I shall represent him with, what you might think, will be the inevitable result. In the meantime - something else you might not know - the police have discontinued any prospect of proceeding against him on a count of murder. I can tell you there is another suspect whom I also represent and who will face a trial and who has absolutely no connection to Giles. As for his expenses, we have yet to debate any irregularities, and we have yet - and if you have your way, never will - hear his explanations and seem content to try him in his absence without giving him the right to be heard. Nothing has been proved and I daresay never will. If this motion is carried, it will have consequences. Firstly, and you might want this, it will ensure the continued reign of Pickles here as our head of chambers and all that that entails. Secondly, and more importantly, it will irrevocably finish Giles. And thirdly, and this might come as no surprise bearing in mind our history of litigation, he will inevitably sue us in malice for dismissing him without any opportunity to put his case. He will say envy, ambition, falsehood and lies. Think about it. While you have the chance. Might he not be right?"

"Thank you Wallace. Very informative. Anyone else?"

Pickles looked enquiringly around.

"Very well. Do I have a seconder?"

"Point of order." McIntosh was on his feet. "Whilst I endorse everything that Wallace has so eloquently said, I move an amendment."

"What is your point of order?"

"You take the amendment first."

Pickles seemed to be looking into the distance. He brushed the lapels of his silver suit, sighed, and narrowed his eyes.

"So what is your amendment?"

McIntosh didn't falter. He must have been thinking on his feet. It's what he's trained to do.

"In the absence of Mr. Giles Baring and pending resolution and or clarification of the following outstanding matters, namely (1) an acquittal by jury of an indictment alleging violence," he paused "is someone writing this down? Thank you Browne-Smythe. (2) his admission to bail in a murder enquiry, (3) pending disciplinary proceedings and (4) an independent audit of chambers' accounts, his membership of chambers be suspended forthwith. Note: suspended not terminated. Any appeal to be lodged at chambers within twenty eight days. Have you got that Browne-Smythe? Perhaps you'd care to read it back."

With many a sideways glance at Horace, Browne-Smythe did as he was told.

"Well. There you have it. Thank you McIntosh."

Horace indicated to Humphreys who on cue joined him on the top table and, as they say in quiz shows, they immediately began to confer.

"Yes. Yes" he continued. Another one thinking on his feet. "Yes. Apparently you might be right. I will take the amendment. Assuming there's a seconder of course.

Thank you, Wallace. Very well …" Horace could barely suppress his annoyance, "I'll put it to the vote. In favour?" He glared around the room. Was this Whitebait Chambers at its best? Expressing sympathy for Giles and a sense of what was right. Or was it Whitebait Chambers at its worst? Ducking out of responsibility; putting off to tomorrow a decision that demanded to be made today. One hand after another hesitantly half went up.

"Obviously carried" Horace threw his pencil down, "I shan't bother recording the number against."

Chapter 36

I sat at home sipping, how I wish it were true, devouring a bottle of wine. It was dark and cold outside in the garden - I'd not got round to replacing the bulb in the porch - and dark and cold inside my kitchen lit (and simultaneously heated) by the fluttering flame of a gas ring that I was too indolent to turn on full. Suddenly I was startled by a heavy persistent banging on my door, Sandy barking and snarling at a shadow through the glass.

Oh for Christ's sake. What time is it? Who the fuck can this be?

"Sandy. Sandy …" I shouted trying to kick him away, "wait a minute. I shan't be a minute. Going to look for the keys."

You never know, it might be a lady. It might be Pauline. It might be Clematis. It might be anybody. I pulled up my trousers checking the zip, and straightened my hair in the mirror. The banging started again even louder - shaking the door in its frame.

"For God's sake wait a minute." It didn't sound like Clematis. Might it be Rodney instead? I went to the side window and, slightly parting the curtain, anxiously peered outside. No it wasn't Rodney. Whoever he was, he wasn't big enough. And he wasn't wearing fucking shorts. He had his overcoat turned up at the collar and his trilby pulled down over his eyes blowing his hands against the cold before turning back to the door.

"I know you're in there" he shouted through the letterbox, "I'm giving you five seconds and then I'm coming in."

Ah well. He sounded a bit impatient. There was nothing for it, I was too drunk to run, and anyway there was nowhere to go.

"All right. All right, I'm coming … I'm coming …"

The key spun in the lock, it had been open all the time, and there stood Tomkinson, towering over me, licking saliva from his lips.

"Wallace. You little fucking cunt."

"Charles, what are you doing here? How nice to see you. Come in and have a drink."

"Where is she? What took you so long to open the door?" He strode into the kitchen and seemed surprised to find me alone. "Where is she you fucking little shit?"

"Who Charles? What are you talking about?"

"Pauline. She's left me. Been looking everywhere. Thought she might be here."

"Sit down. Relax and take it easy. You can see I'm on my own."

I poured us both a glass of wine and, brushing a cat off the chair, we sat down on opposite sides of the table.

"She went this morning. Packed a suitcase, probably more than one. Took everything she needs; glasses, credit cards, emptied my wallet, left the usual fucking note. Terribly, terribly sorry, don't want to hurt you, can't go on as we are, need to be alone …" he knocked back his drink and poured himself another, "…got something stronger than this?"

I went to fetch a bottle of whisky and he carried on drinking without bothering to change his glass.

"What do they say these days? Need some time to myself, need to find some space, I can't believe it - totally out of the blue, only the other day told me she'd never been happier and all the time getting ready to go."

"What else did she say?"

"Does it matter? It had been a mistake from the start. Tried to make a go of it but it obviously wasn't working. Well it wasn't fucking obvious to me."

"Yes?" But he didn't need encouragement.

"Oh the usual shit. Better for both of us. Get on with our lives. Still be friends. Never be able to thank me enough for my kindness. Christ, come on. Probably said the same to you."

"No spark in my case."

"Oh yeah. Something about that as well."

"And you thought she might be here with me?"

I felt mildly flattered. He still regarded me as a competitor. Charm in the old dog yet.

"Last resort. Tried everywhere. Her fucking family and parents. Friends, what few she had. Local hotels, train stations, even rang the infirmary, been onto the police. Nothing. Finally thought, God knows why, it might be you."

"Well you were wrong weren't you?" I gestured round the kitchen, dirty pots piled in the sink, a basket of washing parked outside the washing machine. God knows how long that had been there, dead flowers (shades of Laura), going mouldy in a vase, Sandy growling under the table, week old newspapers next to the filthy stove.

"I know it was stupid. Not thinking clearly. Why on earth would she leave me for this? Why would she want to be with you?"

Why does anybody want to be with anybody? Husband, lover, aged parent, dying chum. Whatever the reason they say they do it, they do it for themselves.

Maybe we should work together. As he got drunker I seemed to sober up.

"Look Charles, I might be able to help you." He looked up over his glass. "I know somebody. Bloody good at this sort of thing. The best in his class. In a different league. All right he's expensive, and obviously no legal aid. I can ring him in the morning. Ring him now if you like. He's just the man to find her. She's probably ready to come home anyway. If I know her, pride standing in the way. Might even be pleased to see him. But let's get him started before the trail goes cold. He'll be up and running in the morning. Let me give you his name …"

I half stood to fetch my diary, but he waved me down.

"Oh yes … don't tell me …" I'd forgotten we plied the same trade, "Mr. Casper fucking Jones."

Chapter 37

I called him in the morning while Charles fiddled with the scrambled eggs I'd made him - pushing them round his plate on a raft of black toast.

"Casper. Henry here. Wallace. You know. Ha ha … you know me better than I think … Yes, well … ha ha .. anyway. I'm sitting here with Charles Tomkinson. You've heard of him as well … Yes … Yes that's great … better we all know one another … ha ha yes .. you don't know him as well as me. Anyway got a job for you. We both have. No. The same job. We want you to find a wife. Ha ha very funny. Not a new one. No. Looking for the old one. Pauline. Oh you know her do you as well? Yes it is isn't it? Very small. Anyway for some reason or other she seems to have done a runner. Yes very good. Ha ha … You're not surprised, that's what she used to be. Yes. A long time ago. Probably heard her and Charles got married. Oh yes. No problems. No. No. Everything going fine. Very happy. Blissful. No Casper. That was a long time ago …" I rolled my eyes at Charles who still for some reason hadn't started eating. He seemed to be inspecting his knife.

"What's it got to do with me? Friendship. Helping out old pals. You might have heard of it. Yes, but not in connection with me. Ha ha. Very funny. Anyway, disappeared yesterday. Note? Did she leave a note? I think so. Yes. Yes. I understand. You wondered what it might say …"

I looked across at Charles, by now inspecting his fork. "Are you sure these are clean?"

"He wants to see the note."

"Tell him he can have it. Here give me the fucking phone."

"No. You get on with your breakfast. You need it. It'll do you good. Yes no problem. Charles can drop it off … yes … yes … when do you think you can get started? Oh, excellent yes … better get going today … any ideas where she might be? Charles tried everywhere … Oh yes hospital, relatives, police - finished up coming to me. Me … oh yes very funny … no, he hasn't looked upstairs … yes … yes … maybe gone abroad … I don't know I'll have to ask him … it's rather delicate, are you sure? … yes … ok … Charles he wants to know if you suspect her of anything …"

He was looking under his plate.

"Of what?"

"You know."

"No I fucking don't. What are you talking about?"

"It's Casper. Wants to know. Is there somebody else?"

"Certainly not. Is he crazy? Jesus Christ. We've only just got married. Why should she want to fuck about with someone else?"

"Casper? No … no. He's adamant. No … no. All right I'll ask him. Charles it's Casper, wants to know … was everything all right between you? You know … you know what he means …"

"Give me that fucking phone. Casper!" he shouted into the mouthpiece. "No. Now you're talking to me. No. Certain. Everything fine. Excellent. Ecstatic. Wallace? Wallace? Don't be stupid. Got more taste than that. No idea. No. Took a suitcase, cards, money, fuck knows what else. No idea. Could be anywhere. That's why I'm paying you. Yes. Money no expense. Get fucking started. Check customs, passport fucking control, Interpol, who cares? I know it'll be expensive. I know how much it costs. What? You want some up front. Jesus Christ. Yes, I'll send a cheque round with the letter. No problem. Get started ok? Get going. And you want a picture? I thought you knew her? Oh yeah. I understand. Yeah. I'll get Freddy to drop one off. Yeah. More recently than that. Ok."

He stood up and sloshed his coffee into the sink. "Thanks for the accommodation." He was carrying his coat folded over an arm. "Be seeing you. Goodbye."

Chapter 38

I rang Casper Jones immediately Tomkinson left.

"Report to me as well."

"I'll report to both of you. All right. Daily. Any ideas where she might be?"

I'd been trying to work it out. My guess was she'd gone to France. Not that she knew the language, she hardly knew her own. But she had some fanciful idea of an idyllic rural retreat in the south. She'd seen a TV programme about Toulouse. The climate, the old buildings, the scenery, perhaps the pace of life, the culture and the food. And of course the nearby airport. The city centre and the shops.

"Ah. One day. One day I'll live in Toulouse."

"Why not Rome or Barcelona? Somewhere with excitement. A present and a past."

She'd regarded me coldly. "I have an affinity with France."

Well perhaps the time had come to find out. I told Casper.

"My guess you'll find her in France."

"Doubt it. Already checked. Took the North Sea Ferry. I'm leaving later. Call you tomorrow. Reckon she's going north."

He called again next morning on a bad and crackling line.

"Traced them … her … to Brussels. She's not pissing about. Stayed at the best hotel."

"What do you mean - them?"

"It seems she's not travelling alone. Hired a car in Rotterdam. Funny choice. An old Riley. Black and maroon. Probably came with a driver. Some young bloke. Not in a uniform. Seems they're getting along just fine."

He rang off before I could explore the detail. I didn't know what to do. Should I tell Charles? Discuss the possibilities? It was somebody to talk to - but when I tried he wouldn't pick up the phone. Did he have the same news as me and wanted to think about it? For some reason wanted to mull it over alone? Why was she going north? Why was she going at all? And why pick an ostentatious car? And what of the driver, if he was a driver, might he be something rather more? The new boyfriend. The reason why she'd decided to leave Charles. The reason why she hadn't bothered with me.

I couldn't think about the Fotheringays or Mr. Eaves and dear old Giles. Why hadn't I told Casper to get a photograph and fax a copy back? I may know him or Charles might. It could be anyone or no one. Another 24 hours before we might find out.

And what was the point of bothering to travel abroad? Wives leave husbands every day and don't go chasing off abroad. They go home to their mother, stay with a friend, book a room in a hotel. What was the point of travelling to Brussels? She knew everyone knew she had gone. The note, the money, the 'sorry' letter explaining why. It must be all over Hull by now. Charles' enquiries had seen to that. She'd gone. So what?

Why was she hiding there?

Casper rang again as he promised. Only about 12 hours late.

"This is getting interesting. Just missed them. I think they're booking ahead. Apparently we're off to Berlin. No. I haven't seen them. I'm going on intelligence. Yes. Blonde hair, dark glasses, flashing the credit card. The bloke? God knows. Much younger. Yeah. Good looking. Spanish type. Down to a pencil moustache."

Chapter 39

I arranged to meet Robin in the Stag at Bay. Only this time it was me that was going to be late. He was already at a table in front of the fire toasting his feet on the fender watching the door and sipping at his double G & T.

"Over here," he waved and smiled, "took the liberty of getting you a wine. Bottle that is. Barmaid's put it in a bucket of ice."

"How very kind." I was beginning to warm to him. Not such a bad chap after all.

"Unfortunately forgot my wallet. Settle up another time. Anyway I've been on to the police. They've done Eaves's drum."

"They've done his what?"

Why do some people persist in adopting the criminal patois? I know for certain that Robin came from a country family, educated in a minor public school. Did he think it leant a racy lift to that plummy accent? A touch of dissolution to his mundane life.

"Turned over his gaff."

"Do you mean they've executed a search warrant upon his premises?" With me it worked in reverse.

"Precisely. And what do you think they found?"

"The missing baby? Giles hiding under the bed?"

"Don't be silly. He'd been doing his washing. Very meticulous our Mr. Eaves. Pulled his clobber out of the drier. Amazing what forensics can do. And wouldn't you know it. Traces of blood on his trousers, a little patch in the crook of his sleeve."

"Don't tell me it's Doreen's."

"Oh yes. I've read the forensic. One in a billion it's not."

"So how did that get there?"

"Well … that's a bit tricky … we were rather hoping that you …"

But it doesn't work that way. Not with me. I take instructions and do my level best to put his case. In effect, when I ask questions, lead evidence, wind-up with the closing speech - I am his voice. Because he can't conduct a trial, I do it for him. When I speak it is coming from him. I wasn't there when he did it, if he did do it, and I depend upon him to tell me what to say.

Of course I can make suggestions, sometimes in a not so subtle way.

'If you were to tell me, for example, that you'd found and touched her body, panicked perhaps and run away. With your reputation perhaps you daren't report it. Put your head in the sand. Wholly irrational. Hoped it would go away. If that is what happened, and of course I wasn't there, it would be better to admit it. Think about it. Am I right? Is that how it was? Is that what you really want to say.'

Is it wrong to suggest a better defence? A fine line, but it depends on how you do it. Telling him what to say is one thing - suggesting what he might tell you is another. Does it matter? I don't know. Both routes inevitably lead to the same predictable end.

'Now you mention it Mr. Wallace. I did stumble across that body. Of course I didn't know she was dead. Could have been drugged or unconscious. My first thoughts were to revive her. But as soon as I saw the blood oozing from her gaping throat it was obvious she was dead. And cold. So cold her limbs were growing wooden. I dropped the body in horror. I can't tell you how frightened I felt. Suddenly aware that to report it would point the finger at me.'

"Yeah," Robin beckoned to the obliging barmaid, "not bad … it might have been that way … Bit of a coincidence though isn't it? He's on the beach and drops a bottle and Giles … well not Giles obviously, somebody like Giles, picks it up and uses it to do her in. Buggers off and disappears and we come rolling back again - discover and handle the body we have previously and thoughtlessly provided the weapon to kill. What sort of jury could possibly swallow that?"

Paul Genney

"A jury of murderers. The sort of jury you sometimes get in Hull."

But it was hopeless. Nobody in the world would acquit him. Not when his previous convictions went in. On the other hand, what will he get if he admits it and pleads guilty? Life imprisonment of course. With a minimum term. Just like dear old Iftiquar Khan. A minimum term before he can apply to the Parole Board. He's never coming out. And if he fights his trial? Pretty much the same. He waits a little longer to get knocked back. What's the difference? Either way he'll never be released. He might as well have a trial, he's got nothing to lose.

And the triumvirate of heroes - me, Robin, and old Chevalier - have everything to gain. A two week trial fighting a 'loser', no pressure, a bit of public relations, and a desperately needed fee.

So next day we trudged back to prison to hear what he'd got to say. More accurately what Robin had previously told him to say. More to the point, how he'd shined up Robin's story to give it a more convincing gloss. In other words what was to be the defence.

Assuming we had one. It's not easy explaining one's fingerprints on a murder weapon; traces of the victim's blood on your clothes.

I also wanted to tell him about Giles. I had to. I had to let him know that, at this stage at least, I also defended the man he was proposing to blame. Tricky. Anyway it was bound to come out one way or another. I'd been giving it some thought. Giles for example. The yo-yoing fingers of fortune had now given him the thumbs up. There was another suspect in the frame. One with considerably greater experience of violence and one with his fingerprints - not Giles's fingerprints - but the fingerprints of this other fellow recovered from the broken glass.

Giles will, of course, be wanting to be out. He will be demanding, and rightly so, a new bail application in the light of the new evidence. What am I supposed to say? Wearing my Giles's hat that is. Substantial and startling evidence that exonerates our man. And then whipping in to the costume department and emerging wearing the headgear of Mr. Eaves in what he will no doubt want to be his bail application saying 'where is the motive?', and pointing the finger at Giles. Very tricky.

Better to put our cards on the table before somebody else did, and put Mr. Eaves in the know.

He already knew. "This other fellow. The one you also represent. I'm told he's on video having a row with this tart shortly before her death."

Tart? I let it pass.

199

"On the one hand …" Mr. Eaves sat behind his metal desk - bolted to the ground for security - and toyed, as usual, with the pros and cons, "I accept the unfortunate presence of my fingerprints on the glass."

"On the neck of the broken bottle as I understand it," I told him, "palm prints in the way one might hold a weapon. Palm prints. Not fingerprints in the way you might hold a bottle to drink from - or as you said in your police interview, throw away and discard. Palm prints wrapped around the neck. A rather different proposition you might agree."

"Yes. Better to be realistic about what one inevitably has to face …" he seemed to be thinking "… on the other hand this other chap, this fat barrister pal of yours, had a motive. From what I hear this girl was something of a 'goer'. Had been his girlfriend. Wanted to chuck him up for somebody else … yes?"

How much did this evil bastard know? Did he know about me and Doreen? Did he know Doreen was pregnant? Did he know more than me and Robin? Did he know the father of the child?

"I'm told they had a bit of a row, and he chased her onto the beach."

"True. Perfectly true" I told him, "the Prosecution will say that's what put her in your way."

"Yes. Yes they will won't they? They'll say running off from a confrontation with the angry Baring - I think that's what he's called - Baring, yes Baring. She came running down the beach and unfortunately, unfortunately for her that is, chanced to collide with me."

Would we ever know what had happened? I looked into those cold indifferent eyes.

"Yes straight into my hands. Rather luckily for me."

Robin and I waited for him to continue.

"Yes the prosecution will say that for some reason she stopped and spoke to me. She didn't know me. Why would she stop? To ask for help from this pursuing boyfriend, ex-boyfriend? It was dark down there. Perhaps to ask the way? Perhaps she didn't stop. Perhaps I stopped her. One hand over her mouth. No sound. Perhaps already unconscious I silently dragged her away."

"Yes they might paint that scenario. You know the form. Better to leave that, if they think it's important, to the jury. Warn them not to speculate. For all we know they will say she may have run straight into your arms. May have known you in some way. Recognised you from the past. Paused to exchange a word. Sought out your society as a buffer against the charging

Giles who, for all we know, might have been gaining ground. We don't know. That is precisely what they will say. And we never will. Because you killed her and left your palm print - how often do I have to say it - palm print on the glass."

"Palm print? Palm print? I don't know why you attach so much importance to it. After all I could have used the neck to throw it and I'm hardly going to hold it between finger and thumb. No. No. That's not important. What you don't know but what I do and what eventually the police will … it is inconceivable to me that they won't … inconceivable .. you know of course they want to interview me again?"

I didn't. Robin did.

"Perfectly normal in a serious enquiry like this," Robin informed him, "been on to my office. Want to do it today. In fact after we've finished. That's why it's rather important we establish what you want to say."

"Not really …" Mr. Eaves began to smile, "not really. You've done your best. Both of you. You did a good job in Sheffield. But this I'm afraid is rather different. Rather more difficult. Impossible really. You don't know but I know … Yes. It's not the palm print that's significant. Although I agree with you Mr. Wallace it is unfortunate. I agree we would rather, given the choice, have fingerprints than palm. But that isn't the point. Not really … those palm prints … of course they're on the neck of the bottle. But what I know, and I daresay the police now know because forensics will have told them, is this … rather difficult to explain in all the circumstances … those palm prints on the neck of this fucking bottle ... or what remains of it … are actually in her blood."

Chapter 40

I'm not going into chambers, and I'm not going into court. The truth is I have nowhere to go. No girlfriend, no welcoming smile and warm body, nobody to listen to my excuses, nobody to advise me what to do. One of the rewards of mundanity is that you have a home to go to. A real home with another human being. I wanted to burrow into bed against a warm bottom - who cares what's in her brain.

But I had nobody. Laura far beyond me, Clematis probably in London, visiting Oil Court Chambers with Rodney, Doreen rotting in her grave. And where was Pauline? Going round the world in eighty days.

Casper was on the phone. I sighed as I recognised his voice on the usual discordant line.

"They're off again. After another noisy evening. Sounds like they're having fun."

What a malicious bastard he is. I wonder if he reports to Tomkinson in the same crowing vein?

"Really. Where are you off to now?"

And then it hit me. It was obvious. Not so far to me and probably never to Tomkinson - but Casper must have had an idea all along.

"Casper have you seen her face?"

"Course I have. Don't be silly. Can't get too close of course. She knows me. Or I think she does. Got to keep a distance. Don't want to blow our cover do we?"

"No of course we don't. Not for this money. Not for an all expenses paid round the world trip. So tell me exactly how close have you been?"

"Other side of a restaurant. More of a huge dining room, a hundred yards away. Kept behind them in the car. Well behind. Lost them once or twice. Saw them outside their room, saw them kissing in the lift."

"But have you seen her face?"

"Course I have."

"So what is she wearing?"

"Sunglasses. Never takes them off. Often a headscarf. Now she's bought a hat."

"Casper. It's over. I'm ringing Tomkinson - you're coming back. It's not Pauline. Of course it isn't. You've been trailing someone else."

"No I haven't. Don't think I don't know my job. I've checked the hotel registers, looked at the booking ticket to cross the channel. What do you think I am, a moron? Been to the garages, dropped in at the shops. Dropped a few euros in the right places - wait till Tomkinson gets my account - checked the number on the credit card and this'll surprise you, it's a match. Of course it's Pauline. Blonde hair, decent legs, bit of an overblown figure, getting a bit fat round the thighs."

"Of course it looks like her. No point if it didn't. But I tell you, I know it and I suspect you know it, you've been following somebody else. So forget it. Turn your stupid arse round. This is it, it's over. Casper, you're coming home."

I finally got through to Tomkinson but Casper had already let him know.

"What do you think you're playing at? Of course it's Pauline. I've told him to get back on the job."

I tried to be patient and explain as best as I could.

"It's *Bleak House* revisited."

"*Bleak House*. What are you talking about.. Where the fuck is that?"

"It's not a place, it's a book."

"A book. What are you talking about? Thinking of going to the library? Who wants a fucking book?"

"It's a famous book. One by Charles Dickens. One I assumed you'd read."

"Listen Henry, I'm not in the mood for reading. What I want is Casper to bring her back."

"Well he won't find her in St. Petersburg. My guess is the south of France. And why don't you go to the library. *Bleak House*. Why don't you get a ticket and take it out?"

"All right. Tell me slowly. Save me the time and effort ..." I could hear him gritting his teeth "... what's this all about?"

"Lady Dedlock, knows a detective is following her. Hot on the trail out of London he chases off up the Great North Road following a lady looking just like Lady Dedlock - same walk, same ways, same figure and wearing her hood and her cloak. But it's not. Of course it isn't. She's stayed in London. He's following somebody else. Get it? This blousy female may look a bit like Pauline, say she's wearing a wig and, I ask you, dark glasses and a headscarf covering half her face. Our incompetent hero has been chasing half way across Europe, God knows where it might have ended, following somebody else. Having a wonderful time. Can you see the fat bastard sitting down at the table, his napkin tucked under the lowest of his chins, ordering à la carte, hoovering up the finest wines and buggering off to a club. For nothing. Absolutely nothing. Pauline's taken off and - she can't resist it - she's also taking the piss. Going in the opposite direction, probably paying cash. Your cash. Having a bit of a laugh. And when she's ready and you're bankrupt, she'll cheerfully come drifting back."

"You mean it's not Pauline?"

"Of course it isn't. A mate of hers. Somebody she hired from a circus. An actress on the dole. How do I know? Who cares? Somebody pissing about with her boyfriend. A moustache, I ask you. Think about it. No discretion. Noisy arguments. Amorous public encounters. Does that sound like Pauline?

Or does it sound like - and this may take some mental effort - somebody deliberately leaving a trail that even Casper could follow. Somebody Charles, I hope you're following the reasoning, somebody else."

He hung up on me. No doubt for a fuller discussion with Casper. I sat in my grandmother's old rocking chair. Why not? We'd had it as a decoration sitting at the distant head of the table, piled with cushions, a home from home for the cats. The joints creaked reassuringly as, bracing my legs on the stone floor, I rocked it to and fro. What to do? I looked at the clock. Not even midday. Casper no doubt on the phone to Tomkinson discussing the subtleties of *Bleak House*. I daresay even with those two - no - disregard Casper - that bastard knew all along - the penny was finally starting to drop.

I expected Tomkinson to ring me back. What was taking so long? I eyed the half-full bottle, the remnants of the night before. Was it too early to start? It's never too early and it's never too late, I reached across for a glass.

Chapter 41

Jas rang me later. Much later. I woke up and looked out the kitchen window at the garden gathering shadows in the dusk.

"It's tomorrow," he sounded excited. "I know you've not much on."

"I haven't got anything on."

"But I have. I want you to come across. Court three in front of Judge Irvine. My first case. I'd like you to be there."

I was touched. How generous to want me there to share his magic moment, to thank me afterwards for everything I'd done. I felt a surge of pleasure. "That's very kind," I told him, I was feeling quite bucked up, "I wouldn't miss it for the world."

Next morning I got in bright and early, slicked up for the show. Shiny shoes and stiff collar, I'd picked a rose from the garden and wore it in my lapel. Out of habit I strolled through chambers to the clerks' room to check my pigeonhole and, I confess it, also out of habit, to glance in those of everyone else.

As I suspected. Why do I bother? I nearly turned away. But what was this? Some fool had sent me a holiday postcard. Very amusing, I couldn't care less. But if they'd taken the trouble - I idly picked it up and glanced at the photograph on the front. Stone horses plunging through a fountain.

Where the hell was that? I flicked it over and read the message, in that childish unmistakeable hand. 'Fancy a trip to Toulouse?'

"Come on. Come on." Jas was in a hurry, also immaculately dressed. "Got to see my punter. I've asked Robin to come as well."

It was a lovely day as we walked along the cobbles, Jas swung his blue bag over his shoulder and softly hummed a tune.

But I couldn't concentrate on him. My mind was away over the Channel in the sunnier fields of France.

"Harry. Harry. What's the matter with you?"

He punched my arm and laughed. "Cheer up. You'll enjoy it. The happiest day of my life."

We walked across the square and he bounded up the steps ahead of me as my mobile went off in my pocket. I checked the number but I didn't recognise it. Jas pushed the doors open and disappeared inside. Should I answer it or leave it? I hesitated, unable to decide. What the hell, it might be Pauline - I walked back into the square.

"Why didn't you ring me?"

"Because I only just got your card."

"What? I sent it a week ago."

"Forget it. What do you want me to do?

"Come over. I put the address on the card. A little village near ..."

"I know. I recognised the fountain."

"Soon as you can. And don't forget some cash."

"What about Charles?" I looked up to see Jas arguing with security. "What are you doing about Charles?"

"Tell you when you get here. Can you come today?"

"Not today. This is Jas's big moment. On his feet for the first time ... I'll ring you when I get out of court."

There was a sudden flash of light and the doors of the court blew outwards and came cart-wheeling towards me down the steps. The fire alarm was whining in the background. I could hear screams and shouting; the occasional rapid bursts of an echoing series of bangs.

"Listen to me Pauline." I was shouting over the pandemonium.

"They've blown up Hull Crown Court."

Pleading Guilty – **Paul Genney**

Wallace is full of passion. He is angry at the changing world around him. He is angry at the Bar, with its charter marks and political correctness, the CPS for its gross incompetence and at the people running his chambers for their lack of loyalty to the clerk who had set up their chambers and helped to make them well paid lawyers.

He is full of love for his wife, their family and bohemian lifestyle. He is also in love with Pauline, a solicitor's runner. The more frustrated he becomes with the world around him the more besotted he becomes with Pauline. The law courts give way to love in the afternoon. When Pauline cools, Wallace overheats and his life ends in turmoil. Like his clients, he is forced to plead guilty to letting his life spiral out of control.

"Genney's easy union of humour and tragedy makes this an appealing debut."   Sarah Sheerman in *The Big Issue*

"Genney has a sure touch and is able to fuse undoubted humour with a compassion for the people who find themselves caught up in the uncertainties of the criminal justice system, and his chapters upon developing family tragedy are genuinely moving. Pleading Guilty introduces us to Henry Wallace, Horace Rumpole on circuit, and a welcome acquisition to the fictional Bar."
                                           John Cooper in *Criminal Bar Quarterly*

A thoroughly enjoyable and thought provoking book."
                                                        Judge Michael Mettyear

£9.99   ISBN 978 1 903517 57 4   242p   B. Format

Gabriel's Bureau – **Mikka Haugaard**

"A deliciously twisted tale of darkness, espionage and murder. A gripping read, with an edginess so often hard to find in a debut novel."

BJ in *Buzz Magazine*

"As much as you'd think being a spy would have its perks, Gabriel's Bureau illustrates the all consuming pressure of the job and the danger that follows from knowing a little bit too much. Having previously worked for Soviet intelligence, Gabriel has used his contacts to set up his own detective agency and when an acquaintance from the past seeks his help he finds himself unable to say no. The consequences are immense as he investigates the seedy London underworld of art dealings where he learns power is money and death is inevitable when art changes dirty hands. As we follow his quest for the truth, the story focuses on the complex life of Gabriel himself, bringing together his past, his present and his intriguing relationship with his wife and the man 'who is Russia', Oleg. The prose is fluid and poetic... Likewise, there are a few gems in the storyline that throw up a great deal of mystery and intrigue. A seemingly cold and unfeeling novel, which perhaps isn't a million miles away from the life of a private investigator."

Angela Singh in *The Big Issue*

"A book of greys and muted colours. Reading it on the train I became infused with the gentle melancholy you get when reading a John Le Carre and it would be near perfect read for a wet Sunday with a bar of chocolate and the gas-fire on. Harking back to Cold War spy novels, with a lone hero, who used to work for the KGB and is now based in London with his invalid wife, Gabriel's Bureau is full of puzzles and enigmas, with an intriguingly labyrinthine plot, played out against the backdrop of a seedy underworld... an intricate and thoughtful book."

James Nash in *The Leeds Review*

£7.99   ISBN 978 1 903517 31 4   258p   B. Format

The Dream Maker – **Mikka Haugaard**

"Rachel and Tina are best friends. They write a novel and, although Rachel does most of the work, the book appears with Tina's name on the cover, and is a bestseller. The fame is Tina's and the money is shared. The novel becomes a trilogy and there's enough cash for a Georgian mansion, where Rachel invites artists and writers to stay for free, including Jules Le Comte de Braband, who dresses all in yellow, down to the bottle of whisky bulging in his pocket. The real hero of this novel is the hero of Rachel's novels, Max. In bed with Mo, her lover who is half her age, Rachel tells Max's stories, interspersed with episodes from Rachel's life. Max, in Rome, is hanging out with a 13-year-old girl and heading for disaster. Max, like Rachel had been, is vastly wealthy and can't go anywhere without a security entourage. The most human among them is Trevor, his chauffeur, but the quality that makes him human suggests a pessimistic view of humanity. From her bed, like a latterday Scheherazade, Rachel reflects that "occasionally a rambling tale is what you most want... because you've done with shape and structure". In fact, there is shape here, and structure, and although we know what is going to happen to Max, we don't know what will happen to Rachel and Mo. Haugaard writes with great wit, flair and invention. I'm already looking forward to her third novel."

Nicholas Royle in *The Independent*

£7.99   ISBN 978 1 903517 56 7   176p   B. Format